PRAISE FOR
SID JOHNSON AND
THE WELL-INTENDED CONSPIRACY

"This captivating book blends elements of a historical drama with an intimate portrait of life during the 1850s. It is a tale of human courage and will, as well as an exploration of the displacement and destruction of the Kanza Nation along the Santa Fe Trail . . . Well-researched and detailed . . . an intense and immersive experience akin to those found in adult historical fiction. A stunner"—The Prairies Book Review

". . . an adventurous journey in a wagon train heading west. You can practically taste the dust from the trail as you join young pioneer hero Sid Johnson and his friends on their harrowing trek. Wonderfully rich in history, this is a tale not to be missed!"—Alan Orloff, Anthony and Agatha Award winning author of the YA thriller, *I Play One On TV*

"This book will raise important questions about our country's history while keeping the reader engaged with adventure and suspense"—BookTrib

"a finely-crafted and well-told story that includes an amazing amount of trail history, the diversity of people on the route, and dealing with Mother Nature in addition to the mystery of the stolen letter"— Leo E. Oliva, Santa Fe Trail Historian

"rich fodder for classroom discussion and historical analysis of the pioneer experience, with its requirement for kids to step up into new responsibilities. Libraries and readers seeking historical fiction that embraces intrigue, discovery, and growth will follow Sid's journey to California in *The Well-Intended Conspiracy* with avid interest, whether the book is chosen for its leisure read attraction or for its living history"—D. Donovan, Sr. Reviewer, Midwest Book Review

Sid Johnson
and
The Well-Intended Conspiracy

Frances Schoonmaker

The Sid Johnson Series
Book 2

AucTus Publishers

www.auctuspublisers.com

for Jon Dunlap
and his students who asked for a book
about following the
Santa Fe Trail and beyond to California

TABLE OF CONTENTS[1]

---

1. Chapter titles are all stops on the Santa Fe Trail starting at Council Grove in Kansas Territory. But they are not all of the stops. You can find an interactive trail map at https://www.santafetrail.org/interactive-trail-map/ to follow as you read. It has most of the stops mentioned in the book with information about the trail and links to even more information.

2. Pronounced ar-KAN-zuhs in Kansas Territory

Before: Council Grove, Kansas Territory, 1856

One day as the sun crossed the imaginary arch that marks high noon a wagon train crossed the Neosho River at Council Grove in Kansas Territory. It followed the ancient trading route of native people. Over 700 miles away, along the same trail, a mule-drawn teamster train reached the summit of Glorieta Pass, the southernmost point of the Sangre de Christo Mountains in New Mexico Territory. About 125 miles to the east of Council Grove, a Missouri River steamboat approached Westport Landing. It carried passengers and goods bound for the ancient trail. Meanwhile, a party of Kanza Indians neared Council Grove from the north, avoiding the trail.

The last wagon in the train crossing the Neosho River was driven by a boy nearly tall enough to be a man. The wagon held everything his family owned. It was part of the Stokes Company, one of the few immigrant trains to follow the Santa Fe Trail. They were headed to California.

The teamster train belonged to a trading company. Its wagons were loaded with fur, colorful wool blankets, and Spanish silver. On the way to Independence, Missouri, it would return with cargo to be sold in New Mexico Territory.

The steamboat carried passengers and cargo. As it docked, a boy dressed almost entirely in black shouldered a wooden frame that carried all his belongings. His pockets were empty. His money was stolen sometime after he boarded in St. Louis. He was bound for Santa Fe.

The Kanza were on their way home. Before the Europeans came with their treaties, the Kanza shared hunting grounds from the Mississippi River to the Great Plains with the Pawnee, Wichita, and Osage tribes. Now they were limited to a reservation only a fraction the size of the lands their fathers had known.

The Neosho River behind him, Sid Johnson slid from the wagon seat to take his place beside the lead yoke of oxen. Wind from the southwest dried the water that streamed from them, clearing dust kicked up by thirty wagons. He took a deep breath, savoring the sweet smell of prairie air.

The captain of the teamster train, Ramon Rios Hernandez, looked up at the sun. In another hour, he would give the order for his train to pull over for nooning and the day's only cooked meal. The tortilla with sliced onion and beans, eaten on the move shortly after dawn, was no more than a memory, leaving him with an empty space in his stomach.

The sun warmed Abraham Biermann's black clothing as his eyes swept the docks. No one was waiting to meet him. Resigning himself to another meal of beef jerky and hard tack from his provisions, he set out alone, following the busy trail to Council Grove. Hopefully, he'd meet wagons from his brothers' trading company on the way.

Hunger was no stranger to Ta Lezhé, who led the Kaw party. For two days the men had hunted for horses stolen by one of the bands of bushwhackers lurking in Kansas Territory. They couldn't afford to lose any more horses. Without horses, there would be no hunting. They needed horses to trade for food and supplies, too. Last year's corn crop had not yielded enough to see them through the winter. Ta Lezhé's people were starving. And wagons kept coming, some of them with settlers who helped themselves to Kaw land and their corn.

Before the Stokes Company left Council Grove, Sid Johnson ate a hearty dinner of prairie hen stew and dumplings.

He had never known real hunger. There was always plenty to share with the freedom seekers who stopped at his family's farm in Illinois, a station on the Underground Railroad.

Sid hadn't wanted to leave home and everything he had ever known. But being part of a wagon train was more exciting than anything he could have imagined. Still, he wished things had stayed the way they were before their stop on the Underground Railroad was compromised. The farm was no longer a safe place for freedom seekers, and the Johnsons had family in California. So, along with his parents, Benjamin and Sadie Johnson, his younger brother Jimmy, little sister Cora, and her cat Serena, Sid was headed west to Santa Fe in New Mexico Territory where the wagon train would pick up the southern route to California.

1.
Council Grove to Diamond Springs

Ma always said rumors spread like wildfire and can do about as much damage. So, Sid didn't pay much attention to the men talking in grave voices as he freed the oxen from their heavy yokes and turned them loose to graze.

Even though he grew up on a farm, Sid didn't know a thing about oxen when his family arrived at Westport Landing almost a month ago. He didn't expect to be responsible for them, either, but his father was elected captain of the wagon company. He enjoyed leading the team. It gave him something to do.

"Grace is havin' supper with us." Ma looked up from the campfire where a pot of beans simmered. It wasn't unusual for his friend Grace Willis to have supper with them, but the way Ma and Pa exchanged looks told him there was more to it.

Grace seemed hesitant. It wasn't like her. "All I know is Mr. Stokes said he needed a doctor's opinion. He asked Daddy to meet him at one of the wagons. Maybe there's been an accident."

There were whispers as children gathered at the Payne wagon for lessons after supper. Before the others could shush her, one of the little girls blurted out, "My big brother said somebody in one of the wagons has a terrible disease—."

"It could kill everybody in the whole wagon train!" a boy interrupted.

Everything stopped. It became so quiet Sid could hear the crickets take up their evening chorus.

"So that's what all the whispering is about." Mrs. Payne pushed back a tightly coiled wisp of black hair escaping from her lace-edged cap. "I imagine we're hearing a lot of things. But we don't have all the facts yet. It's better not to spread rumors. Rumors scare people. When people get scared, they don't do their best thinking."

Her guarded tone was not lost on Sid. He met Grace's gaze. She hadn't missed it either.

As he yoked their oxen the next morning uneasy talk among the men drifted his way. "The boy was coughing all night. My Missus went over to see if she could help." *What boy?* Sid wondered.

"Sounds like pneumonia."

"Anybody hear what Doc Willis says?"

"I heard the boy was burnin' up with fever. We shoulda left Council Grove sooner instead of waitin' around half the day—"

"Could be scarlet fever—"

"Or smallpox."

"Lord help us if it's smallpox. Might as well start digging graves."

"Thirteen days on the trail. It's an unlucky number. Like I said, we shoulda left—"

"Ben Johnson's over there now. We'll know soon."

There was no stopping the rumors now. Like a thread of swirling air, the word "smallpox" swept from wagon to wagon gathering momentum as it was repeated in anxious whispers. By the time Sid had the team hitched to the wagon, the rumor was like a dust devil twisting and spinning its way throughout the camp.

It was old news when Pa rode past to make sure wagons were ready for departure. Eyes were fixed on him as he looked toward Bill Stokes, Wagon Master, waiting where he wanted the first row of wagons to line up on the trail.

Mr. Stokes looked at his pocket watch, "Seven o'clock sharp." He nodded toward Pa.

Pa called, "First line, move out! Johnson wagon."

Sid gave the command, "Giddy up!"

Pa called the name of each wagon. When the company started out from Westport, wagons waited on the trail until they were nearly all in line. Now everybody knew what to do. As soon as Pa had the second row in position, Mr. Stokes stood in his stirrups, waved his hat, and called, "Wagons roll!" Teams fell in behind as the train moved along. As captain, Pa would bring up the rear on their horse, Sandy.

"You know why we've got four wagons in a row?"—Sid could hear Jimmy talking with his friend Matthew Payne— "Because Injuns is more scared of four wagons in a row. Three wagons don't scare 'em as bad."

"James Johnson!" Ma's voice was sharp. "What is that word I've told you not to use?"

"Indians," Jimmy corrected himself. "Indians is more scared."

"Indians are," Ma said. "If you had been listenin' to Mr. Stokes when we set out, you'd have your facts straight, young man."

"Baba says Indians aren't likely to bother us if we don't bother them." Matthew spoke with authority. His father was a retired army scout.

"How come you keep callin' him 'baba'?" Jimmy asked.

"It's African."

"You aren't African, you're American—"

"But *his* baba was. He came from Africa as a slave. Baba says the wagon train has to look bigger now. There's too many thieves and bandits in Kansas Territory."

"Thieves and bandits?" yelled Jimmy in mock disbelief. "Yoicks! I'm gettin' outa here." Pretending he was on horseback he galloped off to the side of the trail. Rolling his eyes, Matthew grinned and galloped after Jimmy, weaving his way between wagons.

"Mrs. Payne says Kansas Territory has been a magnet for thieves and rogues ever since the Kansas-Nebraska Bill was passed," said Grace, coming to walk with Sid beside Cornflower and Promise, the lead yoke of oxen. "Do you think she'll have lessons tonight if there's danger of smallpox?"

"I dunno," said Sid. He liked studying with Mrs. Payne, though now he didn't much care. He scowled up at the empty bird's egg-blue sky. *Where are clouds when you need 'em?* It was uncomfortably hot for late March. There was no protection from the sun. Trees, when they were to be seen at all, hugged the banks of the occasional creek that wound through the low, rolling hills.

Grace rattled on, "The Kansas-Nebraska Bill gives territories the right to decide if they want to be free or allow slavery."

Ordinarily, Sid liked talking with Grace as he led the team. Sometimes they played word games or talked about places they would see on the trail, like the famous Diamond Springs where they would be nooning. Or they speculated about how the prairie looked in ancient times. He slapped his neck. *Dratted mosquitos.* In all the stories he'd heard about the trail, nobody told him about mosquitoes.

"Mr. Stokes said thugs are coming into Kansas Territory

to influence elections. Then they blame the Indians for all their mischief."

"I know all about that." Sid slapped another mosquito bite.

"The mosquitos were really bad last night. Daddy says when the wind comes up mosquitoes aren't a problem."

"Well, the wind wasn't up last night, was it," Sid snapped. He felt as if he'd fought a battalion of mosquitos.

"You don't have to be so cross about it."

Sure, he was cross. He had a headache. He hadn't told Ma. *She wouldn't let me lead the team if she knew*. He had little to do except walk beside the oxen, anyway, and listen to Grace, except he wished she would just shut up for once.

"It's a glorious morning. Mr. Stokes says we're lucky to have warm weather. Sometimes it snows here in March. The sky looks like somebody turned a big blue bowl over us— where's your hat?"

Sid shrugged.

"Looks like you left it on the wagon seat. I'll get it for you."

Grace handed him the hat. Sid didn't even thank her. Turning on her heel, she walked away. He was just as glad.

By the time the train reached Diamond Springs, his head was throbbing. All Sid could think about was the cool shade cast by the deserted station house and its buildings. He hoped there really was cold water bubbling up from the springs like people said.

Unfortunately, the shade was taken by a teamster train. The Stokes Company would be nooning in the sun. Diamond Springs wasn't overrated, though. Water gushed from a hollow in the prairie, running over stones before it poured into Otter Creek. Sid longed to throw himself down by the water the minute he unhitched the oxen. But Mr. Stokes called an emergency meeting of the men while the women prepared dinner. Since he led the Johnson team, Sid had to attend.

"One of our families has smallpox," Mr. Stokes said. "We need to stay calm. If anyone starts running a fever, tell me. Doc will see 'em. If Doc is tied up, Miz Johnson will have a look"—Ma didn't have any formal medical schooling, but back home she had done everything from setting broken arms to delivering babies—"if a wagon has to drop out because of the pox, a couple of volunteers will stay with 'em till they're settled off the trail with plenty of supplies and their wagon is marked."

"Don't seem right, leaving them behind," someone spoke up, his voice rising above worried talk around them.

"It's because smallpox spreads so fast. We wrote it in our company bylaws. Doc Willis will tell the family how to take care of each other. Once folk are well, they can join up with another group. Won't be a day pass without traffic goin' both ways."

"And if they don't get well?" called another voice.

Mr. Stokes said no matter what happened, there was a plan for dealing with it. "I was hopin' to make Lost Creek tonight"—they usually covered 12 to 15 miles a day—"but if the grass is good the other side of Six Mile Creek, we may stop earlier so we can take stock of our situation."

"How are people reactin'?" Ma asked when they returned to the wagon.

Pa's face looked worn and drawn. "People are scared."

"I should think! Let's just hope they act sensibly."

Sid didn't hear the rest. He crawled into the wagon and fell asleep without stopping to eat.

Later, Pa looked in. "You all right, Son? Your ma says you forgot your hat this morning. Too much sun can be hard on a fellow. I'll see to watering and hitching up the team."

The wagon was moving when he awoke from a fitful sleep.

"Mrs. Johnson, I can't find Sid anywhere." It was Grace.

"He's just that tired. He fell asleep when we stopped for noonin'. Hasn't been awake since."

"Tell him I hope he feels better. Come on Jimmy. Cora, get your bonnet. We're going to catch grasshoppers. We're meeting Matthew and Lydia over at their wagon. Mr. Payne made a cage for them."

Jimmy snickered. "A cage for Matthew and Lydia?"

"No, silly boy," said Grace, "for the grasshoppers."

"Silly boy! For grasshoppers." Cora's shrill laughter went straight to Sid's pounding head.

It's too hot . . . He faded into sleep again.

How long he slept, Sid couldn't have said. He didn't know when the train stopped or that Pa talked to Dr. Willis in worried tones. He wasn't aware of thrashing about all night. He was only vaguely aware when Ma discovered red spots on his tongue, face, and arms the next morning. When it was time for wagons to roll, they stayed behind. Someone took Pa's place as captain. The word "smallpox" was posted on the side of the wagon. Doc Willis and Jim Payne stayed behind to help them get settled.

Mr. Payne insisted they follow the trail until they could find a better location. "You can't count on the water at Six Mile Crossin'. Too many animals contaminatin' it." He led the oxen to a low hill overlooking a small creek that ran parallel to the Santa Fe Trail before bending back on itself. "This looks like a good spot, Johnson. You're well on the way to Lost Spring, near a good water supply, and close enough to the trail to join up with another company when the boy's well."

None of this registered with Sid. He didn't think about anything, not for a long time.

The first thing he noticed when he awoke was voices.

That was before he moved; before he decided if he wanted to move. He felt like he was in flames all over. His parched throat burned like fire. But he couldn't make himself swallow when Ma tried to give him something to drink; it hurt too much. Saliva dribbled out of his mouth, wetting his face. His head felt like it would split apart. He didn't want to feel anymore. He wanted to go to sleep and never, ever wake up again.

"I'm not getting a pulse." Sid could feel the doctor's hand on his wrist, then on the side of his neck. "I don't think he's going to make it. I'm so sorry."

Later, the only way Sid could explain what happened was to say it felt like he was a cork popping out of a bottle. For a few short moments, he seemed to float above everything. He could see himself lying on a bed under a canvas shelter next to his family's covered wagon. He didn't burn and itch anymore. Ma and Pa knelt beside him along with Dr. Willis and Mr. Payne.

Dr. Willis looked at Ma and Pa and shook his head. The doctor took his hands and folded them across his chest. Tears washed down Ma's face. "No, no—"

"He's gone, Sadie." There was a catch in Pa's voice. "We can't help him now."

Why were they all so sad?

Dr. Willis covered him with a cloth. "You'll need to quarantine another couple of weeks before you can travel, Ben. We won't leave until we've helped you bury Sid."

But I'm not dead. Am I?

Later—he wasn't sure how much later—he was aware of being inside himself again, of every searing, burning breath, of blistering pain. Everywhere. *Thirsty. So thirsty.* He couldn't get the words out.

He could hear everything around him. Ma sobbing. Pa

talking to Dr. Willis and Jim Payne. "You'd best get on back to the wagon train. You're needed there. I can dig my boy's grave—"

I don't need a grave.

"—He was my first son. I have to . . . I *need* to do this for him." Pa's voice caught again. "If Cora and Jimmy come down with it, we know what to do. Sadie had the pox when she was a girl. I was vaccinated a long time ago. Besides, I've never been sick a day in my life. We'll be fine."

"God bless you, Doc Willis," Ma sobbed. "I know you did everything you could. I don't know how we can stand it. It feels like our whole world is fallin' apart."

I'm here, Ma. I'm not dead. Sid wanted more than anything to say it. Yet, he couldn't.

"You aren't by yourself, Mrs. Johnson," Mr. Payne spoke gently. "The Good Lord is with you. Sid was a fine boy. If it hadn't been for Sid, our Matthew and Lydia woulda been sold into slavery"—Sid tried to make sense of what they were saying. He was too feverish to remember a run-in with bounty hunters back in Council Grove—"I'd be in chains, too, if it weren't for him. You're gonna miss Sid somethin' awful, but you have two fine children who need you. You'll get through this because you have to."

"I'd like to read something from the Good Book before we go." Dr. Willis began, "The Lord is my shepherd—"

"I shall not want," Mr. Payne joined in.

The next time Sid awoke, Ma was saying, "Oh Ben, can't we wait until mornin' to bury him? I can't bear the thought of it."

"There, there, Sadie. It can wait till evening. It's too hot out here anyway. Awfully hot for this time of year."

The last thing Sid heard was Ma's worried voice. "Why Ben Johnson, you're burnin' up with fever!"

2.

Near Six-Mile Creek

Galloping. The whinny of horses. Strange voices. Someone dismounting—was he awake or dreaming? He must be awake. Nobody could hurt so much in a dream. Sid scrunched his eyes more tightly shut. Even the light hurt.

A man spoke. "We saw the pox sign on your wagon, Ma'am. We're out of Fort Riley. I'm Sergeant Jacob Peters. Anything we can do?"

A soldier's voice stood out. "Diggin' graves is no job for a woman."

Sid wanted to tell them he didn't need a grave, but he couldn't get the words out. It was hard to breathe with the cloth over his face. He grabbed at it, but he couldn't seem to pull it off.

The next thing he knew a man knelt beside him. "This boy isn't dead. He's all tangled up in the bedclothes." Big hands eased him up slightly and began spooning something fiery hot into his mouth. He sputtered and coughed.

"Quickly, give him some water," the voice urged. "The whiskey will help him get it down. Sometimes the pox hurts so bad people will die of thirst rather than swallow."

"Oh, Sid!" Ma gently put a cup of water to his lips. "It's like a miracle, Dr. Adams. There wasn't any life in him."

"Sometimes it's nearly impossible to tell," said Dr. Adams, "The boy's in a coma. Just thank the Good Lord he's alive. He's running a high fever. Got to get him cooled down."

All kinds of fuss went on around him: men talking in the background; cool, wet cloth on his forehead; more whiskey and water; more coughing; more painful swallowing. What was real and what was a dream? He wasn't sure. Did Pa have smallpox, too?

Sid wasn't aware of falling asleep again, only of waking. It was dark. Stars were so close it felt like he'd bump his head against them if he sat up. He tried to remember why he hurt all over. Why wasn't he in his own bed upstairs? *Thirsty, so thirsty.* He'd been about to get a drink from the big dipper hanging by the water pail in the kitchen when something Ma said brought him to a halt. "God bless her, I hope she made it to safety." Pa said war was coming. It had something to do with why he was sleeping on the ground in a place he'd never been before.

Another time he thought the barn was burning. He had to tell Pa the barn was on fire. *I'm on fire!* He began slapping the flames, trying to put them out.

"I know it must itch somethin' awful, Sid, but you can't be scratchin' the sore spots." It was Ma. "Here, Private Turner made us some prairie hen soup"—who was Private Turner?—"he's gonna help you sit up."

He was pretty sure he was awake. Every spot on his body was covered with blisters. They were even on the palms of his hands and the bottom of his feet.

"We'll be headin' out with first light, Miz Johnson," said Sergeant Peters. Soldiers sat around the campfire. "Looks like Mr. Johnson should be up and about in a few days. It will take the boy longer.

"There's a Kanza village across creek. Be a good idea to steer clear of it. They've been hit hard by the pox. Couple of years ago 400 Kanza died on the Council Grove Reservation. It's flared up again. Can't seem to stamp it out. They don't have any natural immunity."

"I sure appreciate all your help, especially gettin' our Cora and Jimmy vaccinated."

"We set up a picket line for the horse," said Sergeant Peters. "She'll have more room to graze than on the tether. The milk cow and oxen aren't so temptin' to thieves. They won't wander far."

Dr. Adams spoke up, "You don't remember me, Mrs. Johnson, but I'd know you and Mr. Johnson anywhere. I was known as Hezekiah when we met."

"Hezekiah?"

"It was near twelve years ago. My Sissy and I were on our way to our people in Chicago. Couldn't have made it without you. Men were pounding on your door, dogs baying. I thought we were goners."

"Well I declare!" said Ma.

"Mr. Johnson took us to a place in Alton. He was stopped twice. We were near scared to death. Thought they'd pull the wagon apart before it was over. If it hadn't been for the Underground Railroad, we'd still be in Kentucky picking cotton."

"And you a doctor now. What about your sister?"

"Sissy's up in Toronto, married. Has two little ones about the age of your two youngsters. I apprenticed to a doctor in Chicago and joined the army when he did."

"I remember now," said Ma. "I don't think I've ever been so scared—two little children separated from your parents. We heard they sent the best slave tracker in Kentucky after you."

"Back then, free states could protect us," said Dr. Adams.

"And you took the name Adams?"

"Sissy and I decided to take the family name of the only two presidents of the United States who haven't owned slaves: John Adams and John Quincey Adams. I'm right sorry to know you left Illinois, to tell the truth. The Underground Railroad along that stretch has helped a lot of people."

"It wasn't an easy decision. Bounty hunters burned our barn. We were compromised as a stop on the Railroad. We have family in California. So, we decided to go west."

"Lot of folk up north don't hold with slavery," said one of the soldiers, "but they don't hold with us either. They're afraid we'll mingle too much and contaminate the white race."

"I wish I could say otherwise," said Ma. "I've seen some things nobody ought to have to see. I expect you've seen far worse. But you're right. Mr. Johnson would say it explains the Compromise of 1850."

"You mean the 'Bloodhound Bill?'" said Sergeant Peters. "Gives slaveholders the right to set their dogs on people in free states."

Ma sighed. "Some folk seem to think the good Lord made a mistake when he created us in different colors."

"I beg to differ, Ma'am," said Sergeant Peters. "Some folks think the Lord created black folk to serve the rest of us. I'm headin' a party of five soldiers, all volunteers. Look at us—three of us black as the night. Why do you think they sent us out from Fort Riley to deal with smallpox along the trail? Fact of the matter is, there are officers in high places at Riley who own slaves."

"I can't argue with you," said Ma. "All I can do is tell you how grateful we are for your help. You've saved my son."

Sid didn't stay awake for the rest of the discussion. He couldn't even appreciate the meaning of it until much later.

*****

He awoke with a start. Jimmy sat staring at him from

behind the "do not cross" line Ma had drawn around his bed.

"Who's Essie Ban and how come she's cross with you?"

"What?"

"You been sayin' Essie Ban's cross. Over and over. You look like somebody painted you with polka dots."

"He's gonna have a lot more dots in the next day or two," said Ma. "All those blisters and sores will be formin' scabs. That means they're healin'. And it means you could get the pox if you're near them, even if Dr. Adams did vaccinate you."

"Serena wants to see Sid," said Cora, holding on to a short-haired gray tabby cat.

"Cats don't get smallpox. But she doesn't need to be rubbin' her fur up against him. She could spread it to you."

Sid was awake more every day. But he didn't feel any better. The itching was more severe as his blisters began to form scabs. Ma said once scabs fell off, he could travel. "Your Pa's gonna be up any day now."

"Come on you two," Ma called. "Jimmy, you can lead Sandy. Run get her. Here, Cora, you carry a bucket. We're goin' to the creek for some water, Sid."

There had been days when the Stokes Company traveled all day without finding fresh water. They could have been stuck in one of those dry places, having to depend on water from their water barrel while it lasted. There was plenty of grass, too. They were in tall grass country, the Flint Hills of Kansas Territory.

Sometimes they returned from the creek with stories of Osage and Kiowa people passing at a distance. Once they told him about seeing a whole company of Indians—men, women, and children—passing by on the other side of the creek. It looked like they were moving an entire village.

Sid watched as they left. What had Jimmy meant? He

didn't know anybody named Essie Ban.

Suddenly it hit him. *Esteban's Cross*. It was a code name. Like something he'd dreamed.

It wasn't a dream, though. They had been on the steamboat *Loulabelle*, traveling from Alton, Illinois to Westport Landing in Missouri to meet up with the Stokes Company when he first met William Gallagher. He had seemed like a nice man so, when he asked, Sid couldn't see any harm in taking a letter to Mrs. Gallagher in Santa Fe. That is, until he had overheard two men threatening to kill Mr. Gallagher. They wanted the letter.

He had forgotten about it. But Mr. Gallagher found him in Council Grove. "I wasn't entirely forthcoming," he had confessed. "If it were an ordinary letter, I could send it by post. But the letter contains important history about my wife's family." He said the men who had threatened him, Bayless Sly and J. J. Gordon, were after it because they imagined the letter held the secret to a vast treasure. "That's why I asked you to deliver it. The letter is more precious to my wife than gold." Mr. Gallagher promised he would come for it or send someone for it if there was any reason to think the letter put the Johnsons in danger.

If someone else came for the letter, they were to say, Esteban's Cross. *That's what I was sayin'*. Not Essie Ban, but Esteban's Cross. The letter was still in his box of toy soldiers where he had hidden it. He was too tired to think about it. He watched a hawk lazily circling overhead as he drifted off into sleep.

*****

"I see you're awake, Sid. Pa's been out huntin' along the creek since before dawn." Ma bent over the fire, adding rice and some greens to a pot.

Sid was in less pain now that his blisters had begun to dry. But he still itched like fury.

"Jimmy said he's gettin' tired of prairie hen soup, but—now where have those two little mischiefs gone off to?" She looked out toward where their milk cow, Buttercup, and the team of oxen were grazing.

Sandy was on her picket line closer to the wagon. She raised her head abruptly, ears forward.

"She's watchin' somethin' down by the creek." Ma frowned. "Don't tell me Jimmy and Cora slipped down there when I wasn't lookin'. I expressly told them . . ."

Sandy's ears twitched back and forth. She was either trying to hear something or troubled by what she heard. So was Ma.

A ear-splitting cry rang out from the creek sending the oxen and Buttercup on the run. Sandy strained at the picket line. "Dear God, what can it be?" Ma grabbed Sid's gun.

Jimmy came tearing up the gentle slope from the creek as fast as he could run, screaming like a banshee. Close on his heels was a Kanza Indian carrying Cora under one arm and holding a bow.

Before he reached their camp, the man set Cora down. In one smooth movement, he turned around, put an arrow to his bow, and let it fly.

Screaming, Cora ran to Ma.

Jimmy tried to say something. He was so out of breath it was impossible to understand him.

Ma didn't stop to comfort them. "Get her in the wagon, Jimmy. Both of you, *stay there*!" An enormous wolf came bounding up the hill, teeth bared.

The arrow had found its mark, but the wolf came on, leaping straight at the man.

A second arrow flew as the man twisted to one side,

escaping the snarling jaws by a hair's breadth.

With a thunderous growl, the wolf whirled around facing him again.

The man jumped back as he released another arrow. It caught the wolf midair, bringing it to the ground.

The wolf twitched and lay still.

Ma lowered the gun. Cora began crying hysterically.

The man's eyes swept over them. He went straight for Sandy. He was on her back before they realized what he was doing.

"Sandy!" cried Ma. "Oh, no! Sid, he's taken our Sandy. What am I gonna tell your Pa?" she stifled a half sob. "I should be grateful. He saved the children and we've still got the team."

But they didn't have the team or Buttercup. The livestock would be across the trail by now, running blindly.

"I reckon Buttercup will come back when it's milkin' time," said Ma. Shoulders sagging, she put the gun back in its place.

"What did that Injun go and steal our Sandy for?" asked Jimmy, still standing on the wagon seat. Cora danced up and down, arms in the air, crying and begging to be held.

Ma put her hand to her forehead, shaking her head. "Indian, not Injun. I don't know, Jimmy"—she reached for Cora—"maybe he needed her more than we do. But it couldn't have happened at a worse time."

Suddenly Jimmy began jumping up and down on the wagon seat again, yelling, "Here he comes. Look! Here he comes."

Sure enough, the man was riding around the livestock, directing their stampede into a circle, gradually moving them over the brink of the hill and back toward camp. When the livestock began slowing down, he herded them closer to the wagon, but well away from the wolf. He dismounted, picketed Sandy, and approached the wagon, stopping several feet away.

Jimmy, still jumping up and down in excitement, tried to say something. "Wait Jimmy." Ma pointed to the smallpox sign on their wagon.

"*Ami*," the man said, raising his hand, palm out toward them, middle and index finger together. Sid didn't know a great deal of American Indian sign language, but Mr. Payne had taught signs to some of the children in the Stokes Company. "He's saying 'friend.'" He croaked more than said it. It was still hard to talk.

The man held out a bare arm, pointing to a line of deep smallpox scars along his arm, across his chest, and on his face. Then he crossed his hands on his chest. Fingers spread, thumbs up, he moved his hands back and forth across his chest.

"Means sick," said Sid.

"Yes, I can see he's had smallpox." Ma made the sign of friend, pointing to him and to herself. "I hope I'm sayin' the right thing." She put Cora back in the wagon.

The man signed something that looked like rabbit ears and moved his hand up. This was followed by hands on the chest again and the up and down movement.

"Lordy, I don't know what he's sayin', but he's tryin' to help us," said Ma. "I wish your Pa was back. A rabbit hoppin'? The wolf was after a rabbit?"

Jimmy yelled, "Wolf! The wolf chased Serena up a tree on the other side of the creek. She was growling and hissing at him—"

"And she was all fluffed up," Cora shrieked, "and that bad wolf was jumpin' at her and he had soap bubbles in his mouth."

"Wait children," said Ma. She made the rabbit ears sign and

pointed toward the dead wolf.

The man made a hook with his index finger and brought it down. "Yes, he says 'yes,'" said Sid.

Pointing to himself, the man lifted his hand up almost even with his eyes, palm side down, pointing his middle and index fingers out. "See!" yelled Jimmy.

Then with thumb and index finger together, the man moved his hand up.

"Little," said Sid. He wished he knew more words. It was like charades with them trying to guess what the man was signing.

But Jimmy had more to say. "He saw the wolf, he saw the wolf! The wolf couldn't get Serena. I said to run. But Cora wanted Serena to come. Then he yelled at us."

Sid wasn't surprised. Cora had gone to great lengths to smuggle the cat aboard the steamboat *Loulabelle* when they left for Westport Landing and the Santa Fe Trail. She'd be too worried about Serena to realize her own danger.

Cora burst into tears again, holding out her arms to Ma.

"I need you to stay in the wagon with Jimmy," said Ma.

"She'll come home," said Jimmy, confidently, patting his sister on the shoulders. Cora threw her arms around him and sobbed. Jimmy, uncharacteristically, put his arms around her and held her.

The man stood there, brow furrowed. He made the sign for wolf again. Then he pointed to the wolf and made the same sign he'd made before, moving his hands on his chest, followed by the wolf sign.

"Wolf was sick," said Sid.

"Let me have a look at that wolf," said Ma.

"The wolf was slobberin'," said Jimmy, still holding Cora, "like he had soap in his mouth."

"Soap bubbles"—Ma looked at Sid, eyes widening—

"hydrophobia. And your Pa somewhere out along the creek! Sid, can you tell the man I'm goina look at the wolf?"

Sid pointed to Ma, quickly making the sign for see and for wolf.

"Stay in that wagon, Jimmy, and keep Cora there," said Ma. "If either of you take one step out until I say so, I'll have your hides"—it wasn't like her to threaten that way—"He's dead," she called. "Three arrows straight through him. It's hydrophobia. No doubt about it. Poor thing. He must have been in such pain."

The man stood back watching. He made a clenched fist, opening it quickly and moving it upward, then the sign of the wolf.

"Fire," said Jimmy. "Mr. Indian wants you to burn the wolf."

Ma nodded. "He's right. We have to burn the body to keep the sickness from spreadin'."

The sound of bells, cracking whips, and calls in Spanish signaled the approach of a teamster wagon from the west. Two of the teamsters rode over astride mules, stopping well short of the wagon as their train went on. "All is well, Señora?" called one of the men. "Name is Ramon Rios Hernandez"—he nodded to his companion—is "Luis Marie Diaz. Need help?"

Ma pointed to the smallpox sign on the wagon. Señor Hernandez nodded, eyeing the wolf. They moved closer, stopping a safe distance away.

"This man just saved my children from a mad wolf."

The teamsters dismounted and came closer, staying clear of the wagon. Señor Hernandez began making signs to the man, who signed back. Then Luis Marie Diaz began speaking rapidly to him in another language. Sid hadn't begun to study French at school, but he was pretty sure it was French.

But how come the Indian man was speaking French and not English? He wished he could ask Mrs. Payne. She would know.

"English is not so good, Señora," said Señor Hernandez. "Señor Diaz no speak English."

"Your English is good enough," said Ma. "I'm afraid I don't know any Spanish."

The two teamsters conferred rapidly in Spanish. "These man is Kanza," said Señor Hernandez, "Name Ta Lezhé."

There had been an outbreak of smallpox among his people. They were starving. Men who had survived the pox were too weak to hunt. "Ta Lezhé is hunt, he see los niños. Los niños see lobo"—he paused momentarily—"wolf, see wolf. Niña no leave el gato."

Ta Lezhé saw Serena narrowly escape the rabid wolf on the other side of the creek, knowing it would be a matter of seconds before it turned on the children. The shallow creek between them would be no deterrent. But the wolf was too far away for him to get a good shot. He cried out, trying to scare the children into running back to the wagon. If they ran, the wolf would attack, giving him a clear shot well before it could reach them. But Cora froze in her tracks.

Ma nodded gravely. "Please thank him for savin' my children. Tell him we're the Johnson family on our way to California. My eldest son is still sick. My husband is out huntin', too. And thank him for savin' our livestock."

Turning to Señor Diaz, he spoke rapidly.

Señor Diaz spoke to Ta Lezhé, and made a fist, palm up, opening it quickly.

"Fire," said Sid.

"We help," said Señor Hernandez. The men left for the creek to find wood.

"Serena!" Cora reached out her arms to Ma.

"I wanna go. I can help!" Abandoning his role as comforter, Jimmy jumped from the wagon.

"Don't you set one foot closer to that wolf, Jimmy! You can help by feedin' the fire under the stew. The men will be hungry." Ma lifted Cora down from the wagon. "Serena will come back. She knows where her home is."

The men returned from the creek carrying armloads of wood. Pa was with them, a wild turkey in one hand and an armful of wood in the other.

"I was headed back along the creek when I saw the men." He handed the turkey to Ma and set to work helping build a pyre around and over the wolf. Mr. Diaz began circling the pyre, emptying a bucket of water around it.

"He's doin' that to keep it from spreadin'," Jimmy called. "Can I help now, Ma, please?"

"No, Jimmy. We'd best stay outa the way. The men know what they're doin'."

He remembers what we did to keep the fire from spreadin' when bounty hunters burned our barn. Sid wished he could help, too.

Pa took coals from the campfire and started a blaze. Once the fire was going, Ma called, "Ben, come get somethin' to eat and bring Ta Lezhé."

"Si," said Señor Hernandez, nodding. "Ta Lezhé hungry."

"I would offer you and Mr. Diaz some food, but the pox—"

"Is nothing, Señora. We have food. We watch fire."

Squatting down next to Pa, Ta Lezhé put his hand out, palm up. "Means 'give,'" said Jimmy, squatting down on the other side of Pa. Cora stayed behind Ma's skirt, looking out.

Ma gave them each a bowl of soup, serving Ta Lezhé first. "Here Cora, you give them some cornbread." She handed Cora a plate heaped with hot cornbread. "Serve Mr.

Ta Lezhé first."

Cora stood frozen, holding the cornbread. Ta Lezhé looked at the cornbread, then at Cora. Sid noticed how his eyes seemed to soften as he looked at Cora.

Pa nodded to her. She stepped forward, holding out the plate. Ta Lezhé took a piece, smelled it, and took a bite. He seemed to approve.

While the men were eating, Ma tied up little bags of sugar and of roasted, ground coffee. Ta Lezhé had another bowl of soup, more cornbread, and a cup of coffee. "This man is really hungry," said Ma. "I'm gettin' him some food to take with him."

When Ta Lezhé finished, he pointed to Ma and Pa. "Johnson," he said, and made the sign for friend. Ma and Pa both held up two fingers to say friend, too. So did Jimmy and Cora.

Ta Lezhé held his open palm vertically, thumb up and moved it out from his body. "He's goin' now," said Jimmy. "That means he's goin'."

Ta Lezhé slung his bow across his back. He left carrying dried beans, cornmeal, sugar, coffee and the wild turkey.

"Bye-bye!" called Cora, waving to him as he walked away. "Thank you, Mr. Ta."

"Thank you, Mr. Ta Lezhé," called Jimmy.

Ta Lezhé turned back. Putting down the large sack Ma had given him, he waved, spoke to Mr. Diaz, and went on his way.

"Well I never!" said Ma. "I thought the worst when he started off with Sandy. Shame on me. I wish we could have given him more food."

"Small game in this whole area is over-hunted," said Pa. "His people must be suffering."

"I can't help thinkin' how people complained about the

Kanza beggin' for food," said Ma. "God help us. All we've done is bring them disease and sufferin'.""

"Huh?" Jimmy looked puzzled. "We just gave 'em a whole big sack of food."

"Your Ma is talking about something bigger, Jimmy. It has to do with the United States Government and how we have taken so much Indian land they can't take care of themselves."

"Then why don't we give it back?"

"It's not that simple, Son. I can vote and tell my elected representatives what I think is right. We can speak up when we see something that's wrong. And we can do small things, like share our food.

"But right now, I need to know about Serena. Did the wolf bite her?"

"No. She saw him first and ran up the tree."

"Are you absolutely sure?"

"The wolf was chasin' her, and snappin' his big teeth," said Cora, wide-eyed.

"I tried to tell her wolves don't climb trees," said Jimmy.

Pa talked with Señor Hernandez, who said Ta Lezhé was sure the wolf didn't bite Serena. They looked for other tracks when they were collecting wood at the creek, but there was only one wolf. Pa hadn't seen any tracks along the creek until he reached the men, either.

"I can watch the fire now," said Pa. "You men best be getting back to your train. I can't tell you how much we appreciate your help."

"Thank you so much for your kindness," said Ma, "I was tryin' so hard to understand before you stopped to help."

"La mamá say, no repay kindness. Give kindness," said Señor Hernandez. A broad smile stretched across his face.

"Your mama is wise," said Ma. "You can't repay kindness.

All you can do is pass it on."

"Where'd the teamster train go?" said Jimmy as the teamsters left.

"They'll be at Diamond Springs," said Pa. "Those men gave up their chance to get some rest and a good meal to help us."

Sid slid back down into his bed, kicking back the blanket Ma kept trying to put over him. He couldn't stand being under it, even at night when it got really cold. *Useless. I'm completely useless.* If he had died, they'd be on the way to California. They'd be better off without him. He wished they'd never set out for California. If the barn hadn't burned, they'd still be at home helping freedom seekers, not sitting on some lonely, wind-swept hill waiting for another disaster.

3.

TO LOST SPRING

Dust rose on the eastern horizon late one morning. Teamster train traffic on the trail was constant, though immigrant trains going west usually took the Oregon, California, or Mormon Trails. Sometimes immigrants paid to travel as far as Santa Fe with a teamster train. It wasn't unusual to see a single wagon or groups of two or three immigrant wagons, but Pa wanted to join a company.

Now that Sid could travel, Pa yoked the oxen every day and walked them around. He was restless to be off. He wanted the team to be ready.

"It's a wagon train!" Jimmy was the first to identify the approaching wagons as an immigrant train. "You shoulda seen that teamster train goin' east, this mornin', Sid. There musta been a hundred wagons! Betcha there's 50 wagons in this one."

Feeling for his hat, Sid crawled out from under the wagon where he had fallen asleep. "I'll take your word for it, Jimmy." Though he was strong enough to help with chores, he was not ready to jump up and count wagons every time a teamster train passed.

"Well, boys," Pa said, as they watched the wagons approach, "if we don't find a company soon, I'm a mind to set out on our own and find one along the way even if we have to go as far as the Arkansas River."

"How come it's the Ar-*kansas* River and not the Arkan-*saw* River?" Jimmy asked.

"I dunno, Jimmy," Sid said, attempting to make a joke, "maybe people in Kansas Territory don't want to see what Arkan-*saw*."

Pa was too preoccupied to appreciate a joke, even a bad one. "If we wait much longer, we won't get to Santa Fe until late spring. Crossing that desert to California is no picnic from what I hear. I'd rather sit the summer out in Santa Fe than tackle the desert in July."

As the wagon train came nearer, they could see it was an organized company. Wagons stretched out five abreast.

"I hope they're good people," said Ma.

A couple of men on horseback rode out ahead of the train. "Reckon they'll be checking us out, maybe offering to help." said Pa. "I take that as a good sign."

"People have been awful good," said Ma. "While you and Sid were gettin' through the worst of it, not a day went by without somebody callin' out to see if we needed help."

The men dismounted well away from the wagon. A tall, wiry man approached, tipping his hat to Ma. "Names Jeremiah Davies. This is Cornelius Ryckman. We're with the Wood Company. You folk the Johnsons?"

Pa nodded.

"Our Wagon Master, Isaiah Wood, met some soldiers out from Fort Riley over in Council Grove before we set out. They said to look out for you folk, thought you might be ready to join up with a company."

"Anything we can do to help?" Cornelius Ryckman tipped his hat to Ma. He was an imposing figure, taller than Pa, slightly roundish in the middle. Straw-colored hair stuck out from under his hat. Sid could tell from the way he sat in the saddle as the men rode up that he was a skillful horseman.

His bright blue eyes seemed to be filled with good humor.

Pa introduced the family. "We're ready to get back on the trail."

"If you've no objection, Mr. Johnson, I'd like to have a look at the boy," said Mr. Ryckman. "If his scabs have fallen off, you're welcome to fall in. I have to tell you, though, Isaiah Wood runs a tight company. If you have a problem following our company covenant, it won't be the right place for you."

"What Ryckman is getting at is lots of folk going West just want to *go*," said Mr. Davies. "They don't want a wagon master and an organized company. No hard feelings if you don't fall in with us."

"Well," said Pa thoughtfully. "I reckon it depends on what you mean by organization. We were with the Stokes Company. Bill Stokes ran a tight ship, but it was fair."

Mr. Ryckman winked at Cora. "I hear your brother had more spots than a ladybug. Think he could show an old fellow like me what they look like? Wait a minute! That's a very nice nose you have, young lady. I could use one like it." Before she could protest, he stooped down, slipped the first two fingers of his hand over her nose, and gently pulled. His thumb was peeking out as he pulled his hand away. "Best nose I've seen lately. Wonder if it fits me." He acted as if he were trying to put it on. "Ah, shoot! Doesn't suit me at all. Guess I should give it back." Wide-eyed and uncertain, Cora stood frozen in place.

"I know that ole trick," said Jimmy.

"You do? Ah shoot! Guess I'm found out." He showed Cora his thumb. "Let's have a look at your big brother.

"Could you show me your arms, Sid?" Mr. Rickman wanted to see his stomach and back, too. "Looks like that Negro doctor was right. You've had a bad case. You're good to travel. Some Negros are right good at doctoring. Comes natural"— Ma flinched but Mr. Ryckman didn't seem to notice—"I've got a boy about your age. Named Cornelius after me. We call him Connie. I expect you'll meet him. There's a group of boys. You won't want for friends."

Sid couldn't help liking Mr. Ryckman. But he didn't like the disdainful way he talked about the soldiers who had been so kind to them.

"What about his bedding, Ma'am?" asked Mr. Davies. "You're need to burn it before you move on."

"Yessir. We've already done that. *Doctor* Amos of the scoutin' party told us to burn all the bedclothes and the clothes Mr. Johnson and Sid were wearin' once the scabs fell off." Sid didn't miss the way Ma said "Doctor."

"We're stopping for nooning directly," Mr. Davies nodded toward the passing wagons. "Ride over with us Mr. Johnson. You can have a word with Isaiah Wood, our Wagon Master. The boy's fine, Ryckman?"

Mr. Ryckman nodded, turning to Ma, "You tell this pretty little girl of yours to take care of that nose. Wouldn't want her to lose it."

Jimmy, who was busy showing Cora how to do the trick, laughed outright.

The men waited on horseback while Pa saddled Sandy. "I don't know, Sadie," he said quietly. "It could be a good thing. I don't like the attitude Ryckman has about the soldiers. I know we aren't gonna get away from people with wrong ideas, but still—"

"No, Ben. Not everybody in the Stokes Company welcomed the Payne family. Some of 'em wouldn't let their children sit with Mrs. Payne for lessons on account of her being black. And her bein' a highly educated schoolteacher. But we won't be able to find the perfect company this side of heaven."

Pa swung into the saddle. "Sid, you and Jimmy get the oxen yoked and hitched to the wagon. We'll be ready if we decide to go."

"Wow! They gotta bunch of horses." Jimmy pointed to the rear of the wagon train. Sid judged there must be at least 15 and some cattle.

While Jimmy was trying to count horses, Sid looked under the wagon seat. His box of toy soldiers was still there. He didn't play with them anymore, but they were precious to him. His grandfather had made them. The only other toy he brought with him was a bag of marbles. His slingshot didn't count as a toy.

Underneath the wooden soldiers was the letter he had secretly promised to deliver for Mr. Gallagher. *Wonder if it really is the key to some treasure?* It was tempting to break the seal and have a look. He put it back. It wouldn't be right.

Pa returned from the wagon train smiling. "I think Isaiah Wood is cut out of the same cloth as Bill Stokes. I like him. Jimmy, could you get Buttercup tethered behind? And Cora, better get Serena into her basket."

When Jimmy and Cora were busy, Paw lowered his voice, "The Payne wagon is part of the Wood Company. I talked with Mrs. Payne."

Sid knew it had to be bad news when he saw Pa's furrowed brow. He had no idea how bad.

"The Willis wagon had to pull out of the Stokes Company. Mrs. Willis came down with the pox and died."

Ma gasped. "You don't mean it!"

"Jim Payne and Doc Willis stayed back to help them get settled like they did for us. Hiram Swathmore murdered them. Poor Mrs. Willis saw the whole thing. They left her to die."

"Lord, have mercy!" Ma cried. "I never trusted Mr. Swathmore, but I didn't think him this bad."

Pa shook his head. "The Swathmores took the Willis wagon and Grace with it. Disappeared somewhere to the south, probably Oklahoma Territory. All Doc's medical books and supplies dumped on the ground. A scout of some kind—a Mr. Bright I think Mrs. Payne said—found Mrs. Willis and their dog before she died."

Grace kidnapped? Her parents dead? And Mr. Payne? Sid felt like he was taking one hard punch after another as he struggled to comprehend what Pa was saying.

"Bright promised he'd find Grace and take her to her grandparents in St. Louis. He caught up with the Stokes Company. Mrs. Payne and the children went back with him to see the graves and pay their last respects. She decided to make room in her wagon for Doc's medical things and find a wagon train that would take her west. Bright took her back to Council Grove and introduced her to Isaiah Wood.

"You've got to take your hat off to that kind of courage, a free Negro woman going west with a baby and two youngsters? It says something for Isaiah Wood to welcome her. I can't speak for Cornelius Ryckman, but he's only one man. They set up a covenant like we did in the Stokes Company. And Mrs. Payne said she can't wait to see you."

"I expect she'll need a hand drivin' her team and takin' care of that baby," said Ma, wiping her eyes. "We can help. Lord knows I spent enough time with that Swathmore baby—wretched woman, bone lazy. Poor Grace. You can bet that's what she's doin' now, takin' care of the baby while that lazy, no-good woman sits back and whines."

"Now Sadie—"

"Don't 'Now Sadie,' me. It's the God's truth and you know it, Ben Johnson. I never met a more triflin' woman in my life. Poor, dear Grace."

"Be that as it may," Pa spoke gently, "Mrs. Payne is determined."

"What happened to Old Shep?" asked Sid.

"The dog? I don't rightly know."

It was a nightmare. Worse than a nightmare. He thought of the evening they joined the Stokes Company. Grace had stood with Old Shep, looking all forlorn as she watched them pull into the campground. The way her face lit up when he greeted her made him think they would be friends. Things would never be the same again. He checked to see if he was wearing his hat.

Grace Willis had an easy life in St. Louis. Going West was a bigger change for her than it was for him. He'd lived on a farm. She was from the city. She was younger, too. He was used to hard work. Grace had been pampered. *I didn't even thank her for gettin' my hat.* He couldn't stand it. Tears burned his eyes. He touched his hat to make sure he hadn't left it on the wagon seat.

4.

Lost Spring Camp

Mr. Wood rode up to meet them, tipping his hat to Ma and directing Pa to a place alongside a cluster of five wagons. He had the unmistakable leathery look of someone who has spent years outdoors. Brusk and straight to the point, Isaiah Wood might have been taken for stern and unfeeling, except for a kindly look in his eyes. "I'm putting you with the Reid group. Clarence Reid's your elected captain. He'll be over directly to introduce himself. Be about an hour before I call for the men to hitch up."

Pa said Mr. Wood put them in the same group when he found out they knew Mrs. Payne. She came over to meet them carrying baby Anna on one arm and a pan of fried apple pies in the other. Matthew and Lydia were on either side carrying beans and cornbread. "I've already made dinner," Mrs. Payne said. "I thought it would be nice to eat together."

Pa grabbed the pan of pies as Ma threw her arms around Mrs. Payne and the baby in one expansive hug. Jimmy and Matthew crawled under the wagon straight away. "Serena missed you," said Cora as she and Lydia scrambled into the wagon to find the cat. It made Grace's absence feel even more sharp and painful.

Washed over with grief, Sid pulled his hat down and leaned against the wagon wheel. *Somebody needs to go find her*. The instant the thought came to him, he realized he couldn't do it. *I'm no match for Mr. Swathmore*. It left him feeling even more helpless, discouraged, and useless.

"Jim Payne was a good man." He could hear Pa through the cloud of despair settling over him. "We'll never forget what he did for us."

Sid felt a hand on his shoulder. It was Mrs. Payne. "Sid, I'm so glad you are alive and well. I know you'll miss Grace. Don't underestimate her. She has a lot of courage. Mr. Bright, the man who was such a help to me, is looking for her. I feel confident he'll find her and get her back to her grandparents in St. Louis."

"Yes, Ma'am." He fumbled for words. "I'm sorry to hear about Mr. Payne. He was a good man." There didn't seem to be any way to improve on what Pa had said.

"He was that." She smiled at him with sad eyes. "He thought a lot of you, Sid. I'm glad we'll be in the same company again."

"What happened to Old Shep?"

"He stayed with Mrs. Willis until Mr. Bright came. That's all I know."

"Maybe he went to find Grace."

Mrs. Payne nodded. "That sounds like Old Shep."

It did sound like Old Shep. Old Shep wouldn't let anybody hurt Grace. It was a small comfort. He clung to it.

"Name's Reid, Clarence Reid." A wiry man with bright blue eyes and skin that had seen more than its share of sun shook hands with Pa. "Thought I'd get over and meet you folk. Miz Payne, I see you beat me to it. Reckon you folk have some catching up to do.

"This is Miz Reid. 'Spect you women folk will find a lot to talk about." His stern face lit up as he smiled affectionately down on a jolly-looking woman, almost his opposite. She was short, fair-skinned, and almost as round as she was tall, partly because she was expecting a baby.

"I'm countin' on a boy to help Mr. Reid with the work. I was thinkin' he'd be born in California. But I don't know. I'm gettin' awful big."

Mrs. Payne turned to Ma. "I've told Mrs. Reid you're an experienced midwife."

Ma and Lila Reid hit it off immediately. Mrs. Reid was quite a bit younger. But like Ma, her people moved to Illinois from Kentucky. "Seems like it was gettin' crowded for us farmers. My Clarence says to me, 'Lila, I've half a mind to go west.' Course he's been all over these parts, back before I made him settle down."

A wry smile flickered across Mr. Reid's face. "I trapped all across this country at one time. Far as the Rockies. One day, I looked one of those poor critters with his foot in a trap straight in the eye. Can't say as I know what happened, but I couldn't do it anymore. So, I quit. Went home and chased Lila till she caught me."

Lila Reid gave him a loving smile. "I figured if we was goin' to California, we'd best get on with it before the baby comes."

"I reckon you all know Mrs. Payne's a teacher," said Mr. Reid. "You too old for all that, Sid?"

"Sid and I are well acquainted," said Mrs. Payne.

"We want our youngsters to take every opportunity," Pa said. "Folk ought to be able to do more than just read and do sums in this day and age."

"You got a point there. Seems like the older ones don't take an interest. We're mostly youngsters in our group. There's some older boys in the company, 'bout you age, Sid. Ryckman boy and his friends . . . ." His voice trailed off as if he were about to say something else but thought better of it. "Folk pretty much stick to their own group of wagons. We're a big company."

"One of the things I liked about Isaiah Wood," said Pa, "he has it organized so it doesn't feel so big."

Mr. Reid nodded. "I'll say this for Miz Payne, she's plucky, driving a team all day with a baby on one hip and two youngins to keep track of. We all pitch in and give her a hand when she'll let us. Jeremy Sawyer spells her off. He's Clayton Sawyer's grown boy. They're in our group."

"Come now, Reid, we have to give the fair sex more credit for bein' able to look after themselves." A short, rather compact-looking, clean-shaven man tipped his hat to the women and shook hands with Pa. "Howdy, you must be the new folk. Glad to have you with us. Name's Joiner, Al Joiner."

"Al Joiner is one of our elected captains," said Mr. Reid. "You met Cornelius Ryckman and Jeremiah Davies. I expect Harold Sinclair will be over directly."

Mr. Joiner shook Sid's hand. "Good firm handshake, Sid. I like that." Turning to Mrs. Payne, he said, "No offense in my remarks, Miz Payne. I expect a lot more women would show pluck if us men gave 'em half a chance."

Mr. Reid slapped his hand across Al Joiner's back, "Stirring up trouble amongst the women folk, are you, Al?"

Mrs. Payne and Mrs. Reid looked at each other and smiled knowingly. "If Al Joiner had his way, we women would have the vote," said Mrs. Payne.

Mr. Joiner grinned. "We hold these truths to be self-evident."

"We're hitching up here directly," Mr. Reid said. "Don't let us interrupt your dinner. If you can find any extra firewood, you might wanna bring it along. It's gonna be slim pickins out in the open country.

"Johnson, I'm putting your wagon next to Miz Payne. We're the third group from the end today. Not a nice welcome, but we'll have a better turn in a couple of days when our group leads out."

"Good," said Pa. "We'll have a chance to see how you do things."

"Isaiah Wood is particular about how things is done, but it keeps us on the trail. He's a fair man. Everybody but little ones walks unless they're sick. It's part of our covenant. Sid, feel free to get in the wagon when you need to.

"So, Joiner, what can I do for you?" The two men walked off, deep in conversation.

Pa said they organized the train in Council Grove. Mr. Wood divided them into groups of 10-12 wagons. Each group elected a captain who reported to Mr. Wood and served as the council for the whole company.

"It feels like we've found the right place," said Ma as the call came to yoke up.

Maybe. Sid wasn't so sure. Nothing would ever be as good as the Stokes Company.

Pa told him to ride Sandy. He felt foolish riding when he was used to leading the oxen. It was a miserable afternoon. When the company halted at Lost Spring for the evening, he threw himself on the wagon seat as soon as he had taken care of Sandy. He was too exhausted to think.

"Can me and Matthew play with your soldiers?" Jimmy climbed up on the wagon.

"Not so fast." Sid grabbed him by the seat of the pants before he could pull the box from under the wagon seat. Maybe it wasn't the best place to keep Mr. Gallagher's letter.

"Please? You don't play with 'em."

"No, but they're mine. You can play with 'em only, and I mean only, if you take care of 'em. I give 'em to you. You don't help yourself. And you give 'em back before supper so I can inspect 'em."

Matthew gave Jimmy a questioning look. Jimmy shrugged.

"Jimmy knows what I'm talkin' about. Left to him, they'd be under a tree back in Westport."

"We'll take good care of 'em, Sid," said Matthew. "I promise."

Sid opened the box. There was the letter. Safe. He handed the soldiers out one by one. "Matthew gets Minutemen. You're Red Coats. The box is off limits."

As the boys scurried under the wagon, Sid studied the envelope. *Señora Catalina Lucía Esteban-Valdéz Gallagher, Santa Fe, New Mexico Territory*. The last thing he needed was for Jimmy to find out and blab about it all over the company.

Later, close to supper time, Sid interrupted a strategic battle between the Red Coats and Minutemen. Jimmy fussed, but Matthew said, "Come on Jimmy. Let's go find the Lost Spring before it gets dark. It's not really lost. It just doesn't show up sometimes when it's dry."

"Yeah," said Jimmy. "Let's be Minutemen." They raced off, shooting imaginary muskets at an imaginary enemy.

Ma and Mrs. Payne decided to prepare meals together. Sid didn't pay much attention. He was lost in the gloomy cloud that hung over him like the clouds overhead that threatened rain.

"Sid, you might want to go for lessons this evenin'," said Ma. "Jimmy and Cora are going. Maybe you'll make some friends."

Sid said he didn't feel like it. It wouldn't be the same anyway.

5.

THE FLINT HILLS

"Sid, we talked it over last night," Pa said right after the morning bugle call. "I think you're strong enough to take charge of Mrs. Payne's team till nooning. I have our team in hand. There isn't much to do but walk anyway. She could sure use the help, especially since it rained last night. The trail is likely to be muddy. Somebody can spell you this afternoon."

Ma dished up oat porridge. "With little Anna teethin' and all. Babies get fussy when their teeth come in."

"If you're up to it, Sid," said Mrs. Payne. "It would be good for the team to have a steady presence. Anna is taking more time. Jeremy Sawyer has been bringing the oxen in and hitching them up for me. Some of the men spell me off when he can't. But Jeremy needs to be free now to scout. I don't want to hold him back."

"Me 'n Al Joiner's been teaching Jeremy since some of us set out together from Independence." Mr. Reid paused briefly at their wagon. "The boy's not afraid to learn. I told Isaiah Wood he ought to take Jeremy on. He won't find a better teacher than Wood. Man could follow a weasel in a thunderstorm.

"But I didn't stop by to horn in on things. Miz Johnson, could I have a quick word? Lila has been having morning sickness . . . His voice faded as he and Ma conferred.

"I talked with Jeremy last night," said Pa. "He'll be over directly to get you acquainted with Mrs. Payne's team."

It didn't feel like he had any choice in the matter. But he didn't want to let Mrs. Payne down. Besides, Jeremy was already at her wagon.

"Glad to meet you, Sid." Jeremy Sawyer gave his hand a firm shake like he really meant it. Nearly a head taller than Pa, Jeremy had an easy way about him. "Not that you can't yoke a team of oxen, but cattle are social. You need a proper introduction." He gave Sid a broad grin. "You don't need me telling you. I hear you grew up on a farm, too, and led your team in the other company."

It was a relief to find the Payne oxen together and waiting to be yoked. When they saw Jeremy, the oxen headed toward him. Some teams had to be rounded up either because they wandered too far or because they weren't interested in doing any work. Jeremy nodded as if he read Sid's mind. "You never have to go chasing them down. They're a good team."

He singled out two big, sturdy oxen. "Sid, I want you to meet Justice and Righteous, your wheel team. Justice and Righteous, this is Sid. They're a well-disciplined yoke. These big fellows probably wouldn't brave a river if left to themselves, but they trust their lead team. They'll brake the wagon. That's what counts in your wheel team. All the Payne oxen have interesting names. Something to think about."

Jeremy introduced each yoke as if he were at social event and making sure Sid met all the important guests. Courage and Dependable were the middle team; Jeremy described them as smart and faithful. "Courage could lead if it came to that. He's one smart fellow, aren't you, Courage." Hope and Faith were the lead team. "Hope is your nigh ox"—the one on the left that he would walk beside.

"You're a lot like our Cornflower and Promise," Sid said

as he fixed their yoke to the chain connecting them to the middle yoke and to the wagon.

"I love this team," said Jeremy. "They aren't skittish. They're well-trained. You can use voice commands, body signals, or the whip. Sometimes I just point the whip. Hope knows exactly what to do. She's a real leader."

"You're scoutin' now?" Sid wasn't sure what to say. He didn't want Jeremy to think he was just a pesky kid.

"Yeah, I figure I'm one lucky fellow. When I had the chance to learn more about scouting, I jumped at it. Reid, Joiner, and Wood are the best in the whole company. I thought I was pretty good at tracking. Bottom fact is, I don't know much more than a greenhorn compared to them."

"What's it like goin' out with Mr. Wood?"

"I've learned a lot," said Jeremy. "Funny thing, you think you've learned all there is to know about something—shoot, I didn't know the first thing about scouting in this prairie. Ground here in these hills is shallow, full of flint rock. Grass isn't as tall as it will be by fall, but it's plenty tall. You interested in scouting?"

Sid nodded.

"Maybe I can give you some pointers. I expect you already know a lot being from a farm."

Sid felt his spirits lift. He liked Jeremy. Learning to scout would be great. Plus, the Payne team seemed to accept his authority and responded to his commands. He didn't have to whack any of them on the rear with the whip.

The novelty of guiding a new team soon wore off. His spirits sagged. Grace wasn't there to walk with him, chattering about everything and nothing. With a flush of guilt, he remembered how he had cut her off the last time he saw her. He felt for his hat. Now she was stuck somewhere in Oklahoma Territory with those horrible Swathmores. He choked back his feelings. He didn't want to look like some big, blubbering kid.

Mud and mosquitoes. That's all the Santa Fe Trail was. And miles of empty nothing.

The oxen waited patiently as he unhitched them at nooning. "Everybody ready for a little rub?" He tried to sound enthusiastic as he gave each yoke of oxen a rub around the ears and along the back of the head before turning them loose to graze. "I'm sorry you don't get a drink with your dinner. Doesn't look like there are any good puddles left."

"They can make up for it at Cottonwood Creek," said Mr. Reid as he let his team go. "We'll be there before nightfall if the trail's dried out ahead."

Two boys rode past, looking at him as if he were some kind of inferior being. *So much for makin' friends*. He thought of Jeremy Sawyer's offer. Jeremy wouldn't have time for a useless kid like him. His hopes faded into the gloom hanging over him.

Pa placed a strong arm across his shoulders. "How'd it go, Son?"

"It was fine."

"You look like you could use some rest. Are you going to be up to leading the team this afternoon?"

"I'm fine."

The afternoon was a repeat of the morning, slogging along the wet trail beside Hope, the lead ox. Getting nowhere. Grassland stretched for miles to the far horizon. Sid felt for his hat. Would they ever get to Santa Fe, much less California?

He didn't much care.

He wasn't sure how long he had been staring out in the distance when Mrs. Payne joined him. "I've just put Anna down for her nap in the wagon. Lydia and Cora are looking after her. I can spell you off now. I should walk with the team part of the time, or they'll think they don't have to pay any attention to me."

Sid didn't know what he would do with himself if he had a break. In the Stokes company it was always an adventure. Grace never ran out of ideas. Sometimes they helped the younger children catch insects to identify or collected interesting rocks or played tag. Now there wasn't anything to look forward to.

Mrs. Payne seemed to read his mind. "If you don't need to take a rest, why don't you walk along with me while I guide the team? Maybe we could work on Mark Antony's speech from *Julius Caesar*? How far did you get in memorizing it before you left the Stokes Company?"

It wasn't what Sid expected. He'd learned the whole speech by heart, but he hadn't thought about it since.

"There are a couple of girls in our school group who are working on it. Maybe you can work together. Now, why don't you say it for me?"

Sid felt like a piece of dead wood as he began:

Friends, Romans, countrymen, lend me your ears.
I come to bury Caesar, not to praise him.
The evil that men do lives after them;
The good is oft interred with their bones—

"Don't go any further. You're giving me words, but you're delivering them as if you are disconnected from what you're saying. This speech of Mark Antony's is one of the best pieces of persuasive argument in the English language. I want you to *feel* it."

"Yes, ma'am." Sid knew what she meant. He just couldn't do it. He couldn't feel excited about anything.

"Don't worry. We'll work on it. The feeling will come. It's

such a good story. It was one of Mr. Payne's favorites." She sighed. "I used to read to him after the children were in bed."

It was a while before she spoke again. "The evil that men do lives after them."

The way she said it caught Sid by surprise. It wasn't bitter; it had a sad ring to it. What was it like for her, knowing her husband was murdered? *What would Ma do if anything happened to Pa?*

"I enjoyed our little school in the Stokes Company, Sid. We have a nice school group here, too. It's such a large company. I thought maybe there would be another teacher and we could divide up the older and younger students. But it's just me. Young people your age don't seem to be interested in school. Their families keep them busy. More little ones about Cora's age come. In fact, you might be able to help me."

Sid didn't know what to say.

"It's hard to keep the little ones busy while I'm working with others. I wonder if you could give me a hand this evening? I have something for them to do, but they need supervision. You'd be very good at it. I've noticed how patient you are with Cora and Lydia. What do you say?"

Before he had time to say anything, cries from the back of the wagon announced that baby Anna was awake. "Oh my." Mrs. Payne handed him the whip. "Sounds like I'm needed elsewhere. Thanks for walking with me."

Mrs. Payne was easy to talk with. He thought of Mr. Payne—how brave and good he was. And Grace. Where was she now? Was she safe? Ma said it was wrong to hate, but he hated Mr. Swathmore. *I can't help it. I HATE him.*

He felt to see if he was wearing his hat.

Mr. Wood called a halt for the evening before they reached Cottonwood Creek. "I promised you a drink," Sid told the oxen as he unhitched them. "We didn't get that far. Now there's no water for you until tomorrow."

Mr. Reid gave him a pat on the back. "Well done, Sid. It was slow going in that mud. There's some woulda pushed on. Isaiah Wood is right. Better to hit Cottonwood Creek in the daylight. It's a rough crossing. You want your oxen to be up and moving before a challenge. I guess they're a bit like some of us. Takes 'em a while to wake up and get going. Don't worry about the oxen. They can go a piece without water. It's the horses, they can't go much more than a couple of days before it starts to show. It's gonna be a real challenge once we're in the desert."

Sid didn't want any more challenges. He wanted to go back home. It wasn't fun anymore. He tugged at his hat.

A group of about a dozen Kanza men and women approached them. "Here we go again," said one of the men, "swarming like flies. Begging for food. I don't see how Wood can dole out something every time a bunch of 'em comes up."

Sid first met native people asking for food well before Council Grove when they were with the Stokes Company. Ma said it was right to share. But how would they have enough to make it all the way to California if they gave something to everybody who asked? There seemed to be a lot of Indians asking. Mr. Stokes had considered them a pest more than a threat and advised people not to give them anything. "Giving 'em a handout encourages begging. Be firm but kind."

Apparently, Mr. Wood had different ideas.

Somebody said, "You'd think they'd have some self-respect."

"That's not how they see it." Mr. Reid seemed to be able to speak their language. He said something to the Kanza and pointed toward Mr. Wood. "It's their way to share what they have when somebody needs it. They'd give away their last kernel of corn if need be. They expect the same from us. Truth is, they don't have food because folk like us have been taking it."

"I can't go that far, Reid," another man spoke up. Others nodded in agreement.

"How are they supposed to have enough food?" said Mr. Reid, unruffled. "Look, we have a treaty with the Kaw granting them land. But it was their land to start with. Some wagon trains passing through help themselves to their crops. Our livestock graze down the grass. Used to be buffalo all through the Flint Hills. You hardly see them now till durned near the Little Arkansas River. The Kaw depend on buffalo. Not to mention small game."

"I reckon they knew what they were doin' when they signed those treaties," said somebody else.

Mr. Reid nodded. "You've got a point. But then we caught them in desperate straits before that treaty in '46— floods had wiped out their crops two years in a row. They were starving. Seems like as Christians, we shoulda been offering a helping hand. Instead, we shoved them off the best land and took it for ourselves. The minute they land in one spot and try to make do, we want it. Last count I heard, over 30 families moved in on Kaw land around Council Gove. Federal agent tried to evict them. Squatters burned him out. He took his family and left. Government didn't do a thing. More squatters are moving in every day. That isn't even the half of it. But I'm not here to talk politics. I don't know about you men, but I'm ready for my supper."

As Sid walked with him back to the wagons, Mr. Reid muttered, "Lord, give me strength. Whole system's wrong. Treats them like they don't have a right to exist, Sid. We leave the Kaw homeless and starving, then folk criticize them for asking for food."

*****

Mrs. Payne's school met by her wagon right after supper except on Saturday and Sunday. Sid would have backed out of helping her if he could. It wouldn't be like the Stokes Company. But he'd promised.

As children began to gather, he could see why Mrs. Payne wanted help. Most of those who met for lessons were much younger than Sid. Parents seemed to think older ones didn't need any more schooling or they could pick up where they left off once they got to California. It was that way in the Stokes Company, too. Ma thought there was more to it. "I expect some folks think Dorcas Payne is tryin' to get above herself. People tell you slavery is wrong, but they still don't think folk with black skin can do anything but pick cotton or wash clothes."

There were seven little ones in the group Mrs. Payne assigned to him—a handful of mischief. He immediately took to the Davies twins. Tobias looked like a miniature edition of his father, one of the two men who invited them to join the company. Ella Sue, his twin sister, had large eyes, a freckled nose, and heavy braids tied with red ribbons.

He was busy helping them organize pebbles into groups of 10 when two girls about his age arrived. Was he the only older boy?

When Mrs. Payne introduced them, Bitsy Clark giggled. Ethel Sinclair surveyed him as if she were sizing up the competition.

Mrs. Payne asked the three of them to meet with her once the younger children were busy. She asked so many questions Sid wondered if there was anything left in his head. Ethel came out ahead of him in arithmetic, but he bested her in Latin.

They were about even in grammar, though he diagramed a complex sentence faster than she did. Thankfully Mrs. Payne didn't ask him to recite Mark Antony's address.

Bitsy had been to school, but Sid didn't think it had done her much good. She was silly like some of the girls in school at home. He figured the only reason she came was because Ethel Sinclair came, and it gave her something to giggle about. As soon as Mrs. Payne gave them an assignment to do, Ethel began going over everything again with Bitsy. "Maybe Sid can help me," Bitsy said in a sickening-sweet voice, giving him a big smile and batting her eyes.

Sid felt the red creeping up his neck.

When Mrs. Payne called all the children to meet, Jimmy was eager to ask a question. "How come they call this the Flint Hills?"

"Anybody know the answer?" Mrs. Payne asked.

Sid raised his hand. He wouldn't have known if he hadn't talked with Jeremy. "Because there is so much flint rock in the shallow soil."

"Exactly. U.S. Army Captain Zebulon Pike passed this way in 1806. He gave it the name Flint Hills because the limestone rock just below the soil is full of flint rock. We are in tall grass country. It may not look that tall now, but by fall, some of this grass will be 10 feet tall."

"Yoicks! That's bigger 'n Pa."

"Yes, Jimmy, taller than anybody in our company."

6.

COTTONWOOD CROSSING

Cottonwood Creek looked tame from a distance. But its long, sloping banks and deep bed made it a Santa Fe Trail crossing spoken of with respect. Wagons had to be pulled through its mud and rock bottom by the sheer strength of mules or oxen.

Shortly before noon they reached the creek. Mr. Reid gave instructions, "Isaiah Wood says we double-team and go across single file. Every team does double duty—some teams may need to do triple duty. We're not going in today's traveling order. We'll be last group. Every able-bodied man who isn't leading, be ready to help as needed. Be a lot of coming and going, hitching and unhitching."

Grace woulda ask about able-bodied women. Sid felt for his hat.

"Sid, I'm having Jeremy take Miz Payne's team across." Mr. Reid didn't offer any explanation. Should he be relieved or disappointed? Back in the Stokes Company, he'd led their team across plenty of streams, though they hadn't ever double-teamed. If it was anybody but Jeremy Sawyer, it would be hard to take. Now he would have to sit in the wagon like the women and children.

Men on horseback herded cattle and horses into the creek. "Mighty fine-looking horses," said one of the men watching them cross, "but every one of them is a target for thieves. Puts all of us in danger." He didn't say why they had so many horses.

They ate a cold dinner watching a steady stream of wagons cross. By the time it was their turn to prepare for crossing the sun was on its arc toward the western horizon. Mr. Reid said they were hitching three teams to the wagons now. "Once you set out, keep 'em moving. Only way in this mud."

"It's getting treacherous," said Pa as Sid helped him hitch the team to their wagon. The team had already helped two other wagons across. "The bottom isn't quicksand. But it's slick as glass. There are pockets of mud that want to grab and hold on."

Smoke from cooking fires rose on the other side where people prepared supper. Sid was impatient to have it over. But Mr. Reid said their wagon was to go last of all.

"Come on Jimmy! We get to go next," Matthew called. The boys scrambled up on the wagon seat with Mrs. Payne. Jeremy rode Freedom, Mrs. Payne's horse.

"Reid wagon follows Payne," Mr. Reid called. "Sinclair, you're third team for the Reid wagon," Sid figured Mr. Sinclair must be Ethel's pa.

"Johnson, see to the third teams as soon as they bring 'em over. I'm taking Miz Reid across on horseback." Mr. Reid rode his horse alongside the wagon where his wife waited. Pale-faced and wide-eyed, she said almost without expression, "I'm goin' in the wagon."

Mr. Reid, who always looked as if nothing could take him by surprise, seemed completely flummoxed. "I . . . Lila, I don't want you jostled around in that wagon. The baby—"

"No," Mrs. Reid said quietly. She didn't budge.

Ma intervened. "Miz Reid, it'll be easier on horseback with him holdin' you. It won't be a smooth ride in the wagon. They're sayin' the bottom's gettin' slippery."

"I'm stayin' in the wagon."

"I'll ride with her if that helps," said Sid on an impulse.

Mr. Reid gave Ma a look admitting defeat. "Thank you, Sid. I'd be obliged."

"Right," said Ma. "Bring the featherbed, Sid. Do you have a featherbed or blanket, Mrs. Reid?"

Covered wagon seats were not all built the same way. In the Johnson wagon, the seat was inside and above the wagon box with foot room in a boxed-in platform attached to the outside of the wagon. It felt like being inside the wagon. In the Reid wagon, the seat stuck out in front of the wagon box with a platform for footing below. There was an armrest on either side. While sturdy, it felt more like being outside the wagon.

"Here, Sid." Mrs. Reid patted the featherbed-covered seat. "We'll have a soft seat."

Ma took her featherbed from Sid, spreading it over Mrs. Reid's lap. "Try to stay relaxed, Miz Reid. The featherbeds will soften any sudden jolts. Sid, sit yourself right next to Miz Reid—"

"Where I can grab on to you if I need."

Ma nodded. "If the wagon lunges, grab around her at the shoulders. You'll be fine Miz Reid."

"Ready?" called Mr. Reid. She nodded.

The Sinclair team was in lead position with Mr. Sinclair on horseback driving them. Al Joiner rode next to his team, hitched in the middle. Mr. Sawyer, Jeremy's dad, rode alongside the Reid team closest to the wagon.

"Move out!" Mr. Reid called. He rode to the right of the wagon where he could supervise without being in the way.

Mrs. Reid grabbed the armrest with her right hand and Sid's arm with her left. "Here we go, Sid. Thanks for bein' my strong arm." She tensed, then relaxed as the three strong teams pulled straight and true, sighing in relief as the wagon settled in the water without a jolt. "We aren't entirely floatin', Sid. That might be easier. Not on the teams, though. The teams have the hardest work."

"We're in good hands, Miz Reid."

Once they were well into the creek, water lapped the wagon bed and came nearly to the necks of the oxen. Nothing but the platform for their feet stood between them and the swirling water inches below. "It's better than I thought it would be, Sid. Best not to look down. One big bump and we'd be in the river. Such brave animals."

Whips cracked. The wagon creaked. Clapping and cheering broke out behind. "Look, Sid," Mrs. Reid let go of him to clap. "Miz Payne's wagon is already across. We're nearly halfway"—the wagon wheels began to slip on the muddy bottom—"oh-h-h, here we go!"

Sid threw his arms around her shoulders, bracing his feet against the footrest as the wagon skidded. No time for panic. But for one terrifying moment, he thought they'd be catapulted into the water.

"Keep 'em movin'!" Mr. Reid yelled from somewhere behind.

"Head up!" called Mr. Sinclair. Three teams of oxen lifted their heads higher, straining toward the far bank.

The wagon tilted to one side, then the other. "Hang on, Miz Reid!" Sid pulled her back against the seat. One jolt and they'd be in the water. *Don't let us fall in . . .*

Mrs. Reid bit her lip, clinging to the armrest.

"We're gonna be fine." He tried to sound confident. "Pa said to expect some slidin'."

"I know, Sid." The wagon shimmied back into line. "Whew-w-w-w! That was close. We're almost there. Mr. Reid insisted on havin' armrests on the wagon seat. Good thing, too. Have you seen those wagons with seats stickin' out front and nothin' to grab ahold of? And he added that board across the footrest so as I'd have extra support goin' downhill. He's the best of men. Always lookin' after me."

From the creek bank behind them, Pa called for the next wagon to move out.

"You'd think this was my first time to cross a river. It's the baby. The bigger the baby gets, the more Mr. Reid worries. I didn't mean to be disrespectful of my own husband in refusin' to ride with 'em. Lord knows. But I can't be ridin' on horseback. The last thing my mamma said before we left home was, 'Don't you go and ride horseback, Lila Reid. You could hurt the baby' and I've been"—they went flying forward as the wagon abruptly jolted to a halt. Sid grabbed Mrs. Reid, jamming his feet against the platform, pulling back with all his strength. Just in time. He eased Mrs. Reid back into the seat. But he was fighting against gravity. The wagon tipped toward the right front wheel leaving them at a perilous angle.

"Your Ma knew what she was doin' when she surrounded me with featherbeds! Hope I don't have to go floatin' like a goose. Do you think a featherbed would float?" She gave a nervous laugh.

Whips cracked. Mr. Sinclair urged the teams forward. *Come on.* Sid held his breath afraid to move.

The wagon didn't budge. Water lapped at their feet. They had to move, and fast. There wasn't time to be frightened. "Up here, Miz Reid. We've gotta move up and balance the wagon."

"Mrs. Reid! The baby!" someone on the far bank screamed so loudly they heard it over the sounds of water and the straining oxen. Mr. Wood headed toward them. "Get Miz Reid and the boy off that wagon!" He motioned to the wagon behind them, "Keep moving! Give her a wide berth."

The wagon seat was only about four feet wide, but Mrs. Reid was wrapped in a featherbed. She couldn't move. Sid stood on the narrow platform, clinging to the back of the seat with his back to the team and the water. With one hand, he helped Mrs. Reid pull off the featherbed.

Gripping his arm, she stood, mouth set in a determined line. "Upsy-daisy!" She let go of Sid, grabbed the back of the wagon seat with one hand, and slowly turned.

Jaw set, Sid eased backward toward the high end of the seat, reaching for her hand. But Mrs. Reid was bending over the wagon seat, clinging to it with one hand as she struggled to heave the featherbed into the wagon with the other. "I can't have your Ma's good featherbed ruined."

Hang the featherbed! Unless they balanced the wagon, it could capsize. It was no time for reasoning. "I'll get it." Sid let go of the wagon seat, swept up the featherbed with both hands, and hurled it into the wagon bed, nearly falling after it. "Whoa-oa-ho!" Almost losing his balance, he grabbed the seat in time to keep from crashing into Mrs. Reid, who clung on with both hands.

"That wasn't my best idea." She sheepishly took his free hand and inched toward him, leaving the featherbed she'd been sitting on. The wagon shifted slightly and began slowly dipping down again.

Meanwhile, Mr. Reid had dismounted, and thrown himself against the right front corner, trying to stop the wagon from tipping over. Mr. Sawyer was off his horse and climbing over the hitch between the wheel team and the wagon. "Hold on Sid. Steady, Mrs. Reid. We'll hold her up."

Sid didn't dare look for fear of losing his balance.

"Grab a rope, Sid." Al Joiner rode in close. "Get it on her, right under her arms. It'll give you some support, Miz Reid."

He caught the rope with one hand. *What he means is keep her from goin' under if we fall in.* Mr. Joiner kept the rope taut, but not too tight as they eased their way. It felt like trying to walk backward up a slippery hill, with no grass or roots for footing. At the opposite end, Sid stood upright letting Mrs. Reid grab the armrest and ease past him. She sat, clinging to it to keep from sliding back. "We did it, Sid," she panted. "Don't you go and fall in."

Sid planted his feet on either side of her, back to the water. There wasn't much room. The wagon had stopped sinking but they hadn't balanced it; any movement could cause the wagon to fall over on Mr. Reid and Mr. Sawyer.

"Easy, Lila"—how could Mr. Reid sound so calm?—"Mr. Wood's coming to get you off. Stay where you are, Sid. No sudden movements."

"Feels like the wheel's hit a hole," Mr. Sawyer called. "Limestone's crumbling around it."

Men were on their way to help, carrying wooden planks and shovels. "Brace yourselves," Joiner called. "They're gonna wedge some planks under that end for support. Wagon may shift again." The men arrived, setting to work propping up the wagon at the fallen corner. The wagon tilted up slightly, but they were still at a precarious angle.

Mr. Reid let go and climbed onto the wagon tongue by sheer force of will against the water and mud pulling at him. "Sid, lock that wheel on the left."

By this time, Mr. Wood's horse was even with the men working on the wagon, "Miz Reid, I'm coming around. Be ready to hand her to me, Reid."

"You're doin' fine Lila," said Mr. Reid. "Sid, we're goina haveta change places without upsetting the apple cart."

Time stopped.

Sid edged his way down the seat. Mr. Reid eased up onto

the platform. The creek lapped the lower end of the wagon seat. Mr. Wood's horse sloshed toward the back of the wagon. Mr. Sinclair spoke softly to the lead team. And somewhere on the opposite bank, a baby cried.

"Wagons, wait up." As he rounded the wagon, Mr. Wood's voice boomed out from behind them. "Johnson, I want your team. Get 'em out here and hitched in the lead."

Mr. Reid balanced on the platform towering over his wife. Sid perched on the seat next to her, his feet too close to the water for comfort.

"Stand up on the seat now, Lila." Mr. Reid sounded unruffled like it was something he did every day. But sweat beaded on his brow. "When I say, 'Now,' you lean forward and put your hands on my shoulders. I'll swing you over onto Mr. Wood's horse. Joiner, give her some slack on that rope. Sid, you be ready to slide into her seat and hold on. Gotta keep this thing balanced."

Mrs. Reid looked like a little bird perched on a fence as she stood on the wagon seat. Mr. Reid's hands steadied her at the waist.

Sid braced himself. Too many things could go wrong. He bit his lip. *Don't let her fall.*

Mr. Wood was almost even with them, Mr. Reid watching his every move.

"Ready Lila?"

She smiled at him.

Just before he was opposite them, Mr. Wood nodded. Sid held his breath.

"Now!" In one smooth motion, Mrs. Reid dropped forward, hands on her husband's shoulders. He grasped her under the arms, and swung her out over the angry water and into Mr. Wood's arms. The horse never stopped. Al Joiner tossed the end of the rope to Mr. Wood.

Sid found himself sitting in the spot where Mrs. Reid had stood. How he got there and how Mr. Reid had kept his balance, he couldn't have said.

"Now, let's get you off, son." Mr. Reid's voice was reassuring.

Mr. Joiner rode up alongside the wagon. "Here, Sid, I've got you."

Trading places wasn't nearly as frightening without Mrs. Reid there. Sid climbed out of the wagon, bracing one foot on the wheel, and hopped on behind Mr. Joiner.

They could hear Pa's commands as he brought the team.

"Reckon there isn't a stronger team in the company," said Mr. Joiner.

Across the river, eager hands helped Mrs. Reid down. A cheer went up from both sides of the creek as she patted her large belly and waved. Mr. Reid wiped his forehead on his shirt sleeve. "What's the situation over there, Sawyer?"

"Got her braced. Wheel's fine. Axle's still good. Haveta dig out and see what we can do about getting the wagon across without the back wheel falling in."

"Mr. Wood sent me for Sid." It was Jeremy. "We're to help get the rest of the wagons across. It's gonna get dark fast. Can't afford to have anybody left on this side."

"Who said you can't change horses in the middle of a stream, Sid?" said Al Joiner as Sid slid onto Freedom behind Jeremy.

It wasn't until he dismounted back on the eastern bank that Sid realized his legs were shaking. He wasn't sure he could stand.

Ma put her arm around him, giving him a quick squeeze. "We couldn't see a thing. Probably just as well."

"Next wagon move out," called Jeremy. "Stay to the right. Mr. Wood says wait till they're pulling out on the far bank before the next wagon goes."

They watched as Pa dismounted and waded to the head of the team, water up to his chest. His calls to the oxen floated out over the water as he guided them into place. The wagon was tipped back upright. Men who had been working with shovels stepped back. Others came in on horseback, carrying rock to fill in the hole where the limestone had broken away.

"How they can do anything in that muddy water is anybody's guess," said Jeremy.

Somebody on horseback led Sandy away from the team. It looked like Pa was going to wade beside the team. "Getty-up!" His call drifted over the water. He didn't crack his whip. He didn't have to. Cornflower and Promise, the lead yoke, strained forward. Cornflower was a real leader. It wasn't just her strength; something about her seemed to calm the other teams.

Sid stood on the wagon seat for a better view.

With a mighty surge, the oxen moved forward. There was a sucking sound as hooves pulled free from the muddy creek bed. A great swirl of mud rose as the wagon moved forward inch by hard-won inch.

On the far bank, cheers broke out as Cornflower and Promise stepped out of the water onto the slippery bank. Suddenly, Pa skidded on the treacherous mud. Unable to right himself, he slid into the creek with a loud splash.

No! Sid caught his breath. It couldn't be happening. Their team was trained to obey body commands but stopping on the muddy slope would be perilous. If they didn't, they could run over Pa.

"Gee!" Mr. Sinclair called out, directing the oxen to swing clear of where Pa fell. Sid strained to see. The wagon pulled up away from the bank, safe at last. But where was Pa?

Mr. Wood led his horse into the creek, holding an uncoiled

rope attached to the saddle. He reached down and pulled Pa's head and shoulders up above the water. Sputtering gray-brown water and streaming with mud, Pa threw up his arms for the rope.

"It's not quicksand," said Jeremy, standing beside Sid, "but it might as well be. It's mighty hard to get out of that mud once you're in it."

Cheering broke out again as Mr. Wood and Pa struggled up the bank, covered with mud. Jeremy sent the next wagon across.

Pa rode Sandy back across the river, bringing the team. Ma, who had remained stoic through it all, said, "Lord of glory! If you aren't a sight, Ben Johnson. How am I ever gonna get the mud out of your clothes?"

Pa grinned. "Thought I was gonna lose a shoe."

"Sid and I'll hitch the team, Mr. Johnson," said Jeremy.

"Sid, think you can lead 'em across?" asked Pa. "I'm about winded."

"Are you sure—"

"I'm sure. The team knows you and you've got two good teams behind to help. Can't think of anybody I'd trust more." Pa handed him Sandy's reins.

Theirs was the only wagon remaining. Mr. Davies, whose team was in the middle position, said, "We're ready when you are, Sid."

Jeremy rode into place beside the wheel team.

Sid swung into the saddle. "Getty-up!" It was both terrifying and exciting. Cornflower and Promise didn't falter at the edge of the river. Wagon wheels slipped on the treacherous bottom, causing the wagon to shimmy and tilt. "Steady," he called. *Please, please, just let us get across.*

Then, glorious moment. Cheers went up. He had brought the final wagon across. He breathed a sigh of relief that went all the way to his toes.

Many hands helped to unyoke the oxen. They were set free to graze with the other livestock in a natural corral made by a bend in the river.

A teamster train waiting to cross in the opposite direction passed as the sun set.

Some of the men from other wagon groups came around with Mr. Wood to shake Pa's hand and his. Mr. Wood tipped his hat to Ma. "Sid, you were steady under pressure out there, can't think of many men who could have done better."

Sid felt red creeping up to his ears, thankful it was too dark for anybody to notice.

"It was a team effort," Pa said.

Mr. Ryckman brought a boy with him who looked like a younger edition of himself, tall and fair-skinned with a bright pink face. Blonde hair stuck out from under his hat. "I was telling you about my son, Connie," said Mr. Ryckman. "I thought it was about time you two met."

Grinning, the boy extended his hand. "You're the boy who had the pox."

Sid nodded.

"People was sayin' Miz Reid wouldna made it if you hadn't been there to steady her—guess you're like your father. That was really somethin', Mr. Johnson. Your team saved the day."

"Took a lot of people working together," said Pa.

"So, where've you been hidin' yourself, Sid?" Connie's mannerisms were just like his father's. The only noticeable difference between the two, except for about four inches and a bunch of years, was that Connie spoke with a slight drawl, while his father sounded like he was from somewhere back East.

"I haven't been here that long. Guess we haven't crossed

paths.

"There's a group of us that play marbles just about every noonin'. You play?"

Sid nodded.

"You any good?"

"I have my good days and my bad days."

"Fair enough. I'll come lookin' for you next time we play."

"Good," said Ma. "Maybe that will perk you up a bit."

They were finishing supper when Mr. Reid sent for Ma. The baby had decided not to wait for California.

"We'll have a cup of cocoa for her when she gets back," said Mrs. Payne. "Mr. Payne always liked a cup of cocoa at night."

It must have been two hours later when they heard the unmistakable cries of a newborn baby. Ma returned tired but smiling. "Baby's premature. But he's gonna be fine. I knew she wasn't gonna make it all the way to California."

That night a cracking thunderstorm swept over. Cottonwood Creek was overflowing its banks by morning. If Mr. Wood hadn't insisted on getting all the company across before nightfall they would have been stuck on the other side. They were lucky to find the Wood Company.

*****

Some immigrant companies didn't travel on Sunday. It depended on the Wagon Master. Some observed Sunday for religious reasons. Others, because the Wagon Master believed a day of rest was good for the animals. The Wood Company observed Sunday with an early morning service led by Preacher Jones. Ordinarily, the train would move on afterward, but they were going to lay over until after nooning to let the oxen rest, inspect the wagons, grease wagon axles, and make repairs. Many of these jobs were routinely done at nooning or in the evening, but the Cottonwood crossing was harder than expected.

Right after breakfast, when the company met for Sunday service, Mr. Wood made an announcement. "Sometime in the night, five of the horses belonging to Cornelius Ryckman were stolen. I sent Clarence Reid, Al Joiner, and Jeremy Sawyer out before dawn this morning to track them. I am not optimistic after that thunderstorm. I don't want to hear any talk about who was responsible. If you saw something, come talk with me. The men on guard did not see or hear anyone and there isn't enough evidence on the ground to say."

After that, Reverend Jones read from the Bible and said a few words. Then Mrs. Jones led them in singing a hymn.

Enoch Jones and his wife Miranda looked familiar. Where had he seen them before? Sid couldn't place them until Pa said, "Remember the couple in a horse and buggy that passed us on the way to Shawnee Mission, back before Council Grove?"

Mrs. Jones laughed when Pa reminded them. "Gracious me, heading out to Santa Fe alone wasn't the best idea we ever had. Most nights we found a company to camp with. First time we were out on our own with the coyotes yapping and wolves howling, I says to my Enoch, 'I'm not going all the way to Santa Fe with wolves snapping at my heels. We're finding a company and that's that.' Thankfully, we met Mr. Wood in Council Grove."

Reverend Jones grinned. "Miranda Jones is a mighty force to be reckoned with when she makes up her mind."

"You kept your head yesterday, Sid," said Mrs. Jones. "It must have been terrifying. Mrs. Reid said she would have ended up in the river if it hadn't been for you."

That night Sid thought about what she said. Back home in Illinois, when they'd read Uncle Luke's letters about going to California, it sounded like one big adventure. Adventure is pretty exciting when you read about it, or maybe when you think about it afterward. *But being in the middle of an adventure isn't so easy.*

*****

Connie Ryckman came as promised. When the weather was nice, boys often played marbles in the schoolyard back in Illinois. Sometimes Sid won. Sometimes somebody else won. It was fun either way. He'd selected half a dozen marbles and a larger marble, his shooter or taw in anticipation. It would be fun to play again.

Connie had an easy way about him. Maybe they'd become good friends.

"There's six of us. You have to watch Frog. He's a sly one. Take every marble you own if you aren't careful. The others are so-so. Sometimes it's just raw luck with marbles."

A stocky boy extended his hand. "Billy Elston. Heard you was about to hang up the fiddle for a while there. They said you had the pox."

Connie introduced the others. "That's Frog Barton, Eli Mason, Dale Goodall, and Squeaker Warwick."

Squeaker held back from shaking hands. "Lost your manners, Squeaker?" asked Connie.

Billy guffawed. "You ain't gonna get the pox from shakin' hands."

"How'd ja know?" Squeaker asked in a shrill, high-pitched voice.

"It's been weeks, bird-brain."

It was easy to guess how Squeaker got his nickname. He had a pinched look like somebody had closed a door on him.

Billy, on the other hand, was built like a prairie buffalo. His head and wide shoulders were out of proportion to spindly legs and arms. He looked familiar, though Sid couldn't think where they might have met.

Like most boys his age, Eli and Dale looked tall and stretched out like somebody had pulled them from both ends.

"There's a slew of boys around," said Connie, "but these are the ones you wanna know."

"Come on then, Sid, show us whatcha got," Billy motioned to a spot by the circle they had drawn in the dirt. "Everybody puts in three mibs to start. If you get shot out of the circle, put in another mib until you run out. We play for keeps."

Playing for keeps didn't feel right. Better to play by their rules this time, though, if he was going to have any friends. When he got to know them, he'd have his say. Good thing he hadn't brought his best taw.

"Startin' with your commoneys?" The way Billy said it sounded like an accusation.

Squeaker was in perpetual motion, managing to squat down by the circle in one spot and move all over at the same time. His eyes darted here and there, like a cornered weasel. He snickered. "Gotta watch Frog, he'll clean you out."

Frog didn't say a word. He sat on his haunches like a frog ready to leap. Maybe that was how he got his nickname. That, or the way his eyes kind of bulged out.

Frog went first. He aimed at Sid's marbles, hitting one and knocking it into another marble with such force it hit another. They flew out of the ring taking another on the way, his taw close behind.

"Good shot!" said Sid.

Squeaker snickered. "He gotcha, Eli. Lost a mib. Sid lost two."

Eli shrugged. "Think we don't know it?"

Frog's face was expressionless. He was good, but how good?

"Your turn Sid, see if you can get your mibs back," said Connie. Nobody explained how they decided who went when. There were a lot of things they hadn't explained.

"It looks like I have to send my taw out of the ring, right?" With marbles, the rules largely depended on those playing, but you needed to know them. He'd have to see how each of the boys played without losing his taw or too many marbles.

He usually knuckled down when he shot, a slightly different way of holding his taw than Frog had used. It gave him more control. Better wait until he knew what other people did. He was a good shot either way. He played it safe, sending two marbles out of the ring, his taw safely behind.

"Bad luck, Eli!" yelled Squeaker. "One more and you're out. You gonna haveta buy mibs."

"Think he gives a boondoggle?" Dale scowled.

It was Connie's turn. He passed up a really good shot to take aim at Sid's marbles and took one. Sid replaced it. Billy was bound to see the good shot.

He passed it up.

So did Dale.

So did Eli.

And so did Squeaker. A shot like that didn't come along often. One solid hit could take all of Connie's marbles and more.

Frog was too good a player to miss it. But he aimed for Sid's marbles instead. *What kind of Tomfoolery?* If he'd been back home, Sid would have gone for the good shot. Maybe they wanted to see how good he was. He'd learn more about how the other boys played if he passed it up, too.

Billy had an ugly grin on his face as Sid picked off one of Frog's marbles. Frog remained expressionless.

One good shot and Connie could save his marbles. But he took another of Sid's marbles. *Why?* By the time it was

Frog's turn again, the good shot had shifted slightly, but it was still there. Frog let it go.

Sid was running out of marbles. Time to go for the good shot. Moving around until he was in position, he lined up his taw and flipped his thumb with all the force he could give it. Marbles flew.

Nobody cheered. The boys at home would have cheered, even if they lost marbles. Red crept up Connie's neck as he grimly replaced lost marbles. "Get him, Frog."

It was war after that. Eli and Dale were out of the game before their next turn. Squeaker shot wild. The only danger he posed was accidentally interfering with a good shot. Frog systematically dismantled Sid, taking all of his marbles in one calculated shot after another. Then Frog's game went downhill. Connie won.

It was a puzzling game. He wasn't sure he had learned much, except that Squeaker was at the bottom of their social ladder. Connie was at the top, followed closely by Billy. Dale and Eli were slightly above Squeaker. He couldn't decide about Frog. He wasn't sure he liked any of them that much. *Then what can you tell after one game of marbles?*

"See you tonight?" Connie asked. "Us six hang out after supper."

"I'll ask my Pa."

"Sure, if you gotta ask," said Billy.

"I don't have to, but—no, wait. I help Mrs. Payne with lessons." It was the wrong thing to say.

"Oh! He does lessons!" Squeaker mocked. "Thought lessons was for girls and panty-waists," Billy sneered.

Sid could feel himself going hot all over. One thing for sure. Billy knew how to get his goat.

Connie eyed him critically. It was hard to know how to take Connie. He'd have to give it some time.

7.

NEAR RUNNING TURKEY CREEK

Sid was unhitching the oxen for nooning when Connie and Billy rode past. They brought their horses to a stop, dismounted, put their heads together as if they were conferring, then walked his way. "Hey, Sid," Connie broke into a smile. "Billy 'n me are gonna' do a little scoutin' over by those bushes up there. Wanna come along?"

He hesitated.

Billy's lips curled in a sneer. "Reckon he's afraid he'll miss his dinner."

"He's got a point, Billy. I don't wanna miss dinner either. We won't take long. Billy 'n me do this all the time for practice. Come on, we'll be back before the biscuits are done."

"Sure." After all, Ma and Pa wanted him to make friends.

They headed toward a dry creek bed where tenacious wind-whipped bushes competed for water hidden beneath the soil.

"Gotta gun?" Billy eyed him.

Sid met Billy's hostile glare. "I don't carry it when I'm leadin' a team."

"We carry guns," said Connie. "Ridin' with the horses means you haveta be on the lookout. I reckon if the men who were guardin' the other night had been awake, we'd have had some dead Injuns instead of losin' five horses."

Sid flinched, but he didn't say anything.

"Come on," said Billy, "times wasting."

"Let's head on up," said Connie, "maybe go as far as the rise on the other side. See what we can see."

It wasn't far, only a few minutes from the encampment. If he'd been leading, Sid would have followed the faint outline of a trail left by deer or antelope. Connie cut straight through knee-high grass, sending up a cloud of insects, walking too fast to do any scouting. Near the bushes, he slowed down.

Behind them, the camp looked like a collection of toy wagons with curls of smoke drifting up from miniature campfires. A deep stillness surrounded them, broken only by sounds of the wind, insects, and their own clumsy movements.

The bushes hugged a dry, sandy creek bed. Connie stooped low, following the creek bed. "Let's take this like we're lookin' for horse thieves. I'd like to find those horse thieves."

"Coyote tracks," said Sid, studying the sand.

"Yeah, those." Billy was dismissive.

"Coyote for sure," said Connie.

"Let's get a look on the other side of those rocks up ahead, Connie," said Billy. "Be just the place for a bunch of Injuns to sneak up."

"That's what I'm thinkin'." Connie stooped lower.

They didn't know the first thing about scouting. *Playing games, like Jimmy and Matthew.* Still, Sid was glad to be with his new friends.

Connie motioned for quiet, creeping up to an outcropping of gypsum rock on the far side of the creek bed.

"We'd have had 'em if there was anybody here," said Billy.

Sid cringed. While they gloried in their successful campaign, he dropped to the ground. He hadn't grown up on a farm and gone hunting with Pa for nothing. Maybe he could teach them a thing or two about tracking. For one thing, you sure didn't go crashing around, then get quiet at the last minute. He eased past the rocks and bushes where he could get a good view of the plains beyond.

Connie lunged ahead. "Hellfire and damnation!"

Coming up fast was a small band of Indians on horseback. As they drew closer, Sid could make out a party of six in full war dress.

"They've got our horses!" said Connie. "Bunch of dirty Kaw. Comin' for more. We gotta get back to the camp and warn my dad."

"We got our guns," said Billy. "There's only 'bout half a dozen of 'em. We can pick 'em off before they get here."

"No!"—Before Sid could stop him, Billy took aim and fired.

The Kanza were out of range.

In an instant, they brought their horses to a stop. A man in the lead held something up.

"It's a broken arrow," said Sid. "He's holding up a broken arrow. He wants peace."

"That's all you know," said Billy. "Dirty Injuns are always doin' that so they can get the jump and scalp everybody, right Connie?"

Connie wasn't there. He was running back to camp waving his arms and yelling, "Indian Attack!" Mr. Wood would calm things down, except when the company stopped for nooning, he'd gone on to check the trail ahead, taking Mr. Joiner and Jeremy Sawyer. Mr. Reid would know what to do, but he was only one group captain. Sid didn't know the company well enough to predict what others might do. He had to act fast before Billy started shooting again.

The Kanza party inched closer.

Catching Billy off guard, he wrenched the gun from his grip and stood up in full view of the oncoming warriors, holding the gun up with both hands.

"Are you off your mental reservation?" Billy tackled him.

In the split second it took to fall Sid recognized a face: Ta Lezhé.

"Give me my gun, you stupid fool." Billy was on him, knee in his back, arm around his neck.

He couldn't defeat Billy. All he could do was keep him from shooting again. "Broken arrow, Billy," he panted.

The hold around his neck relaxed slightly.

"I know him, Billy. I know their leader. He saved my life—"

Billy was up and running for camp before Sid could explain.

"Ta Lezhé!" Sid called, pulling himself up.

Ta Lezhé brought his horse to a stop just short of Sid, pointing to himself, to the horses the men were leading, then to the wagon train.

They're returning the horses. Sid didn't know how to explain what he feared might happen. But if he walked with the men to camp, maybe it would show that the intentions of the Kanza were peaceful. He pointed to himself with his thumb, to Ta Lezhé with his forefinger, and made the sign for walk—two fingers down and "walking."

Ta Lezhé and the other men dismounted. As they approached the camp, sun glinted on gun barrels pointing at them. Connie's doing, probably made it sound like thousands of Indians were attacking. *Don't let anybody shoot. Please, God . . .*

Before they had covered half the distance, three men came to meet them: Mr. Reid, Mr. Ryckman, and Pa. They weren't carrying guns.

Mr. Reid talked rapidly with Ta Lezhé. "These men have also lost horses to thieves. Two of their younger men saw the company crossing Cottonwood Creek and stole the horses to make up for those they've lost. The men are returning them. We're into Pawnee, Cheyenne, and Arapaho territory now. They're enemies of the Kaw. They've taken a big risk to return the horses. They have gifts to show their sincere apology. I explained that the shot was fired by one of our boys who panicked and acted rashly. I invited them to share a meal. They'll present the gifts to you, Mr. Ryckman. I suggest that you give them coffee, sugar, and some cornmeal and anything else you can spare unless Isaiah Wood returns and says otherwise."

"Tell the Kanza that I am grateful to have the horses back," said Mr. Ryckman. "It will be our honor to have them share a meal with us. I'll have the missus collect some gifts. And tell them that I am sorry for the gunshot. Our boys are inexperienced."

They had a longer than usual nooning. Mr. Wood returned. He seemed to know Ta Lezhé. Like Mr. Reid, he spoke the Kanza language. Mr. Ryckman received a clay pipe, and a buffalo hide. Mr. Ryckman gave them a blanket, dried beef, and a large sack of beans. Mr. Wood gave them coffee and sugar.

There was one disruption in the proceedings when Cora ran over calling, "Mr. Ta, Mr. Ta!" She stopped short of the circle of men, suddenly turning red and running back to hide behind Ma's skirt.

Pa explained how Ta Lezhé saved the children from the rabid wolf. There were nods and sounds of approval from all the men—Kanza and Wood Company.

Later, Mr. Reid said, "That may have done more to improve attitudes toward our brothers than anything else could have. Good thinking, Sid. I'd like to think the Kaw could have approached our camp without conflict if you boys hadn't been out there. It's hard to say. Some of our people live in fear."

"They were in war dress," said Mrs. Payne. "It would be unsettling to see them riding up like that."

"It was their way of showing respect. It's like you dressing in your Sunday best to do business with somebody."

As Sid thought about it, he realized he had accepted a lot of praise he didn't deserve. It wasn't a great risk to stand up as the Kanza men approached. He knew Ta Lezhé. The Kanza took a bigger risk in walking to the wagon camp. The question was, had he made an enemy of Billy? The boys were a tight-knit bunch. They'd been together since Council Grove. And Billy seemed to have a grudge against him.

About an hour after nooning they crossed Running Turkey Creek. There was hardly enough water to make a big splash and no wood except for a house of logs and turf and a supply wagon. "Set up by a fellow name of Charles Fuller," Mr. Reid said. "Government's been giving land to folk willing to set up waystations and postal stops. Lot of folk are riding with the mail stages these days. Gives 'em regular business."

"Huh? I thought all this land belonged to the Indians," said Jimmy.

8.

MIXED GRASS PRAIRIE

The air was cold and crisp when the wagon train set out the next morning. Cloud masses floated above like enormous spoons of whipped cream heaped one on top of another. Sunrise and sunset were something to look forward to on the prairie. The clouds went all pink, gold, and purple. Wisps of pink stretched along the horizon like pulled cotton. Admittedly Sid hadn't paid much attention since Grace wasn't there to go on about it.

He felt for his hat.

A flock of whooping cranes flew over, white bodies shining in the sunlight, long black legs trailing behind. Grace would have been going on about them, too.

The Payne wagon was in the last row on the outside right. When the wind kicked up from the southwest, as it often did, it was the worst place to be in a wagon train. He'd be eating trail dirt all day. So would the team.

To his left Pa called to Cornflower and Promise. Ma and Mrs. Payne walked between the two wagons. Cora and Lydia followed along doing whatever they did to amuse themselves. Jimmy and Matthew came darting through, pausing long enough to ask what had happened to the tall grass that had been the stage for their endless games of conquest.

"We're in mixed grass country now," said Pa. "It will be two or three feet tall when it's had its full growth. You boys

73

are going to have to adjust your military strategy. It looks like a vast ocean out there. Maybe you can be ships at sea."

"Pirates!" said Jimmy.

"Yeah," said Matthew, "and I get to be a black pirate escaping from slavery."

"Me too!"

About mid-morning, Ma called, "Reckon what that is, Sid?" She pointed toward the vast prairie to the north, so flat it looked like somebody had rolled out a gray-green carpet. A cloud of dust swirled on the horizon.

"A dust devil?" But it couldn't be. A thin line of black appeared under the dust swirl, turning dark brown as it grew until it looked as if someone had poured a giant pot of boiling brown water along the horizon.

"Buffalo!" Word swept through the train along with Mr. Wood's orders. The front line of wagons stopped. They couldn't outrun stampeding buffalo. Their only hope was to create a barrier massive enough for the buffalo to avoid. Animals following the train were brought to a space in the middle with wagons closing in around them. Those tethered behind wagons were hitched to wheels in the narrow space between wagons.

A rumble like thunder grew, rising above the sounds of cracking whips, bellowing oxen, whinnying horses, and the frantic voices of children being herded into wagons.

Sid turned the team over to Mrs. Payne and brought in Buttercup, making her fast to the front wheel of their wagon behind Pa and the team. Ma was there to steady her.

He'd been told he had a way with animals, but it was all he could do to control Sandy. She stamped her feet, shook her head, and whinnied as he led her between their wagon and Mrs. Payne's. Freedom was high-strung. He hoped he could manage her on his own.

The earth began to vibrate under his feet.

Suddenly Jeremy Sawyer was there. "I'll get Freedom." He threw Sid another rope. "Get it around Sandy's neck. Mind you make a good knot. Tether may not be enough. We'll have to hold them, too."

Once the horses were secured to the wheels Jeremy extended a hand. "Reid sent me. Hope we aren't here to die together."

Sid wanted to say something funny and confident. "Me too," was all he could muster.

Pounding hooves beat the earth in a booming rhythm like waves crashing on the shore. The cloud looked like buffalo now. Hundreds of them. Heads down, churning dust as they came.

Sandy's nostrils flared as the unfamiliar earthy, smell of buffalo hit them. "Steady, girl."

It was terrifying but thrilling at the same time.

"They're heading right at us," said Jeremy. How could he be so calm? Sid felt like a leaf shaking in the wind.

He could see them now, five unswerving bulls in the lead. Like the point of a broad arrowhead. Aimed at them.

The herd fanned out behind. Would they turn in time? Could they?

"We're gonna be fine, Sandy, we're gonna be fine." *I hope. Let them turn . . . please let them turn.*

Horses screamed. Cattle bellowed. Children cried. Frightened calls of, "Whoa!" "Steady, steady" rose and were muffled by the deafening pound of unswerving buffalo hooves.

Dust hit the wagons carried by the forward force of the herd and a strong wind. Sid's eyes burned. His nose stung and all the way to his lungs despite the handkerchief tied around his face.

The momentary thrill was gone. They were done for.

He was going to die.

He didn't want to die. *Not like this.*

Closer.

Close enough to see their horns and the whites of their eyes.

He braced himself for the impact. Leaning into Sandy, he buried his face, terrified of looking.

But he couldn't bear not to look.

With split-second timing, the point of the gigantic arrowhead swerved. An endless line of buffalo curved past the rear of the train without slowing down. He could almost reach out and touch them. They were close enough to hear their heavy breathing, feel and smell the heat they generated. Sand lashed his hands and face.

The piercing scream of horses rose above the beat of hooves as they strained to break free and run with the stampede. "Steady, Sandy, steady old girl."

Jeremy's voice, as rasping as his own, called to Freedom.

The long line swept past leaving a thick cloud of dust hanging in the air and stragglers, the buffalo unable to keep up with the herd.

"Scared the thunderin' fool out of me!" Jeremy pulled the handkerchief from his face wiping his dust-caked brow with the back of his sleeve as the last buffalo passed. "How about you, Sid?"

Sid couldn't answer. His legs were jelly. He felt for his hat. Still there.

"I thought you were about to be the boy who died twice!" Jeremy patted him on the back.

Sid found himself grinning. "Me too."

Mr. Wood appeared on horseback. "Everybody good back here? Thought for sure they were taking off the back end of the train." He forbade the men from trying to shoot buffalo that lagged or from going after livestock that had broken away. "They're long gone. And we're not hunting buffalo till we need the meat."

"Reckon we did get the worst of it," said Jeremy. "Good horses. They held steady."

Dust settled. Order returned. Sid took his place beside Hope. Up ahead Mr. Wood called "Wagons roll!"

Sometime later, they halted for nooning across from a vast network of prairie dog mounds, larger than any prairie dog towns they had passed. Little prairie dogs romped on the mounds marking the entrance to underground homes. Cora and Lydia crept as close as they could get to the mounds, trying not to alarm the sentinel prairie dogs. But sharp warning cries sent the prairie dogs diving into their holes. They wouldn't come out until another cry signaled the all-clear. Unfortunately, there were too many children playing in the town for the all-clear to sound anytime soon. Cora and Lydia returned looking disappointed.

"Well," said Pa as they sat down to eat, "you have to admit we haven't been bored in the Wood Company."

"Buffalo didn't scare me," said Jimmy.

"Me neither," said Matthew, munching on corncake.

"Scared me," said Lydia.

"What'd ya expect from a girl?" said Jimmy. Matthew nodded.

"Me too, Lydia." Sid gave Jimmy a look. "I was nearly scared to death."

9.

The Little Arkansas River

The Little Arkansas River was another crossing people talked about fearfully. As they approached it one morning, a teamster train came their way. *Gallagher Trading Company* was written on the tall sides of the wagon beds. With all the excitement of being in a new company, Sid hadn't given much thought to the letter hidden under his toy soldiers. He wondered if he would see Mr. Gallagher before they got to Santa Fe now that he was in another company.

Crossing the Little Arkansas was anti-climactic after what they'd been through at Cottonwood Creek. Despite its high banks and swift current, every wagon made it across without major damage.

They nooned on the other side. As he got ready to meet the boys for marbles, Sid promised himself he'd bring up playing for keeps. There there hadn't been a good time. It wasn't a big deal anyway. Everybody had marbles and he never lost so many that he couldn't play. Admittedly, he passed up good shots to let Connie win, but he wanted friends. He still didn't feel a part of the group.

The boys were in the middle of an argument. "I say they were eyin' our horses," said Connie.

"I don't think so." Dale shook his head. "That man was just asking about them."

Billy guffawed. "That's all you know."

"I don't trust a bunch of Mexicans anyway," said Connie. "They wouldn't be askin' if they weren't thinkin' about stealin'. Besides, did you see the name on those wagons? 'William Gallagher?' Oughta tell you somethin'."

"What should it tell us?" Sid asked.

Billy shrugged. "Gallagher's a thief and a cheat."

"Everybody knows," Connie scoffed. "Ask any teamsters you meet. He's a crook. So, who's ready to play?"

It poisoned the afternoon. "Not exactly your best game, Sid," Billy sneered.

Squeaker snickered. "Maybe he's thinking about lessons."

"Yeah, about Bitsy Clark." Billy gave Connie a knowing look.

It was lost on Sid. He was so troubled he hurried back to the wagon and slipped the letter from his box of toy soldiers.

He had resisted the temptation to open it out of curiosity. But if Mr. Gallagher was a thief and a cheat, he'd better know what was in the letter. There was no telling what kind of dirty work he'd gotten himself into. It could put the family in danger.

Taking great pains to loosen the wax seal on the envelope without tearing it, he slid the letter out. He could seal it again and nobody need know the difference. The paper was so old it looked like it might fall apart. It was useless. The writing was in a foreign language.

He argued with himself as the team set out. Mr. Stokes said Gallagher was trustworthy. *But how would Mr. Stokes know?*

When Mrs. Payne came to lead while Anna napped, Sid told her about the letter. "We passed Gallagher trade wagons. The boys said Mr. Gallagher isn't trustworthy. I was worryin' about it, so I opened the letter. I mean, if he isn't trustworthy, there's no tellin' what I could be carryin' for him. I know it's wrong to read somebody else's mail, but I have to know if he was tellin' me the truth."

"And if he wasn't?"

"I don't know." Sid could feel the red creeping up his neck.

"You could just deliver the letter to Mrs. Gallagher as you promised."

"But these men are after it. What if they hunt me down? What if I'm puttin' everybody in danger?" His excuse for opening the letter wasn't holding up under her questioning. "I guess I shouldna opened it."

"Probably not."

"But the boys all said—"

"I suppose it is a matter of who you choose to trust, Sid. Mr. Stokes seemed to think highly of Mr. Gallagher. I'll have a look after lessons. If it seems to be too personal, I won't read it. If something seems amiss, we'll talk it over with your parents and decide what needs to be done."

He thought Ethel and Bitsy would never leave after lessons. Bitsy was especially annoying. "I hear you're really good at marbles, Sid."

Her simpering voice made him want to gag.

"How do you know?" Ethel asked. "Have you been spying on the boys?"

"A little bird told me." Bitsy laughed and batted her eyelashes.

Thankfully, Ethel said, "Come on, Bitsy. I promised your mother we wouldn't stay late."

When she finally looked at the letter, Mrs. Payne caught her breath. "Oh my, Sid! This is very old. It says 'Mission' something—I can't make it out, it's smudged. The rest is in remarkable condition. It's in Spanish." She studied it, eyes widening. "He said it was worth more than gold to her? I can see that. Your Mr. Gallagher was truthful. It's a family history. If I read this correctly, it tells of a black man on the US continent in the 1500s. I thought the first African people in America were slaves in the Virginia Colony in the 1600s. I'd like to read it. The writing is small. It will take me a while. Could I keep it until tomorrow? I'll put it in my Bible. It will be safe there."

Mrs. Payne read her translation of the letter to him the next evening after lessons.

> *My loved and beloved daughter, I pray this will reach your hands. No words can express my profound regret at abandoning you and your dearest mother. Loyalty to king? To God? Duty? Honor? Such are the lies I told to myself. Mark well, it was never for want of love for you or your mother. It was adventure that drove me, that and the lure of a hidden treasure belonging to our family. And what bitter lessons I have learned—*

"Hidden treasure?" Sid gasped. No wonder Sly and Gordon were after the letter.

> *—I had hoped to tell you the things herein upon my return this spring, for I had resolved to be home by then. But there will be no returning. I am weary. The Presidio is no sanctuary from smallpox. The mission has lost half of its natives. I fear I am soon to succumb, for I now show the signs, hence the urgency of this letter—*

"Smallpox?" said Sid. "They had it then, too?"

> *—But to the more important matter: I know now the truth of what I have been told since childhood. I had thought stories of our family were small truths embellished by time. It is not so. The blood of one Esteban de Dorantes, of*

the city of Azamoor in Morocco, runs through our veins. He was a Moor, a slave, a remarkable man; more educated than those who claimed to own him, more gifted in languages than any of them. It is said that he became a believer, converting to the one true Church, but I suspect he remained one of the Moriscos.

Mrs. Payne looked up. "A Morisco is a Muslim forced to convert to Christianity in Spain back in the Middle Ages. A Moroccan Moor would have been black. This is what I find so remarkable, given that the letter is dated 1790.

He was a healer. As our family story goes, after eight years wandering with Álvar Núñez Cabeza de Vaca, Esteban was sent by Antonio de Mendoza to guide the ill-fated expedition of Marcos de Niza.

"Sid, Cabeza de Vaca must have been part of an expedition that was supposed to explore what is now New Mexico Territory or maybe the southern coast. I don't know that history."

It is said that our ancestor acquired turquoise, silver, and native women. (This leads me to believe that he never fully converted from Islam.) As the family story goes, one of these women Esteban named Suna, from the Persian word for gold. We are told that he said, "You are more than gold to me." For he loved her above all others.

Esteban and his party were taken prisoner by the Zuni, who believed he was an imposter for taking on the trappings of a medicine man. Esteban helped the others to escape, including his beloved Suna, who had in her possession a great store of his wealth and carried his child. It is said that she returned to Mexico City, where the child was born. Suna's great beauty must have caught the eye of

Juan Rodríguez Cabrillo, for she and her child, Luisa María, accompanied Cabrillo on his voyage to explore the Pacific coast of New Spain. When Cabrillo died at San Miguel Mission, she and Luisa María remained. The ship and its crew went on to explore the coast.

There is a small chapel near here made of native adobe, lovingly attended by the friars. It was built by the few who remained when Cabrillo's men left. Suna lived out her life here, and it is here where Esteban's treasure is to be found—beautifully wrought silver, turquoise, and an emerald, more precious than all—

Sid caught his breath. "An emerald?"
Mrs. Payne nodded. "Wait till we get to the end, Sid."

When she was old enough, Luisa María was sent to Spain for her education and married well, having found favor among the nobility of the court. She returned to New Spain with her husband, an Englishman by birth and Spanish by his own adoption. He took her name as his own. They found their way to Santa Fe when it was little more than a pueblo at the base of the Sangre de Cristo Mountains, leaving all but the faint memory of Suna and her treasure behind.

Our family clung to the name of Esteban, but I alone held to the legend of Suna and her treasure. My own eyes have seen the grave of Suna in the shadow of the chapel. My own eyes have beheld Suna's treasure. I write, not to inform you of the treasure, but to teach you of your past. The treasure is best left here with Suna, a lesson I have learned to my great sorrow.

Now may such meager blessing as is mine to give rest upon you.

Your loving father who from his heart loves, and esteems, and wishes to see you,

Fernando Esteban Alvarez.
19.09.1790

"There's a note at the bottom, Sid. It's written in another hand:

Fernando Esteban Alvarez died and was buried in the yard of The Chapel of Our Lady of Many Sorrows next to the grave of Suna Esteban as was his request. He was a kind, just, and fair leader, who defended the native peoples against those who would misuse them. He wished to be remembered as a servant of our Lord and faithful to his beloved wife and daughter.

Attested to this 23rd day of September 1790.
Fray Juan Gómez.

"Then Mr. Gallagher was telling the truth," said Sid, "and Bayless Sly was right, too."

"This could be extremely important, Sid. You were wise to guard the letter carefully." Mrs. Payne gently spread out the old letter. "Look, down here at the bottom. This is in English. Curious, don't you think? I'm not sure if it's in the same hand as the note. I think it is. But the ink is different, and it isn't dated."

Sid read it aloud:

A deed. Toothless Crook!
Who rows life unhurt?
He who has ears, let him hear—"I can't read this bit in Spanish."

"It repeats the last line. *El que tiene oídos, que oiga.* 'He who has ears, let him hear.' It's from the Bible."

"It doesn't make any sense."

"It's puzzling." She turned the letter over. "Up here at the beginning, he writes, 'And what bitter lessons I have learned.' Then at the end he advises, 'It is best left here, with Suna a lesson I have learned to my great sorrow.' It could be a warning to the one to whom the letter was addressed, or to anyone reading the letter."

"It sounds like the treasure is buried with Suna."

"Maybe. Sid, there are legends of treasure buried all over the great Southwest. Mr. Payne knew hundreds of them. Hundreds of people have died looking for treasure. The thugs you talk about won't pay any attention to warnings, English or Spanish. If we don't see your Mr. Gallagher before we get to Santa Fe, you must deliver this. Do you have a safe place for it?"

"Yes, Ma'am. I keep it in—"

"Don't tell me. Put it away. Don't take it out again. It is best not to speak of it to anyone, even your father and mother.

"You know, Sid, you haven't seemed like yourself since you joined the Wood Company. It is terribly hard to leave family and friends at home. That makes losing Grace even harder. I know you worry about her. Having smallpox must have been a terrible ordeal for you, too. I was hoping that leading the team and your studies would help you snap back. Sometimes it's routine that holds us together when everything seems to be falling apart.

"You've done so well with the team. I'm proud of the way you've taken to working with the little children. You're a good teacher. Your Latin is coming along nicely. You've helped Bitsy to learn Marc Antony's address. I'm pleased with your grasp of history and mathematics. You've read just about everything I have with me except Dr. Willis' medical books. But frankly, I'm missing the old sparkle you and Grace brought to the Stokes Company."

He didn't know what to say.

Sounds of the camp drifted their way. Someone played a violin.

"Some things are important enough to be sad about. Your parents hoped having friends would help. But Sid, sometimes having friends isn't enough. They have to be the right kind of friends, the kind who lift you up."

He lay awake that night. It felt like he was under a dark cloud. But he didn't know how to get out from under it.

*****

Sid's supply of marbles was dwindling. Only he, Connie, and Frog had any at the end of the last game. How could they go on if they insisted on playing for keeps? He should say something. And maybe it was time to quit letting Connie win.

Eli was drawing a circle on the ground in the shade of the Ryckman wagon when he spotted them. "He's here, he's here," called Squeaker.

"Guess his Pa gave him leave," said Billy.

Everyone was unusually quiet.

Eli, Dale, and Squeaker had marbles again. Maybe they'd kept some in reserve, too. According to their rules, you could play as long as you had a taw to shoot with.

When it was his turn, Sid took the best shot he could see. Dale and Eli wouldn't have stayed in the game long if the others hadn't been gunning for him. It was another way to tell him he didn't belong.

Squeaker never lasted long. Once he was out of the game, he danced around the circle until Connie told him to sit down and shut up. Billy would have been a better player if there hadn't been an unspoken ban on Connie's mibs. In the second round, Billy's taw didn't leave the ring. He was out. Frog ignored Billy's taw to go after Sid.

Sid took Billy's taw and another one of Connie's mibs.

Billy's face turned red. "You and Frog get 'em, Connie."

Squeaker leaned over to cheer Connie on. Connie shot wildly. His taw rolled to a stop just inside the ring without touching a single marble. He was out. Jumping up in a fury, he punched Squeaker in the stomach. Hard. "Made me miss, you stupid jackass!"

Squeaker doubled over. But he didn't make a sound.

The air crackled with tension. Nobody said a word. He should say something, call Connie out. But he didn't.

"Frog," Billy scowled at Sid. "It's on you."

They were so evenly matched Sid thought the game would go on forever. Connie brought it to a stop. "Noonin's about over," he said crisply. "Frog wins. He has the most marbles."

Still expressionless, Frog put all his marbles in a heap inside the circle.

"Who needs to buy mibs?" asked Connie. "You're all out, Dale."

"Heck, I ain't got no money left to buy stuff."

"Frog will trade," said Connie, "How about that beaded pouch you bought off that Injun back in Council Grove? It'll buy you a dozen mibs."

"Make him give up his braces," snickered Squeaker. "Then his pants gonna fall down." He laughed in his high-pitched, squeaky voice as if he'd made an excessively funny joke.

Dale ignored Squeaker. "Pa would hide me."

"Guess your playing days are over," said Billy, "less you come up with some money. Or you can get 'em back the way

Squeaker does." He gave Connie a knowing look.

Dale looked down.

"Eli?" Connie asked.

Eli stood and shuffled his feet. "Guess my playing days are over, too."

"Billy?"

"I'll take a dozen, plus a taw—on credit."

Connie nodded. Frog handed Billy a dozen marbles and a taw, gathering up the rest.

"Reckon you got lessons tonight, Sid," Connie said dismissively.

"Yeah," Squeaker chortled, "Except he's done lost his *old sparkle*."

"Shut up you stupid fool," growled Billy.

They'd been spying on him. Sid felt like he'd been punched in the stomach, too. How much had they heard?

Even before he put away his marbles, Sid checked to make sure the letter was safe. *Enough is enough!* As hard as he'd tried to be friends, it wasn't working.

10.

COW CREEK CROSSING

After they entered mixed grass country, the company almost always formed a large circle at night to contain livestock. Campfires were built outside the circle. Wagon groups adjacent to each other often joined together around a common fire after the day's work was done. Since the wagon groups went in a different order every day, it was a good way to get to know everyone in the company. Bits of conversation, music of guitar, harmonica, and violin floated in the air, punctuated by outbursts of laughter as people found ways to make trail life seem like home.

One night they camped at Cow Creek Crossing, a welcome stop with plenty of wood and water. The Reid and Joiner groups shared a fire. Mr. Wood came to sit with them. He made a point of sitting with a different group every evening. Sid hoped he would talk about his days as a trapper, wandering all over the West. It wasn't long before somebody asked him a question about Old Fort Bent, located along the mountain route of the Santa Fe Trail.

"I sold fur to Charles and William Bent before they ever built the fort. It's in ruins now. We'll miss it and New Fort Bent. We're taking Aubry's Cut Off. It avoids the mountains. Now Old Fort Bent, that was *some* place."

They were in for a good story with a history lesson in the bargain.

"Thing you have to remember about the Bent brothers is that they are businessmen. Traders. William Bent married into Cheyenne royalty, became a member of the tribe and a sub-chief"—wide-eyed, Jimmy and Matthew left their play to sit beside Sid on a log behind the circle closest to the fire—"his wife was Mistanta, Owl Woman, a Cheyenne princess, the daughter of White Thunder. The Cheyenne called him *Schi-vehoe*, or 'Little White Man.' The Cheyenne used to claim all the territory north and south of the Arkansas. White Thunder was a mighty chief and medicine man. He was 'Keeper of the Arrows,' the four sacred arrows of the Cheyenne. I only met White Thunder once. He was an impressive man—razor-sharp mind.

"William and his wife had a room at the old fort, but Mistanta preferred the lodge built for their wedding back in the Cheyenne village. Bent was gone for six months at a time, running his train back to Missouri trading goods. She lived in the lodge when she wasn't traveling with him. She did more to build peaceful relations between soldiers, white traders, and plains tribes than all the big shots they sent out from Washington.

"Bent brought the family back to the fort in the winter. Mistanta had a bark lodge built in the plaza. She died— that was a couple of years before cholera took out half the Cheyenne. I don't think Bent ever recovered.

"Must have been in '47 that Bent burned the fort—"

"Burned it?" Jimmy's hand flew to his mouth.

Mr. Wood nodded. "To the ground. Some say it was because the Army didn't make good on paying him to use it. Some say he couldn't stand the sight of it after Mistanta was gone. Not for me to say. He built a new fort at Big Timbers on the Arkansas. The Cheyenne camped at Big Timbers during the hunting season and in winter. So Bent knew it would be a good location."

"I can tell you, any peace we have with the Cheyenne today? Thank Mistanta and William Bent. Some say he loves peace. I figure he loves trade. Can't have trade without peace.

"Charlotte Green was there back in the days of the old fort. William's brother, Charles, inherited the Greens as slaves. Brought them out from St. Louis. She was one cook to remember. And parties? She knew how to throw a party. Charlotte could dance your shoes off. Called herself 'the only lady in the whole damned Indian country.' Begging your pardon for the language, ladies." Mr. Wood looked around apologetically. "Mistanta would have disputed that. She was the real first lady.

"Mistanta focused on family. The Bent children learned about pancakes and fine china, and they learned about Cheyenne ways. At the Old Fort, children ran everywhere underfoot. Mistanta wanted people to know times were peaceful, and families were safe. It was a great place." Mr. Wood paused to tamp his pipe.

"It couldn't have been so great for the Greens, not if they were slaves." Ma was not one to be outspoken, but when it came to slavery, she refused to be silent. "It's more than disappointin' to find slavery out here."

"I don't hold with slavery." Mr. Wood shook his head. "Charlotte and her husband Dick, and his brother—all three were at the fort—probably had a better life than most. But they weren't free, not till Charles Bent died and set them free in his will. Last I heard, they'd moved back to St. Louis."

"He coulda freed 'em and paid 'em a living wage," said Mr. Joiner.

"The Cheyenne have slaves." One of the men spoke up. "The way I heard it they wagon trains, take captives, and trade them off."

Mr. Joiner shook his head, "It's wrong no matter who's doing it."

A man in the shadows leaned forward. Sid gasped. *Bayless Sly!* One of the crooks who threatened Mr. Gallagher. His stomach in knots, Sid slid into the protective shadows cast by Ma and Pa.

It wasn't unusual for strangers to join them, especially at a popular camping site such as Cow Creek. Travelers going alone or in small groups often camped nearby, sometimes traveling with the train, visiting around one of the campfires at night, and exchanging news and stories. At some point, they went their own way.

Sly spoke up. "Way I heared it, the old fort was runnin' with half-breeds."

Mr. Wood frowned. "Children growing up at the fort were lucky to be in a place where folk knew how to show respect for each other."

Sly squeezed himself into the circle. J.J. Gordon remained in the shadows.

"What brings you gentlemen west?" asked Mr. Joiner.

"Me and my associate, J.J. Gordon, work for William Gallagher Trading Company out of Santa Fe. You know Gallagher?"

A chill ran up Sid's spine.

Mr. Wood nodded. "Honest man. Married into one of Santa Fe's leading families."

"Seen him lately?"

"Not since my last trip through Santa Fe. He's well?"

"Very well. See, I'm his right-hand man; manage the day-to-day work of the company fer 'em. Ask anybody you meet in Santa Fe."

"I'll make a point to do that," said Mr. Wood. "Gallagher's a big name in Santa Fe."

Sly nodded. "Gallagher depends on me. Sent me 'n Mr. Gordon to find a family name of Johnson. They were with the Stokes Company out of Westport, about three weeks ahead of you."

Jimmy gasped. Sid motioned for him to be quiet. Ma sat next to Pa holding the Reid baby. Her shoulders tightened, but neither she nor Pa said anything.

"Stokes Company arrived in Santa Fe. Johnsons wasn't with 'em. They dropped out. One of their children died of the pox. Me 'n Mr. Gordon, has had our work cut out tryin' to find 'em."

"But—" Sid put his hand over Jimmy's mouth before he could finish.

"Nobody's heard of 'em since. We been askin' every company headed this way. Somebody oughta know somethin' about 'em."

"What sort of business did Mr. Gallagher have with the Johnson family?" Mr. Joiner asked, looking Bayless Sly up and down. "It'd help if we knew."

Mr. Sly looked straight at Pa and Ma. "I don't rightly know. Mr. Gallagher kept that to his-self."

"Seems odd," Joiner said, "seeing as how he depends on you for everything."

"It was personal-like."

"My name's Johnson," said Pa—Sid caught his breath— "but I don't know your Mr. Gallagher—"

"Johnson's a common name," said Mr. Wood, before Pa could finish. "You must be looking for somebody else."

"Not safe to take up with folk who've had the pox," said Mr. Reid, yawning widely.

"Wouldn't want 'em in the company," said Mr. Joiner. "Pox gets started, could wipe out the whole train." There were sounds of agreement. It felt like Pa and Ma were being surrounded by a protective fence.

"What do you know about these Johnsons, in case we see 'em?" asked Mr. Wood.

"We ain't actually met Johnson," said Sly. "Has a little tow-headed girl name of Cora."

Sid could feel Jimmy tense. "Just stay down. They can't see us," he whispered. Thankfully, Cora was fast asleep in the tent.

"Ran into the misses and the young 'en in Westport before we knew who she was. Coulda saved a whole lotta trouble if we'd known."

Mr. Wood leaned forward. "If we run into them, I'll send Gallagher word by postal express—"

"Ain't no need to trouble 'bout that. Me 'n J.J.'s gonna be at New Fort Bent awhile. Give us a chance to meet wagons comin' this way. Might catch up with Johnson there."

"That would be the place to find 'em," said Joiner.

"Course, they coulda gone back home," said Jeremy's dad. "Some folks run into trouble, and it sends them straight home."

Mr. Wood stood. "Reckon I'd better head off to bed." He leaned down, shaking hands with the two men. "Glad to meet you. If you see Gallagher before I do, tell him 'Howdy' from Isaiah Wood. You're welcome to share my fire in the morning. Still got coffee. That's more than some can say this side of New Fort Bent."

"That's right neighborly of you, Isaiah Wood," said Bayless Sly as he and J.J. stood. "Might jest do that."

Al Joiner stood, shaking hands with the two men. They towered over him. "I see you're camped alongside the train. Good thinking. Never know what kind of fools is out and about. Couple of honest men like you could get cleaned out in the night. You're safe with us. Wood posts a double watch in these parts. I'm on watch here in a bit. I'll make a point to keep an eye on you."

Mr. Reid chuckled. "Joiner here is a might shorter than some, but you fellas can rest easy. He could shoot the eyelashes off a flea on a dark night. Got some mighty fine men keepin' watch. Get yourselves a good night's rest. Maybe we'll run into you again at the fort."

But they weren't going to the fort. The company was taking another branch of the trail. *Thank God!* It was a small relief, though. How much did Bayless Sly know? Was he at the campfire when Mr. Wood said they would be taking Aubry's Cut Off? Had he recognized Ma?

All around the circle, fires were banked as people made their way to bed. Sid lay down on his bedroll, too uneasy to sleep. Bayless Sly and J.J. Gordon didn't seem to recognize Ma. She was holding the Reid baby. And Cora wasn't there. Maybe that threw them off.

The camp took on night sounds. Occasional snoring came from under neighboring wagons. Oxen and horses shifted as they settled in the center of the circle. From somewhere far in the distance, the spine-chilling howl of wolves cut through the dark.

As soon as he heard Pa's heavy breathing, Sid came to a decision. He wasn't sure what he could do, but he had to find Sly and Gordon.

Slipping out from under the wagon, he darted from shadow to shadow. Al Joiner would be on guard duty soon. He wouldn't get past Mr. Joiner. At last, he saw a small wagon with mules picketed nearby. Had to be them. *Mustn't alarm the mules.*

The bright red-orange dots of burning cigarettes assured him the two men were not settled for the night. He crept as close as he dared. "Now that's just plain stupid, J.J. Been worryin' 'bout you ever since we caught up with Gallagher on that steamboat. Yer goin' soft on me. Gallagher was messin' with your head, talkin' about all he done for you. The thing you gotta remember about Gallagher is he's out for his-self."

"Yeah, but he done helped me get outta debt and on my feet when nobody else was willin' to give me a hand—"

"No 'yeah buts' about it," interrupted Sly. "Gallager's fer Gallagher. He wouldna done nothin' for you if I hadn't made 'em do it. 'You gotta give folk a hand,' I says to 'em. I says, 'Take that Gordon fellow. He's a good worker. Deserves a chance.' Course he done took the credit. Then he up and fires us like that."

"Fired you, Bayless. You talked me into quittin'. Dumbest fool thing I ever done."

"Now don't go gettin' on yer high horse, J.J. That's all water under the bridge. You're in over your head now. No turnin' back. That letter's real important to Gallagher. Smells like treasure to me. Heck, I didn't work for Doña Catalina's family all those years for nothin'. I heard a thing or two."

"Yeah, but it's supposed to be cursed. 'Who rows life unhurt?' Man in St. Louis read that part right out. Can't think 'a no reason to keep lookin'. You do what you want. When we get to the fort, I'm goin' my own way. I'm done. I told you before."

Sly let out a string of cuss words. "'Tootless crook?' Heck, J.J., we both got our teeth. Somebody's idea of scarin' folk off the treasure. Don't run out on me now. We got the chance of a lifetime. A couple of smart fellas like us—like me, anyways—oughta be able to figure out how to get some treasure outta Gallagher for the letter and find the treasure out there in Californee. Then we disappears into Mexico, where we leads the good life."

"If you're so hell-bent on goin' to California, get on with it. I don't wanna go anymore. I told ya, I'm done. Ain't no call to go botherin' folk here. They's good folk. Kind to each other. You heard how they stood up for Johnson. They just wanna find a better place to live, like me when I ended up in Santa Fe. Shoulda stayed."

"Now there's where you got it wrong again. We don't get the letter, we miss a sure thing. Findin' the treasure is a chance deal. Gettin' somethin' out of Gallagher is like playin' with a marked deck of cards. Johnson stole that letter. They was on the same steamboat comin' up the Missouri."

"Lot of folk was on that steamboat."

"Nah, Johnson's got it. They was at the same hotel in Westport. I wouldna known Johnson from nobody, but we seen that tow-headed girl stick her head out of the tent as we was ridin' up. Little girl's our ticket. We nab her, trade her for the letter, and grab a couple of those horses—you seen them horses? They'll bring a handsome price."

Kidnap Cora? Sid's blood ran cold.

"I ain't hurtin' no little girl," said J.J.

"Ain't a gonna hurt nobody, jest grab her till they come up with that letter. Kill that danged cat, too."

"Cat gave you somethin' to remember her by, that's for sure."

Bayless pulled up the sleeve of his shirt, inspecting his arm. "Who keeps a danged cat in their hotel room? Hope the coyotes got it by now."

"I'm through, Bayless. Get that into your head." J.J. snuffed out the butt end of his cigarette. "This ain't turnin' out the way it was supposed to. We was gonna find the letter before Gallagher did, buy it off that crook in St. Louis, and go for the treasure except he got there first. I didn't sign on for nothin' else. I ain't got a dime left. You done spent all my money. I'm goin' home. You're on your own." J.J., threw himself on his bedroll, his back to Bayless Sly.

"We'll see 'bout that," said Sly. "I'm gettin' some sleep. We got an early start tomorrow."

Gripped by fear, Sid eased backward. It was time to talk to Pa. When he got back to the wagon, he slipped his box of toy soldiers out of its hiding place. He sat for a while, trying to think what to do. Then, tucking it under his bedroll, he settled down under the wagon.

He awoke with the bugle call and felt for the box of soldiers. It was there. He hastily returned it to the safe place.

Sly and Gordon were gone.

"Pa, they were the men who broke into our room in Westport." They stood in front of their teams, waiting for the signal to move out.

Pa nodded. "Undoubtedly. But what in thunderation could they want with us? That whole cockamamy story—"

"Mr. Wood lied for us."

"I think he knows a snake when he sees one."

"Wagons roll!" The call came before Sid could tell him about the letter.

11.

NEAR THE GREAT BEND IN THE ARKANSAS RIVER

Thunderheads were gathering on the horizon to the southwest when the train stopped for nooning. They'd be making camp for the night a bit early.

Sid had been through more than one cracking thunderstorm along the Santa Fe Trail. Sometimes the lightning was so fierce it sent fireballs skipping across the ground. Thunder could be deafening. But gathering clouds of another sort troubled him.

He meant to talk to Pa at nooning. But Mr. Wood called for a meeting of captains and asked Pa to attend. Sid tried to reassure himself. After all, Sly and Gordon were going to New Fort Bent.

Until about five years ago, most trains took the 66-mile route through the desert to avoid the Rocky Mountains. But Colonel Francis Aubry discovered a shorter route with more water that avoided the mountains and American Indian hunting grounds. The company was taking Aubry's Cut Off. So, if Sly and Gordon planned to kidnap Cora, why were they be going to New Fort Bent? Did Mr. Wood's talk about the old fort confuse them? When had they joined the campfire?

When it came time to meet the boys for marbles, his

heart wasn't in it. Eli and Dale had marbles. He might have wondered how they got them if he hadn't been preoccupied. Connie and Billy could talk of little else but the two strangers at the campfire. Like they had been there, and he hadn't.

"Mr. Wood came by our wagon last night," said Connie. "Said we'd better post a double guard on the horses. He figures they're after our Thoroughbreds. They're meetin' about it now. My dad won't blink at shootin' anybody tryin' to steal our horses. Me neither. Heck, I'll shoot first and ask questions later."

Sid wasn't impressed. Not after seeing Connie run like his pants were on fire when they spotted the Kanza warriors coming toward camp. He was thoroughly disgusted with the boys and with himself. He was desperate to talk with Pa. But the meeting didn't break up until nearly time to yoke up. *Why didn't I wake him up last night and tell him?*

They hadn't traveled more than an hour when Mr. Wood called a halt. Clouds piling up along the horizon were now a sinister, gray-purple color and closing in fast. The company braced for a storm. Every wagon had to position its back to the wind and pull as close to the next wagon as it could. All the livestock were herded into the circle. The last wagon pulled in to close the gap.

By the time the team was unyoked, the wind had picked up. Greenish-black clouds rolled like water in a hot cauldron. Jagged forks of lightning splintered the sky. Earsplitting thunder followed.

Livestock milled around inside the circle, sensing the danger swiftly closing in. Ma and Mrs. Payne had everyone safely inside the Johnson wagon when Sid and Pa crawled in.

Hail began to fall. Big hailstones, larger than a walnut, hit the unprotected animals. Horses screamed. Oxen and cattle bellowed.

It stopped only to have wind slap the wagon with terrifying ferocity, rocking it like a cradle. Rain hurled so hard and heavy that mist fell on them despite their double-layered canvas bonnet. Baby Anna whimpered.

Suddenly everything went quiet. The silence was more terrifying than the sound of the storm.

"That's no good." Pa peered out of the bonnet closure. It looked like someone had snuffed out all the lights in a dark room.

"Under the wagon, quick," he yelled. "On your bellies." They scrambled down. Ma was last, dragging the featherbed. In less time than it takes to tell, they were packed like sardines in a tin with the featherbed stretched over them.

"Anchor it on your end Sid," yelled Pa. "Pull it over your heads, everybody!" It was the last thing Sid heard before a roar split the silence.

Like some ancient fury, the storm pelted them with nameless objects. The wagon groaned and creaked above them.

The storm's rage was spent in minutes. Driving rain followed like a second fury. The ground shook as terrified livestock broke through a gap the storm had left in the circle.

Sid looked out from under the featherbed. Wagons on either side were undisturbed. Lightning lit the sky, revealing a long, snake-like cloud lashing the earth to the east, sending sagebrush, rocks, and dirt flying. The featherbed was covered with debris—mud, dirt, rocks, pieces of other wagons, even an iron cooking pan that had narrowly missed striking his head.

The rain let up. Shaking off the debris, they crawled out. "Hurry, Ben," said Ma, "There's gonna be some folk injured."

"Sid, get your Ma her doctoring bag and come with me."

"Go," Mrs. Payne urged. "We'll take care of things here. My wagon's still upright."

Baby Anna's face was red from screaming. Cora started to cry, grabbing for Ma. Mrs. Payne reached down, gently restraining her. "Cora, you and Lydia see if you can find Serina. She'll be somewhere in the wagon. She needs you. Matthew, Jimmy, help me shake out this featherbed—"

Sid didn't hear the rest. His eyes swept the circle. Contents of wagons were strewn everywhere. Ma knew what she was doing when she grabbed the featherbed to protect them from flying debris.

The tornado's deadly funnel had dipped down outside the circle, tearing into wagons as it cut a path through the train. Some wagons were smashed to smithereens along with everything inside. Others were lifted into the air and set down elsewhere, unharmed. Some stood on end, looking as if a giant had held them up, shaking their contents to the wind. Others were completely unharmed.

Rain fell again, but they could not stop. They dodged rubble as well as barrels and crates that looked as if gentle hands had carefully arranged them. Heart-wrenching cries cut through the confusion as those who could, freed themselves from the rubble.

A few yards away the empty Davies wagon stood upright in the middle of the circle, its bonnet barely dented. Ma knelt by Mrs. Davies who sat on the ground rocking back and forth. Little Ella Sue rested in her arms, lifeless. Mr. Davies sat with one arm around his wife, the other holding wide-eyed, uncomprehending little Tobias.

Sid could hardly comprehend either. How could bright, happy little Ella Sue, the first in his group of school children to count to 100, be dead?

Mr. Wood appeared, shouting orders, organizing people

who were already helping. "Leave the livestock. Too many people hurt to spare anybody. We'll run 'em down tomorrow. Get these wagons righted so we can find the wounded." He sent people to help with the wagons that had taken the most damage, appointing men to be in charge.

"Reid, you're in charge of helping the injured once we find 'em. See who's in greatest need. Anybody who can help, make yourself known." Mr. Wood joined Ma in tending the wounded who had already been found.

Sid and Pa were among those sent to help the Sinclair group where the tornado hit hardest. It looked as if someone had stomped on the wagons. Sid caught his breath. Ethel was nowhere to be seen. Nearby, Frog Barton stood next to an upside-down wagon. Cries came from underneath. Sid and Pa hurried to help, but before they got there, Frog squatted down, gripped the side of the wagon, and turned it up in one mighty heave. Other hands rushed to the family, bruised and cut, but alive.

"Over here, Mr. Johnson, there's folk trapped under here." Jeremy Sawyer and his father were straining to right a wagon standing on its side propped up by its crushed bonnet stays.

They found a family of six underneath, remarkably unharmed. But the wagon's contents were nowhere to be seen. "It's not even our wagon," said the man, looking around in bewilderment.

"There," said Pa. Cries came from another upside-down wagon. Its shredded bonnet and stays stuck out on either side.

"Help! Please somebody help. We're hurt bad."

"Hold on, we're coming," called Pa.

"Load's still underneath," said Mr. Sawyer. "If we lift her up, we could make things worse."

"There's barrels around," said Sid, "could we brace—"

They were rolling barrels over before he could finish the thought. They propped up the front of the wagon and began easing things out from under bit by bit. Moaning and uncontrollable sobbing grew louder as they cleared a path to the trapped family.

"Behind the trunk, we're back here." The voice sounded familiar.

"Hang on," called Pa. "We're close. Sid, see if you can crawl back there and ease that trunk out. Mind where you move. The whole thing could crash."

Edging his way, Sid managed to grip the end of a small trunk.

"You can move the trunk," called the voice. "It's not holdin' anything up. I'm pinned down behind it."

Sid backed his way out, dragging the trunk through the narrow tunnel they had created until Pa could reach in and help. Behind the trunk, Dale Goodall lay on his stomach under a heap of cornmeal and eggs, wedged between a barrel and a large sack of rice. Sobbing and moaning came from behind him.

Dale winced. "It's my Ma and little sisters. Pa's trying keep the wagon from falling on them."

"Come on then. Let's get you out." Sid swept away broken eggs and cornmeal, took Dale by the hands, and eased him out from under the bag of rice. He backed out on hands and knees. There wasn't room to turn around. Somebody helped Dale to his feet and threw a blanket around him. They'd found the Goodall's tent and set it up.

Sid followed Pa, crawling back under the wagon. Jeremy and his father went around to the back of the wagon so Pa could tell them where to brace it.

Dale's two little sisters were behind the rice sack leaning

up against their father, who bore the weight of the wagon bed. Sid helped them to crawl out. A woman gathered them into her arms.

By the time he was back under the wagon, Jeremy and his father had shifted the weight from Mr. Goodall. "Couldn't support it," he panted. His shoulder was bare. Blood trickled down the front of his torn shirt.

Sid had to back out again so Mr. Goodall could scoot out. "Bring a blanket if anybody can find one," called Pa.

Somebody handed Sid a blanket as he started back. Once the back of the wagon was braced, Jeremy and his father were able to help free Mrs. Goodall. But she was unable to move.

Sid gasped.

She looked at him with vacant eyes, moaning as her swollen arms clung to Dale's lifeless baby brother.

Pa and Mr. Sawyer took her out on the blanket. Sid crawled out after them, his stomach churning. Leaning against the broken wagon he vomited violently. Jeremy patted him on the back. "I know, Sid. I know."

He took a deep breath as the vomiting subsided. "Pull yourself together, Son," Pa called. "We're needed."

The rain washed the vomit from his clothing as he turned to follow Pa. Under the shelter, a couple of men handed Mr. Goodall a bottle of whiskey. "That shoulder's dislocated. Take a good swig. We're gonna haveta pop it back in place." A woman knelt beside Mrs. Goodall, who still clung to the baby. Dale stood where Sid had left him, blanket gripped tightly, shaking as if he were in the freezing cold.

"I'm sorry, Dale." It felt hollow, but he didn't know what else to say. He couldn't tell if Dale even heard him. As he left, he saw Ma on her way to help. Pa motioned him on.

Under Mr. Reid's direction, people who still had them

brought tents to set up so the injured could be moved out of the rain. Mercifully, it was slowing to a drizzle, but it left them freezing cold.

He and Pa found the Joiner wagon in pieces. Pearl had freed herself. Al's head stuck out from under the wreckage. He was trapped. Tears streaming down her face, Pearl was desperately trying to free him. "Don't leave me, Al. Please, please don't leave me!"

Pa knelt, taking Al's pulse at the temple. "He's alive, Miss Joiner. We'll get him out."

"It hit so fast. Wagon collapsed over us. Al pushed me out but it fell on him."

They removed a heap of wagon remains finding Al flat on his back, his upper body pinned beneath a trunk. Pa took one corner and Sid the other. "Don't move him, Miss Joiner. He may have broken bones. Ready, Sid?"

"No! I can do that. He's my brother. I'll care of him. I don't need any help."

It wasn't a job for one person. But Pearl protested as they heaved the trunk. With it came most of Al Joiner's shirt. He was covered with blood. A deep gash traced from his shoulder almost to his waist. Pearl threw her shawl over him but not before Sid saw.

Al Joiner was a woman.

"Never mind, Sid," said Pa.

Miss Joiner looked like a cornered rabbit. "Please. Don't take Al to one of the tents. Please don't—"

"Get your Ma, Sid. Tell her Al Joiner needs to see her. Don't let her send anybody else. Now don't go fretting, Miss Joiner. Let's get that bleeding stopped."

Sid found Ma under a makeshift shelter putting a splint on a girl's arm. Ethel! She was alive. He breathed an inward sigh of relief. Mrs. Sinclair cradled Ethel's head, giving her a drink of whisky. Her eyes clenched shut, she choked down the whiskey, sputtering. "Deep breaths, Ethel," said Mrs. Sinclair. "Take deep breaths. It'll be over soon."

"That ankle looks bad, too," said Ma. "Let's have a look, Ethel. I know it hurts. Keep remindin' yourself it hurts because you're alive. The good news is it isn't broken. Try to keep it propped up."

"So many injuries," Ma said as they rushed over to the Joiner wagon. "Some folk may not make it."

He couldn't bring himself to tell her about Al Joiner.

Pa had found a piece of the tattered wagon bonnet big enough to protect Al from the rain. He held one end and Pearl the other. She greeted Ma with pleading eyes, handing her end of the canvas to Sid.

"I'm gonna need you to keep your head, Pearl. Let's see what the damage is." Ma pulled back the shawl. She didn't so much as blink. "We're goina have to cut the rest of this shirt off. You have a sheet or petticoat? I need some more packin' to stop the bleedin'. I'm about out of bandages. My petticoat's already gone. So many wounded."

"You aren't going to have to tell, are you?" Pearl's voice quaked.

"It's none of my nevermind."

Sid was torn between curiosity and embarrassment. Despite the temptation to look, he didn't. There was too much blood; it made him queasy. Ma worked rapidly. There were other injured people waiting. Soon Al Joiner was a mass of bandages, their secret was hidden under strips of Pearl's petticoat.

Wide awake now, Al Joiner's face was distorted with pain "You'll be fine," said Ma. "It's gonna hurt. You have two broken ribs and a mean wound. They'll give you some whiskey over at the tent."

"Do we have to move him?" Pearl stammered, "I just, it's . . . we don't want—"

"Pearl, get on over there out of the rain. Nobody has time to pay any attention." Ma picked up her bag and was off to where someone called for help.

There was no time for Sid to ask questions as he and Pa carried Al Joiner to the tent where the wounded who had been cared for were being sheltered.

*****

Mr. Wood seemed to be everywhere at once, bandaging, comforting, and organizing the company. One minute he was asking someone to move the few animals that hadn't escaped with the stampede out of the circle to make more room for the tents Mr. Reid had set up for the wounded. The next minute, he was kneeling to bind up a wound while he conferred with Reverend Jones about caring for the dead. "We owe them that last dignity."

In almost the same breath he said, "Johnson, I need your boy if he can read and write." Pa nodded.

"Come with me, then, Sid. We have to find out if everybody's accounted for and has shelter for the night."

The clouds swept over taking the cold drizzle with them. The sun had begun to set. Twilight bathed the train in soft gray-pink light reflected in mud puddles that slowed every step.

Sid followed as Mr. Wood made his way around the circle. He ordered a fire to be built using anything that would burn— wood collected at Cow Creek Crossing, extra buffalo chips held in reserve for the next stop, broken bits of wood that weren't waterlogged and couldn't be salvaged for repairs.

All told, seven people were dead: little Ella Sue Davies and five people from the Sinclair group, including Dale's baby brother. Both parents were killed in one family, leaving two little girls orphaned. Dick Turney, whose wagon was parked next to the Sinclair wagon, was killed by flying debris. Arms around their two little ones, Mrs. Turney sobbed inconsolably. "Dear God, what are we gonna do? What *are* we gonna do?"

Sid could hardly bear the sadness around him. But there was no stopping to give in to grief. As they walked through the disorganized circle, reports came to Mr. Wood. Sid listed a total of thirty-five injured, most with scrapes and bruises, but some with serious injuries, like Dale's parents and Al Joiner. Half of the wagons in the Sinclair group were beyond repair.

"Tornados are the very devil," Mr. Wood said grimly, "They can tear a strip through a whole town, with one house untouched and the one next door smashed to smithereens."

The twilight of sunset gave way to night. The sky looked like a colander turned upside down over the earth with thousands of points of light shining through. A bright half-moon lit the night as they worked on, collecting scattered supplies, treating the wounded, and consoling the grieving.

The first hint of dawn caught Sid by surprise. He was weary beyond description.

Mr. Wood called the company together. "We have witnessed a mighty act of nature. I've asked Preacher Jones to say a prayer."

People stood in the mud, arms around each other, holding each other up. Grief hung thick in the air. Ma was somewhere, still tending to the injured. Sid stood between Pa and Mrs. Payne. He was beyond grief, beyond prayer, beyond feeling. He could have been made of stone. Yet, he caught and held on to something from Reverend Jones's prayer, "Grant us the courage to accept what we can't change. Open our hearts to kindness and generosity, as we recover from this terrible affliction."

Sid's eyes swept the crowd. He didn't see Dale or Ethel. Connie stood at a distance, with his father. Frog Barton was between his pa and one of his two older brothers.

"We'll have to let the ground settle before we can bury our lost company members," said Mr. Wood, "I need volunteers to round up the livestock. We can't go anywhere without our animals"—a few horses were left, unable to escape before the gap was closed—"We're coming up on the Great Bend where the trail meets the Arkansas. I hope and pray the river brought 'em to a halt. Not too worried about theives. Reckon anybody out there is as bad off as we are. But there's plenty out there to harm 'em.

He appointed Mr. Reid to set up a rotation of volunteers to nurse those who needed care. Mrs. Ryckman was appointed to set up a mess where the company would eat, so focus could be on the work to be done. Food supplies that could not be claimed by any of the families were to go to Mrs. Ryckman for immediate use.

"Clarence Reid is in charge until I'm back. Men looking for livestock will come with me. Everybody else get your wagon bonnets back—if you have a bonnet left—wagons took on a lot of water. Let the wind help you dry things out. Take a couple of hours to rest. Miz Ryckman, you decide when the cooking starts."

Mr. Wood stopped him as the company dispersed. "I'll need you again this afternoon, Sid."

When Sid saw Buttercup at the wagon, the realization hit him. All of their oxen, Mrs. Payne's oxen, and Sandy were gone. One milk cow couldn't pull two wagons. Without the teams, they were going nowhere. It was a burden shared by most of the company.

The children were still asleep. The smell of coffee beans

roasting over the campfire greeted them and a pot of coffee, hot biscuits, and bacon were waiting. Had he eaten anything since nooning yesterday? Pa gulped down a cup of coffee and grabbed a couple of biscuits as he hurried to join the men who were searching for livestock. Most of them would be on foot, too.

"I could use a cup of coffee myself," said Ma, nodding to Pa as she set down her bag."

"Could we take somethin' over to Dale Goodall's family?" Sid's voice quavered. He wanted to cry, but he was too tired.

Mrs. Payne, gathered bacon, biscuits, butter, and a jug of milk. "I've been making extras and handing them out ever since the boys got a fire started last night. We'll send along a pot of coffee, too. I'll put the boys to grinding beans soon as they're up. More folk are going to need coffee. Mrs. Reid's here helping me. I made her take the baby and get some rest with the children.

"I milked Buttercup this morning. She was patient with me. I've never milked a cow before. I thought it must not be too hard. I'm not so sure now." She gave Sid a big smile. "Jim Payne must have had a good laugh watching me." Sid didn't have the heart to tell her Jimmy could have done it for her.

"It's gonna be hard on Mrs. Goodall," said Ma. "I don't know how that woman survived. Poor love has both arms broken. One set right well, but I'm worried about the other. Mr. Goodall's gonna have a lot of pain till that shoulder mends. Sometimes I think they shouldn't try and pop a dislocation back in place. Seems like it does more harm than good. But I'm not a doctor."

It took some balancing to carry the pail with food and milk in one hand and a pot of coffee in the other without slipping in the mud. He met other people who were also taking food to the hardest hit families so everybody would have something to eat before the mess was set up.

He found Dale sorting the contents of their wagon. Mr. Goodall's arm and shoulder were bandaged to his chest. He lay in their open tent, eyes closed, his face wrinkled with pain. Mrs. Goodall sat propped up against a small trunk, eyes sunken and red, both arms in splints. Dale's little sisters leaned into her lap.

"Mrs. Payne sent over some things." Sid fumbled for words.

"Ma?" Dale looked into the tent as if he needed permission. Mrs. Goodall nodded.

Sid swallowed hard as he set down the pot of coffee. "My Ma asked if there is anything else we can do for you right now. She said to tell you we have enough supplies to share until we get to Santa Fe if you run short. She'll be around to check on you directly."

"Folks has been awful good," said Mrs. Goodall numbly.

"I'll pour you and Mr. Goodall some coffee, if you like," he said. "I guess Dale will have to help you drink it."

A faint smile flickered across her face. "He's a good boy."

Sid stooped over and poured coffee into the tin cups, handing them to Dale. Dale took one to his father, who sat up slightly, taking it with his good arm.

"There's milk and sugar. Mrs. Payne sent enough milk for the girls and you, if you'd rather have it, Dale. We were lucky. Our cow didn't escape." He couldn't think of anything else that he could do or say, so he left.

Mrs. Sinclair waved as he passed. She looked drained. "Thank you, Sid. Thank your mother and Mrs. Payne."

Impulsively, he walked over. "Anything we can do? Mrs. Payne baked a lot of biscuits."

"No," she began, hesitating, "Well, actually, we could use a biscuit or two if she's already made them." She didn't say so, but he could see she'd been so busy taking care of other people she hadn't taken care of herself.

Mrs. Payne gave him a heaping plate. There was another pot of coffee, too. "Give it to whoever needs it."

Sid sloshed back through the mud. "Mrs. Payne says I'm not supposed to give this to you, Miz Sinclair, until you sit down for a minute and eat."

Mrs. Sinclair smiled wearily, easing herself onto a barrel. "Ethel's still over in the tent with the injured. We don't have a shelter for her here yet. I'll save something for her and share the rest with our folk. You can pour some coffee into that pot by the fire."

"Is Ethel gonna be all right?" Sid hardly knew how to ask for fear she wasn't.

"Ethel is too stubborn not to be all right, Sid. Our family is so fortunate to be alive." Around them lay the ruins of their wagon and its contents. Sid guessed that was what Preacher Jones meant by "Give us the courage to accept what we can't change." He felt for his hat, but it wasn't there. The storm had taken it.

*****

Mrs. Ryckman was a tiny woman, but she organized the mess with the precision of an army general. By noon, children Matthew's and Jimmy's ages were delivering salted beef stew and skillet bread to those who couldn't get it for themselves. A broth made with prairie chicken was sent to all those who couldn't take solid food.

Later, Dale and his sisters came over to return the dishes Mrs. Payne had sent. Dale didn't say anything except, "Thank you, we sure appreciated it." But Cora insisted the girls pat Serena. Dale waited while they climbed up onto the wagon, where the cat was stretched out on her blanket in the sun. A smile flickered across his face, as Cora made formal introductions. "Serena, this is, Molly and this is Emma."

Mrs. Payne wouldn't let them leave empty-handed, even though they had been fed from the mess. She collected some eggs and dried apples. "You may need these before supper. Best have some things on hand. I expect you can scramble an egg."

Dale nodded.

"Put the apples in a pan with a little water and let them simmer over the fire for a bit. That's all they'll need to plump out. Give them a stir so they don't stick. Sid, get him the rest of the milk. Any of your team make it back?"

Livestock trickled back all morning, some on their own, some herded back by the men who were out looking.

"No, Ma'am," he said. "They're all gone."

"Ours, too. Let's pray the men find them. You're going to have to be the man in the family until your pa heals."

"Dale is made of strong stuff," said Ma returning to the wagon. "I could see that while I was workin' on your ma, Dale."

Dale's "Yes, Ma'am," was interrupted by Cora and Lydia. They didn't want their new friends to leave. Emma and Molly didn't want to leave, either.

"Dale," said Mrs. Payne, "the girls are welcome to stay and play for a while if you say so. It would give you a break. They can stay till supper. It's up to you. You're in charge now."

"I reckon they can stay," Dale said, tentatively. The little girls all jumped up and down, squealing with delight. "But mind, you behave yourselves," he added with authority. "And if you're asked to help out, you do it."

Ma smiled, giving him a pat on the back. "We'll see to it. Our girls will keep 'em distracted. I'll be over to check on your folk directly. Looked like they were doin' about as well as anybody could expect."

"You need a hand with that food?" Sid asked.

"Naw," said Dale. "I got it." He started to leave, then turned back. "Thank you, Miz Payne, Miz Johnson. Reckon I'll see you later, Sid." His brow furrowed again but Sid couldn't help feeling that the encouragement had lifted Dale's spirits, even if it was just for a moment.

*****

When he awoke from a short nap, Sid told himself that he wasn't making up excuses to go see how Ethel was doing. Mrs. Sinclair probably needed help with Isla and Maize, the little girls who were orphaned. After all, Ma and Mrs. Payne had been talking about them and wondering how Mrs. Sinclair was going to manage. If he wanted to see Ethel, he'd just go.

She sat with her leg propped up wrapped in a shawl. Her left arm was in a sling, her fingers swollen up like little sausages. "That must hurt a lot." He blurted it out. *Stupid thing to say. Of course it hurts a lot.*

"How do you do, Sid?" said Mrs. Sinclair. "I hope your mother has been able to get some rest. Ethel, Mrs. Johnson said you should keep moving those fingers, even if it hurts."

"I'm fine," Ethel said, gritting her teeth. She slowly wiggled her fingers as if to prove it.

Sid's carefully planned discussion about the orphaned girls left him. "Ma said she set your arm, Ethel. I didn't know you hurt your leg, too."

"It's just a sprain," said Ethel, tossing her head like he'd topped her score on a history test. He couldn't figure her out. He always seemed to say the wrong thing.

"Connie Ryckman said if Ethel needs any help getting

around with that leg all gimpy, he'd be *glad* to help."

Drat. Not Bitsy Clark's super sweet voice!

Ethel rolled her eyes. "There's plenty worse off than me."

Sid tried again. "Ma said you all are takin' in the little girls who were orphaned. We'd be glad to help out. Maybe they'd like to come over and play with Cora and Lydia."

"They know us." Ethel sighed as if all the fight had gone out of her.

"How kind," said Mrs. Sinclair. "What Ethel means is that right now they need things to be as stable as possible without their parents."

"I'm really sorry about Ella Sue Davies," said Ethel. "I know you were fond of her." She abruptly turned her head. But Sid saw tears welling up in her eyes. How would little Tobias get on without his twin sister? He gulped. He couldn't let himself cry, not in front of Ethel.

Mr. Wood's booming voice rescued him. "There you are Sid. Ready to help me take stock of supplies? Glad to see you're sitting up, Miss Ethel. Miz Sinclair, any idea yet about what your folk need?"

"Not any cocoa powder," a wry smile swept across Mrs. Sinclair's face. "There's no rhyme nor reason to it. My cocoa powder was undamaged, but I lost all my baking soda. I wish it had been the other way around. I can't make biscuits with cocoa powder. Still, we've salvaged more than I'd have thought.

"I'm worried about Mrs. Turney. Most of her supplies are gone. She can't take care of the wagon by herself with two little ones and another on the way—assuming we get her oxen back."

"I'm hopeful, Miz Sinclair. I expect we can find one of our older boys to help out. Sid here has taken charge of Miz Payne's team and doing a right good job of it"—Sid couldn't help looking to see if Ethel heard— "she'll have to make some hard decisions. Don't let her be hasty."

"I can help Sid take inventory." Bitsy Clark smiled brightly.

"Thought you had to get back and help your mother," said Ethel.

"Wouldn't want to keep you from your chores, Bitsy," said Mr. Wood.

"Oh, I don't have to rush right back."

Sid cringed. *What a muttonhead.*

"Well then, come along." Mr. Wood didn't ask if people wanted to take care of each other. He assumed they did. Sid wrote down the name of each group, the wagon owner, losses, and what they could share. He tried to ignore Betsy, who repeated everything with, "Did you get that, Sid?" Why did he have to get stuck with her?

Mrs. Clark waited, hands on her hips, as they neared the Ryckman wagons. "Where have you been, girl? I said you could go see how Ethel's doing. Didn't say you could spend the afternoon—and Mrs. Ryckman needing us."

Bitsy flushed. Sid couldn't help feeling sorry for her.

"Didn't mean to keep her, Miz Clark," said Mr. Wood affably. "Bitsy's been helping us take inventory of missing supplies."

Mrs. Clark didn't wait for them to be out of earshot before lighting into Bitsy. "You no-count girl, flouncing about when there's work to do. Can't trust you out of my sight."

Mr. Wood didn't say anything, but his lips tightened.

Mrs. Ryckman was busy making skillet bread. A girl who looked about Jeremy's age stood over a camping stove.

"Morning Miz Ryckman. Morning Patsy." Mr. Wood tipped his hat. "Smells mighty good."

"Good mornin', Mr. Wood. And to you, Sid," Mrs.

Ryckman spoke with a heavy Southern drawl. "Dinner's almost ready. Takes a lot of food.

"Sid, Cornelius Jauncey is behind the wagon over there workin' with our men fixin' the damaged wagons. I'm right proud of the way our boy has been helpin' others. To tell the truth, I was worried how makin' this trip would affect him, but he seems to thrive on trail life."

Sid kept his thoughts to himself.

"Musta taken a page out of your book, Miz Ryckman," said Mr. Wood. "That's mighty fine-looking bread you're turning out."

"We're all doin' our part." She gave them a radiant smile. She was perfectly groomed, though there were dark circles under her eyes. A crisp, white apron covered an immaculately clean dress that matched her bonnet. Sid looked down at his own mud-spattered clothing.

"Our group was spared. There's not a bit of damage to any of our wagons. But the loss of our horses is inestimable—Tennessee Thoroughbreds, our whole reason for goin' to California. There's no understandin' the ways of the Lord. Mr. Ryckman is distraught. I'm prayin' the men will be able to find all of them. Seems like we're surrounded by broken dreams." She turned to the girl. "No, no, Patsy, dear. It isn't quite ready.

"You know, Mr. Ryckman is plannin' to set up Thoroughbred racin' in California. I just don't know what we'll do if the horses are lost. Then I feel guilty for frettin' when I think of others."

Mr. Wood nodded. "Let's hold on to hope, Miz Ryckman. What you're doin' for the Company is a ray of hope in itself. Good food helps folk keep up their spirits."

"I didn't know Connie had any brothers or sisters," said Sid when they were away from the Ryckman wagon.

"He doesn't. Patsy O'Connell is Mrs. Ryckman's maid."

People brought their maids on the trail? But then he'd just learned the Ryckman family had two wagons as well as a horse-drawn buggy where Mrs. Ryckman usually rode.

"Cornelius Ryckman could have formed a company on his own," said Mr. Wood. "Has enough people with him. But he was looking to join a larger company for protection. Smart. Horses are prime targets for thievery. Most of it gets blamed on Indians. I reckon they know a good horse when they see one. But people tend to forget there's plenty of thieving done by outlaws with pale faces.

"Ryckman's folk were willing to follow our covenant. We divided their wagons among the company to keep things democratic. Ryckman is an elected captain, takes it seriously like his misses does. I'm proud of our captains, they're good folk. And I'm partial to good horses. Never seen better. Figured it would be a service to get his Thoroughbreds to California. Sure hope we're able to find them."

Sid was mulling this over, when Connie called, "Y'all's wagon take much damage?" He knelt by a wagon where he was helping Mr. Clark.

"We were lucky," said Sid. "Just got good and wet."

"Father's in a right state over our horses. Mother says we should be grateful we escaped with our lives and our stuff. My father says she's the eternal optimist. Sure hope the men find 'em. Hate to think of some Injun buck ridin' my saddle horse."

Sid recoiled inwardly. Ma said using those words was a way of making Indians seem less than human. Pa said it made it easier for people to justify killing them. He was pretty sure Mr. Wood wouldn't approve, except he was busy talking with Mr. Clark. *But it's what a lot of people say.* Deep inside, he knew he was making excuses, the way he made excuses for not standing up to Connie when they played marbles.

They gradually made their way around the circle. Squeaker's family had been hit hard. Ma was there checking on Squeaker's oldest brother who had broken ribs. "You're gonna haveta sit up and cough. It will hurt somethin' fierce, but you don't wanna get pneumonia. You have a pillow or blanket or somethin' you can hold on to? Makes coughin' easier."

Turning to Squeaker's father, she said, "He's gonna need to sleep sittin' up for a few nights. Your Winston's is old enough to pick up the slack."

Sid looked around. Was she talking about *Squeaker*?

"Boy's not much good for anything," said Squeaker's father. "And I can't be askin' our girls to do a man's work."

Squeaker was busy helping his sisters sort their things. His face went pink.

"Maybe this will give him somethin' worth doin,'" said Ma. "Looks like he's helpin' out now."

"You all right?" Sid asked Squeaker.

"Yeah," Squeaker looked down at his feet.

"I expect Miz Johnson's right," Mr. Wood said. "Winston will step up."

"I tell you what, Mr. Wood," Squeaker's father took off his hat, mopping his brow with a blue bandana. "Some folk are gonna have a hard time making it. I ain't worried. Ryckman takes care of us. But there's some as sunk their last dime into outfitting for the trip."

They made their way to the Davies group. Frog was there, taking a broken wagon wheel off an equally broken wagon. He gave them an expressionless look.

Mr. Davies's eyes welled up with tears when Mr. Wood ask how his group was doing. "We took some real damage. Most of it can be fixed."

Sid caught his breath. *But not Ella Sue.*

Mr. Davies wiped his eyes with the back of his sleeve. He seemed broken, not at all like the man they met before they joined the company.

They were surrounded with acts of kindness, yet a burden of sorrow hovered over the company that even Mr. Wood's hopeful presence couldn't dispel. Some of the families couldn't afford to reoutfit in Santa Fe. And how could someone like Mrs. Turney work a piece of land, even if she got as far as California?

*****

The men searching for livestock had been bringing in animals all day. Like some of the teams, the Johnson oxen were together, except for Gregg who was missing. It was hard to think about Josiah without his yokemate. They were named for Josiah Gregg, who wrote an important book about trade along the Santa Fe Trail in the 1840s.

Pa returned with the last of the men just before supper, staggering with fatigue. He rode Sandy. Mr. Sawyer rode Freedom. Hope was the only one of Mrs. Payne's team to be found. "Well," she sighed, "at least I'm not without Hope. And I have my Freedom. Mr. Payne named our oxen: Faith and Hope, Courage and Dependable, Righteous and Justice—he said we'd never get to California without them."

Sid figured Mrs. Ryckman would be happy. He was riding one of their horses. All but two were accounted for.

The men carried the remains of an ox they'd had to shoot. It had broken its front legs in gopher holes. They butchered the ox where they found it. The meat was needed for the mess.

Pa wearily threw Sandy's reins to Sid. "Here, Son. I think this is yours." He handed him a hat. "It was on a plum thicket like somebody hung it there. There's no rhyme or reason to what a tornado will do."

The camp stirred again at dawn. Pa ate a hasty breakfast. "Maybe you'll find Promise and the rest of Mrs. Payne's team today," said Sid.

"Hope so. The longer they're gone, the less chance we have."

"One thing you don't haveta worry about, Mrs. Payne," said Jimmy. "I can milk Buttercup."

She handed him a biscuit. "That is good news for me and for Buttercup."

Not long after noon, the jingling of harnesses alerted them to a teamster train coming from the east. The trail had been silent since the storm.

The teamsters pulled off the trail opposite the Wood Company. Sid got to go with Mr. Wood to find out if they had any news. Two men came to meet them. Sid recognized them immediately: Ramon Rios Hernandez and Luis Marie Diaz. Their teamster train had been all the way to Independence and was on the way back to Santa Fe again.

"It goes to show how much faster mules are than oxen, Sid," said Mr. Wood, shaking hands with the men.

Señor Hernandez said they were just shy of the Little Arkansas when they saw the storm clouds. Luckily, they crossed before the storm hit. The worst they got was wind and hard rain. The creek was over its banks, though. They brought some oxen and horses they had found on the way knowing they'd belong to a stalled wagon train. Sid couldn't wait to tell Mrs. Payne the good news. Courage and Dependable, her middle team had been found.

As soon as the teamsters had eaten, Señor Hernandez put them to work digging graves, seven in all. Because they were in open prairie, they dug the graves on the trail so passing trains would pack the earth, keeping the graves from being disturbed.

Seeing all of those graves, especially the tiny ones for Ella Sue and Dale's baby brother, was almost more than Sid could bear. He'd come close to being in an unmarked grave on the Santa Fe Trail. How many people were buried there? Melancholy swept over him again, settling like a dark place in his heart.

When the teamsters left, they took letters to be mailed when they reached the next postal express stop, including a letter from Mrs. Sinclair to the grandparents of the orphaned girls, Mazie and Isla. The teamsters also left some blankets as well as some food for the mess.

As they watched them leave, Mr. Wood said, "You know, I've heard folk call teamsters no-good thieves. Some may be. But that hasn't been my experience. I have a hunch it's because they're mostly Mexicans. I reckon they're no better or worse than the rest of us. Take Hernandez. He's on a tight schedule, but he stopped out of human kindness."

"Like he did when Ta Lezhé saved us from that wolf."

"Mm," Mr. Wood nodded. "Digging graves is the hardest thing."

"There's somethin' I don't understand. Mr. Diaz talked to Ta Lezhé. But it wasn't in English—"

"French. It would have been French. The French lived and traded with the Kaw long before the English ever came this way. Ta Lezhé's grandfather was French."

He wanted to ask how Mr. Wood knew so much about the Kaw, but he wanted to talk about Bayless Sly and J.J. Gordon, too. It was more urgent. He took a deep breath and plunged in. "It's a good thing you know Mr. Gallagher. Pa says it frightened away those men who were askin' about our family."

Mr. Wood shook his head. "Don't know him; know of

him. He has a reputation for being an honest man. Bayless Sly had 'crook' written all over him. Soon as I said I knew Gallagher, he started back-tracking. I don't know about the other one. He didn't say much."

"I have what they want."

Mr. Wood raised his eyebrows.

Sid told him everything. "What should I do? My family's in danger. I started to tell Pa, but we got interrupted. Then I guess the storm drove it outta my head."

Mr. Wood looked into the distance. "Most times, I'd say it's wrong to keep something like that from your Pa. The fact he didn't know was in his favor the other night, though. We thought they were after the horses. But kidnapping Cora? That's an ugly turn. Your Pa needs to know."

"Would you keep the letter for me?" It would be a relief to be rid of it.

"Safer with you, Sid. Mr. Gallagher trusted you with it. Most folk don't think children can do anything that amounts to much. In my experience, there's some things youngsters can do better than anybody." He looked Sid up and down. "Not that you're a child, but you've still got some growing to do. When we get to Santa Fe, I'll help you find Miz Gallagher if you haven't heard from him by then. I wasn't shooting the breeze when I said they're one of the best-known families in Santa Fe.

"Best if nobody else knows about the letter. If word got around in the company"—he shook his head, frowning—"Fool's gold. That's what I call it. Easy money. Folks come out looking for treasure at Pawnee Rock. Waste their time digging around at the Caches where people supposedly buried their valuables at night to keep them safe from robbers. Men die in the desert, thinking they'll find Spanish treasure. I reckon Miz Payne's right. The letter's the treasure. The only treasure that means anything to fools like Bayless Sly is the kind that amounts to nothing in the end.

"Let me think on it, Sid. You talk to your Pa. I'll talk to him soon as I get a chance. Little Cora isn't in any immediate danger, not till we get to the fort—"

"We're goin' to the fort?"

"Have to. Some of our families can't wait until Santa Fe."

*****

Shortly after the teamster train left, the men who had been searching for livestock returned. Most of the animals were accounted for, better than anyone could have hoped. Justice and Righteous, Mrs. Payne's wheel team, were among them. But Faith, Hope's yoke mate, was still missing as was Gregg. Other families would also have to make do with one or two less oxen. Surprisingly, all of the horses were found. It was reassuring. If Bayless Sly and J.J. Gordon were hanging around, they'd have helped themselves to the horses.

The biggest surprise was a boy sitting behind Pa on Sandy. The boy, who looked to be about Sid's age, carried a large pack on his back. He was so thin and lanky he looked like he wouldn't make a good shadow. He was wearing a black coat, black trousers held up with braces, and what had once been a white shirt. He had a bedraggled black hat and very worn boots. Pa helped the boy down from Sandy's back. "This is Abraham Biermann. Looks like he has a bad sprain, Sadie. You'd better have a look.

"Mercy me!" said Ma. "Let's get that shoe off, Abraham. Jimmy, you help him. Take off both shoes. They're soaked clean through. Set 'em over by the fire where they'll dry out, Jimmy."

"I did not take off my shoe," Abraham said. "I was afraid I cannot get it back on. I loose the . . ."

"Laces," Ma supplied the word.

"How does it look like?"

"Tell me where it hurts." Ma gently examined the swollen and bruised foot and a raw, angry-looking gash above the top of his boot. "Where are your people, Abraham?"

"My brothers are since five years in Santa Fe." Abe was on his way from New York to meet his three brothers, who had a trading company.

"New York? All by yourself?" Ma's jaw dropped. "Thousands of miles?"

"I travel with a family to the near of Saint Louis. I took a steamer to Kansas. But my money is taken. I was meeting teamsters of my brothers, but I do not have the informations. If I would have enough money, I would wait in Kansas. But I have no money. So, I am by myself going to Santa Fe."

"He talks funny, Matthew," Jimmy said. "He's from England. He probably thinks we talk funny, too."

Sid had to bite his tongue to keep from laughing. Abe looked puzzled.

"Jimmy, Abe is from Germany," said Pa, joining them by the fire. "We met people from England on the trail. They had a different accent, too."

Abe grinned.

"Sid, heat the kettle and get me an onion, please," said Ma. "Doesn't feel like there's a break, but that scrape is infected. You won't be walkin' for a while. Seems like it takes a sprain more time to heal than a break."

"I do not think it is broken," said Abe. "I worry about infection. But I have no fresh water to wash."

"Get me an onion," meant more chopping. Since the storm, Ma had Sid chopping onions in every spare moment when he wasn't helping Mr. Wood. She used them to draw infection from wounds or reduce swelling. Their supply was coming to an end. He set the kettle over the fire and got out the big wash pan and some clean rags.

Before they left the farm, Ma had him help her tear old bedsheets into various sizes of strips for bandage cloth. Jimmy and Cora had helped roll bandages, too. Sid hadn't been able to imagine why they would need so many. He understood now. Ma had bandaged up many an injury on the trail, even before the tornado. Now nearly all the bandages were gone.

Tears ran down Sid's cheeks as he poured water over the onion. If there was a way to chop onions without crying, he hadn't found it. He stirred until they were mushy.

"How in the world did you manage at night?" Ma wasn't making idle chatter. She was interested in Abe, as he liked to be called. She was also trying to keep his mind off the pain.

"I have a small tent. *Had* a small tent," Abe corrected himself, grimacing as Ma gently poured warm water over the wound. "I camp on the trail with other people. But the storm—I was in trouble. No train is in sight. I look for shelter. I put the tent by the near of –*haufen steine*—what is it you say?"

"Near a pile of rocks," Mrs. Payne joined them. "Guten Tag, Abe. I am Frau Dorcas Payne."

"Sprechen sie Deutsch?" Abe's eyes widened.

"Yes, I do speak German, but not so well as you speak English. I am very impressed with your pronunciation. But we're all eager to hear what happened after you set up your tent near a pile of rock."

"Did you see zat cloud? I have never seen—it ran on the ground. It took my tent and me! I went up with the tent and down at the *haufen steine*. The tent is gone. It is raining. The ground is moving—I thought it is buffalo. It is cows. Running! I never know cows run so fast. Ach! I am a city boy. What do I know of cows? Then my foot"—he looked down at his swollen foot—"Mr. Johnson found me after two days."

Ma placed a clean piece of cloth around Abe's foot. "I'm so sorry, Abe. Jimmy, get him some drinking water." She put the mushy, wet onion over the cloth, covering his foot and up above the ankle.

He watched Ma intently. "My Mume use cabbage. She would have me drink onion and honey."

"Cabbage leaves are good," said Ma. "Onion and honey is something I don't know about. Tell me more."

"You must cover half the onion in honey. After an hour you drink. Then you put more honey on the onion."

"Honey would pull the water out of the onion. I'll have to try it. Now, let's wrap that foot up good and firm. Nothin' like an onion poultice—or cabbage—to draw out infection. We'll see how your foot looks this evenin'."

Abe grinned. "You are like my Mama. She helps people. My Mume says it is from their father. My opa—grandfather— vas a doctor."

"Where are your Mama and Papa now?" asked Mrs. Payne.

"My Mama died before we come," Abe winced. His ankle was hurting. "I was then ten years old. Papa is in Germany. He said he is too old to go adventuring. I and my brothers come to America. In New York we have family. They have been living in Brooklin more than ten years. Nathan, my elder brother, says the West is a land of opportunity. So, I am staying with the kazans."

"Kansas?" Jimmy had been listening intently. "We was in Kansas City."

"Cousins," said Mrs. Payne.

"I don't have any cousins," said Jimmy.

"Staying with his cousins, not yours," said Matthew, shaking his head.

"Manners, Matthew." Mrs. Payne gave him a look.

"My brothers are five years in Santa Fe. They send for me now I am older."

Mr. Reid came by. "Reverend Jones is going to say a few words for those who are being buried today."

Ma took off her apron. "I'm so sorry about your Mama, Abe. You're a brave young man to come all this way by yourself. Ben, you and Sid help Abe over to where he can keep his foot up. We'll be back directly, Abe. Our company took a real battering from the storm, too. Come along, children."

Reverend Jones read a few verses from the Bible and asked people to say Psalm 23 together. Everywhere Sid looked faces were streaming with tears. So was his.

He caught Pa afterward. It was a relief to tell him about the letter.

"I wondered what those two were really after." Worry lines wrinkled Pa's face. "From all accounts, Gallagher's a good man. I daresay he didn't intend any harm. I know you promised to keep it a secret, but circumstances alter cases. I'm glad you told Mr. Wood. I think he's right. The letter's probably safer with you than anywhere else. The fewer who know about it the better. I don't like keeping things from your Ma, but she's carrying a heavy load with all the sick and injured. We'll keep a watch on Cora."

Before supper, Ma looked at Abe's foot and declared it improved. "Here's somethin' for you to drink." She'd made him some honey and onion drink. Sid wasn't so sure about it. It smelled awful. But Ma said it didn't taste bad at all.

Abe was good-natured about obeying orders from Ma. But when she offered him a tin plate with beans and pork rind from the mess, he hesitated. "Mrs. Johnson, I do not eat pork."

She looked at him quizzically.

"I'm a Jew. It is not for you to worry. In my pack I have food. I will cook."

"Oh, I'm so sorry. I didn't know. Everything from the mess is cooked with pork fat."

"What about your cornbread, Sadie?" Mrs. Payne asked. "Abe, could you eat cornbread and milk for supper? Mrs. Johnson doesn't have a koshered bowl, but we scald our dishes when we wash them."

"The good Lord must be lookin' out for you, Abe," said Ma. "I make my cornbread with butter. I like the flavor better."

"Mrs. Johnson doesn't use her corn pan for anything but cornbread," said Mrs. Payne.

Abe's face lit up. "I do not know this cornbread, but I am getting tired of beef jerky and hard tack. I learn about plants growing in the near of the trail. I can cook this cornbread for myself." He produced cooking utensils from his pack.

"What's wrong with pork?" asked Jimmy, eyeing his dinner. "Pork 'n beans tastes good to me."

"Jimmy!" said Ma, frowning, as she beat eggs in a metal bowl Abe produced from his pack.

Abe grinned at him. "I am like the Hebrews in the Bible, Jimmy. Our laws forbid us to eat pork. My brothers said not to worry on the trail about rules. But mine onkel tell me to follow the rules. I have hard-tack crackers and beef jerky. Up to now, I have pleased mein onkel and mein brothers. I'm alive and I have not eaten anything forbidden."

"Bible didn't tell me not to eat pork and beans," said Matthew.

Lydia eyes were wide with alarm, "Does it?"

"We follow different rules in some things," said Pa, eyes twinkling. "It'll be all right to eat supper, Lydia."

Mrs. Payne was delighted to know Abe was from Brooklyn,

New York. They chatted as Ma put Abe's cornbread over the fire to cook.

"Colored School Number 2 in Weeksville?" said Abe. "You teach in the best school for Africans anywhere in the near of New York."

"Mrs. Payne has lessons after supper," Sid said.

"Why yes, Abe. Come if you feel like it. I thought it would be wise to start up again this evening. We all need the routine."

"I would like," said Abe. "Maybe you can help me with my English improvements?"

"Your English is remarkable, Abe."

"My Mama was also a teacher of English."

Sid missed the rest of the conversation. He was back to chopping onions. Ma wanted to see the Goodalls before it was dark. He'd heard her talking with Mrs. Payne in low tones. One of Mrs. Goodall's arms was infected. She had a fever.

*****

Dale was playing a game of "button-button" with his little sisters. Sid didn't know what to say. Then it occurred to him, "I expect you get pretty worn-down takin' care of the girls. You can bring 'em over to our wagon. They had fun with Cora and Lydia."

"Ethel had 'em playing with Isla and Mazie. I just now brought' em back for supper. Good thing we have the mess. All I can make is pancakes and scrambled eggs. Pancakes ain't that good if you have 'em every meal."

Sid fumbled for something to talk about. "I don't know when the boys are gonna play marbles again. You can have some of mine. I mean, when we get back to playin'."

"Naw. Got too much to do."

131

"I think I'm out of favor with Connie."

Dale grinned. "Ain't so hard to do. Guess I'm done with 'em for good."

As eager as he was to get back to lessons, Sid dreaded it, too. He helped Abe hobble over to where they met by Mrs. Payne's wagon. Bitsy was helping Ethel. Little Tobias Davies, and the orphaned girls, Isla and Mazie, were with them.

Seeing Tobias without Ella Sue was almost too painful to bear. How could someone so eager and full of life and mischief be gone?

Ethel usually heard the children Matthew's and Jimmy's age read aloud, but she wanted to stay with the younger children since Mazie and Isla hadn't been to school before. Naturally Bitsy wanted to stay, too. Sid cringed. It would be hard enough with Ethel looking over his shoulder. Thankfully, Mrs. Payne needed Bitsy elsewhere. Sid carried a stool for Ethel to the far corner by the wagon where he worked with the little ones, but she tossed her head when he tried to help her.

"Sid," Tobias tugged on Sid's trousers. "They put Ella Sue in the ground."

Sid felt it like a punch to the stomach. "I know, Tobias. I'm so sorry."

Tobias went right to work, following Sid's directions. Soon he came back to lean against Sid. "They put Ella Sue in the ground."

Trying to hold back tears, Sid put his arms around Tobias, not knowing what else to do. Ethel intervened, a pained look on her face, "I'm so sorry, Tobias. Ella Sue is dead.

"It's the same with Isla and Maize, Sid. Mamma says they need to keep saying it and hearing it. It will help them come to terms with the reality."

Like Grace. The thought took him by surprise. Maybe he

needed to keep saying it. *Her parents are dead, and she's gone.*

Ethel stayed until Mrs. Payne called everyone for a group meeting. She let him help her stand, leaning on his arm as they joined the group meeting. Sid figured she must be really hurting to let him help. Bitsy glowered at them.

"Oh good, maybe you can help Sid with his algebra," Mrs. Payne was talking with Abe as the children gathered. Sid didn't know whether he should feel relieved or resentful. Algebra wasn't his best subject, true enough.

"We'll be helping Abe with his English. It is very good, Abe, but sometimes word order is tricky and some sounds. Maybe you can teach us a little German. How do you say, 'Good evening,' in German?"

Abe smiled a broad smile. "You say Guten Abend."

She had everyone try. Isla and Maize seemed to brighten. "Their family immigrated from Germany," Ethel whispered to Sid.

Bitsy scowled. "No secrets!"

Mrs. Payne cut lessons short. Mr. Wood had called for a company meeting after supper. Ordinarily, she sent the younger ones back to their wagons and met briefly with the older groups.

"It was nice to have you join us, Abe," Mrs. Payne said as Sid helped her put things away. "I hope you'll think about staying with the train, if not this one, another. I hate to think about you out there alone. You have the Arkansas to cross. The Cimarron route isn't easy. Mr. Payne said it's desert all the way to Santa Fe. Mr. Wood, our wagon master, says there's been some unrest among the Comanche along that route, too."

"This is what my brothers tell me when they write. Their teamsters go this way. I hope I will meet a Biermann Brothers train. But I am not seeing them."

"The teamsters told Mr. Wood a lot of trains aren't getting in and out of Westport now," said Sid. "It has to do with fighting over whether Kansas Territory will be a free or a slave state."

"I wondered about that," said Mrs. Payne. "We were never out of sight of other trains on the way to Council Grove. There hasn't been much traffic since."

Sid hoped Abe would stay. It had been such a long time since he'd had a real friend. Maybe Abe would be a real friend.

*****

Sid looked up at stars sprinkling the sky. In the center of the circle, the mess campfire was reduced to glowing orange coals. A hush fell as Mr. Wood called the company to order.

"Our captains met earlier. We agreed to change our route in order to stop at New Fort Bent where we can do some restocking. There is a new store at Walnut Creek Crossing before we get there, but we'd pay through the nose. We're better off waiting. Crossing the Raton Pass will tax our animals and our wagons. But there are advantages. There's a more certain water supply. There's plenty of game and we'll need it."

"What about buffalo? We haven't hunted buffalo," one of the men said.

"We'll be hunting buffalo soon. The plan was to use our buffalo hunt to fortify us for that long stretch from Santa Fe to California. We'll need it sooner. Mr. Ryckman, you wanna say a word for the captains?"

Mr. Ryckman stood. "We're all in agreement. The bottom fact is we don't have any other choice. Whatever you may have heard about the Mountain Route, it is much improved since the early days of the trail. It will be a challenge. But we can do it if we work together. If you have questions, talk them over with your captain. I'm proud of the way these men have stepped up to get us through the crisis. I'm proud to be a part of this company."

And what about the women steppin' up? Grace wasn't there to say it. Sid tugged at his hat.

The children were asleep when Ma came back from checking on the wounded. "Sid, chop an onion. Meet me over at the Joiner's. I'm gonna haveta put another poultice on Al Joiner's wounds. Lord help us, I hope the onions hold out till Fort Bent."

"I can help," said Abe.

"You're interested in doctoring? I can use the help, but you need to stay off that foot tonight."

Sid hadn't thought about Al Joiner since he and Pa had rescued—*him? Should I say her?* It didn't feel right. Pa and Ma hadn't said anything, not even to Mrs. Payne.

Pearl had hot water ready when he got there. Ma was already unwinding Al Joiner's bandages. Sid mixed the poultice together and waited, hesitant to enter the tent. "Come on inside, Sid," said Pearl. "You can look the other way while your Ma changes the poultice. There's something you need to hear."

"Greetings, Sid," called Al, "come on into the house of secrets."

"See, it's like this," said Pearl. "Alma and I were schoolmates back in Ohio. Best friends growing up. Alma's folk all died and left her the farm. She married a fellow from over to the next town."

"Biggest mistake I ever made. Ouch, Mrs. Johnson! You trying to kill me?"

"Doin' my best. You're too sassy to kill off so easy."

Pearl didn't even crack a smile. "They had a little baby

who died. He up and sold the farm without saying a word to Alma. Left with all her money."

Sid's eye widened. "Sold the farm?"

"Cleaned me out. Took every penny."

"How could he do that? It was your farm."

Pearl shook her head. "Could and did. The law says once you're married, property belongs to the man. That—I don't have a word for him—left Alma without anything—"

"Except the money from my mamma's estate. Thank God I had the good sense to keep my mouth shut about that when we got married or he woulda had it, too.

"Ah, that feels better, Miz Johnson. You can look now without offending your sensibilities, Sid." Al Joiner was all bandaged up again and had a shirt on.

"So, we started plotting," Pearl said.

"See in the west, we can own our own land," said Al Joiner. "Spanish and Mexican women own land. It's theirs even if they get married. And they get half of everything they own with their husband. So, what the heck? I ain't going to get married again anyway, and Pearly wasn't inclined to sit around with people feeling sorry for her like she was some wilting flower because she ain't married. Can't think of anybody I'd rather be with than Pearly, anyway."

"So, we ran off," said Pearl. "Changed our names. Bought our wagon in Independence. Met Mr. Wood in Council Grove. We said we was brother and sister. If we put our heads together, Alma and I can run a farm. And nobody can up and take it away from us."

"He was a no-good, lazy—if I say it Pearly will wash my mouth out with soap. He didn't give two hoots and a holler about me or the farm. He wanted my money. Man didn't know the front from the back end of a mule. Heck, I grew up doing men's work with Pa. Weren't any boys in our family. I was the oldest. Besides, it's a danged sight more comfortable wearing trousers than those infernal petticoats."

Pearly smiled pensively. "We just figured it would be easier if we told people we're brother and sister. People try to take advantage of women. The only sad thing was saying good-bye to my Mamma and Papa and my brothers, them not knowing. That and Alma losing the baby."

Al Joiner sighed, "I woulda liked to have kids. He woulda left anyway. Just used it as an excuse. Truth is, I wouldna married him in the first place if I hadn't promised my pa to hold on to the farm."

"People have accepted us," said Pearl. "Al's a captain and a scout. We wanted you to know, Sid, because if you was to tell, it would ruin everything. People would start thinking of us differently. I couldn't stand that."

"I danged sure couldn't. You think they'd let me hunt? Heck no. And I've brought in nearly half the game for the train since we left Council Grove."

It was a lot to take in. Why was it right for a man to marry somebody and take everything she owned? And why shouldn't women be able to go west and have land and live their lives the way they wanted? He looked at Pearl, then at Al. Their eyes were fixed on him. "You can count on me. You stood up for us when those two men showed up lookin' for our family, Mr. Joiner."

Pearl gave him a hug. Al grinned, "If you think I'm gonna get up and hug you, think again. Your Ma's done tortured me enough."

12.

WALNUT CREEK

Nearly a week later, the train returned to the trail. Wagons were repaired. Some had to be rebuilt. Teams missing oxen were regrouped. Josiah would have to walk behind the wagon. Without Gregg, he would be thrown off balance in a yoke. Some milk cows were going to be learning how to be oxen. Pa told Mrs. Payne right away that Buttercup could stand in for Faith. Mr. Reid had Squeaker's dad adjust the yoke. He was a good carpenter. With a little work, it fit Buttercup perfectly. "So, Jimmy, you're going to get to see an ordinary cow turn into an ox," said Pa.

"How are we gonna' get milk and butter?"

"I reckon she'll be doing twice as much work as the others." Sid patted Buttercup on the neck. She looked at them with soft brown eyes as if she understood perfectly.

Mrs. Turney decided to stay with the company. "Ain't got nothin' to go back to," she told Mrs. Payne. "I figure if you can make it, anybody can."

Sid wasn't so sure it was a compliment, but Mrs. Payne didn't flinch. "You can make it," she said. "Folks call us the weaker sex, but don't you believe it, Mrs. Turney. There's lots a woman can do, including farming. There's plenty of folk ready to help on the way."

"I can sew. I'm real good at sewin'."

"People always need clothing and mending. I'll bet you

could set up a business in Santa Fe if you don't want to go all the way to California. Mr. Payne said it's a nice place to live."

Later, he heard Ma talking with Mrs. Payne. "You've been cryin' again. I'm so sorry."

"Does it show? I was thinking how hard it must be for Mrs. Turney without her husband. Then I thought of my Jim, and all we'd planned to do." She let out a big sigh.

"It takes time," said Ma. "Give yourself time. Sometimes I think our Sid is still grievin' for Grace Willis. It's hard not knowin' what happened to her."

"At first, I just couldn't accept it. I felt so much hatred toward the Swathmores. But what good does that do? It just poisons me. It won't bring Jim Payne back. I had nearly ten years with one of the most wonderful men God ever put on earth. And I have two precious children who need me."

Ma gave her a hug. "And memories to hold on to."

Sid wasn't sure he could ever let go of hating the Swathmores.

*****

"Gonna play today?" asked Connie. They were on the trail again. Sid didn't feel much like playing, but he said he would be there. Billy looked at him through slitted eyes, as if he were trying to decide where to punch him.

When he returned to the wagon for dinner, Ma was out checking on her patients after half a day of travel. Jimmy was trying to walk with the crutch Pa made for Abe. He wasn't tall enough to get his arm over it. Abe sat in the wagon where he rode with his foot propped up. Serena was on his lap. Cora sat beside him. "Look, Sid! Serena made friends with Abe."

Abe grinned. "I miss the cats of my cousins."

"Mrs. Payne says time to get washed up," said Jimmy.

She had made cornbread served with molasses with stewed dried apples for dessert.

"Abe made cornbread and apples, too," said Cora. "And he let Lydia and me help. And he can eat it because it's in the Bible."

"Do you like to play marbles?" Sid asked as he poured thick top cream over his warm apples. "Some of the boys get together after dinner."

Abe nodded. "I have marbles. I and my friends play. Do they play so good?"

"So-so. A boy they call Frog is good—*really* good. Don't take anything you wouldn't wanna lose. This bunch plays for keeps."

"You never said they play for keeps." Ma had a way of returning at exactly the wrong moment.

"Well, we're all about equal, so it comes out the same," Sid lied, looking down at his plate.

After dinner, Abe selected half a dozen marbles and a shooter from his bag. "So, zey play for keeps?"

"Yeah. I understand you can buy 'em back. But I can't see as how anybody could have money to be buyin' marbles."

"Maybe that's what they mean about the 'lawless' west." Abe laughed, taking the crutch from Jimmy.

As soon as they were out of earshot, Sid confided in Abe. "I just started playin' with these guys." It wasn't entirely true. "I don't know any of 'em that well"—at least that part was true—"they let a boy named Connie win and they hang out after supper when I go for lessons. The other night they were spyin' on us. Makes you wonder what they're up to."

The boys were waiting. "I do not think zey are putting out a red carpet," said Abe.

Should he have invited Abe? Connie and Billy glowered

at them in stony silence. Squeaker was subdued. The sudden memory of Connie punching him caught Sid off guard. He hadn't let himself think about it. As annoying as he was, Squeaker hadn't deserved that.

"Who's your friend?" Connie stood, surveying Abe disdainfully.

"He's—" Sid almost said, "He's not my friend." Catching himself and going red in the face, he introduced Abe. Nobody offered to shake hands. Billy stared at Abe as if he were a circus sideshow freak.

Connie's eyes narrowed. "I usually do the invitin'. We're not lookin' for anybody new."

"It is nothing," said Abe, shrugging his shoulders, "he said you were hard to beat. I like to see. It is not necessary to play."

"Let's see if you're any good then. You go first, then Squeaker, Eli, Billy, Frog, Sid, then me. We play for keeps. Losers, weepers."

It was silent as they placed their marbles in the ring. Abe awkwardly took his position, leaning on one hand, knuckling his shooter with the other. He released its and marbles flew from of the ring. *Woah!* It was a terrific shot. Billy said a curse word. Eli gasped. Connie's face flushed. Frog's expression never changed.

Abe's taw rolled to a halt just outside the circle.

"Ain't fair!" challenged Squeaker, who hadn't even lost a marble. "He cheated."

Abe looked at him curiously.

"Holdin' your taw wrong," sneered Billy. "Shot don't count."

"He wasn't cheating, he was knuckling," said Sid, holding back a surge of anger. "It's another way of holding your shooter. I use it sometimes."

"Not the way we do it," said Billy.

"Lost his turn, lost his turn," said Squeaker.

"It is not a problem. I will do next time." Abe returned marbles to the ring.

"Take the shot over," said Connie. "You play with us, you play by our rules."

"It helps to know the rules ahead of time," said Sid evenly. He felt red creep up his neck. It was like he was seeing the boys for the first time and himself starting to become like them.

When the marbles were in place, Sid held his breath. Abe put his knuckle to the ground, balancing his taw on his index finger the way the boys did. He aimed slightly to the center. There was a snap as the taw hit, scattering the mibs and taking five. His taw rolled clear.

When it was finally Sid's turn, he was with Abe. The boys could think as they liked. He took aim at a cluster of marbles at one side, sending three out of the ring. Frog, Connie, and Abe lost a marble each.

Squeaker looked like a trapped weasel. Billy snorted like an angry bull. "Good shot, Sid," said Abe. Nobody else said anything.

Connie was grim-lipped. He wasn't strategic. The only reason he won was because people let him.

Frog was a better player, more intentional. When it was his turn again, he picked up three mibs without troubling any of Connie's. "Good shot, Frog," said Abe. Nobody said anything.

By the time they finished, Abe was the winner. A pile of marbles rested next to him. He kept his marbles separate. Sid had a pretty good collection, too.

Connie's face turned an ugly shade of puce. Frog, who only lost to Connie, was expressionless. Everybody else looked as if they expected a storm equal to the tornado.

"Reckon it's time to hitch up," said Sid, giving Abe a hand as he stood.

Abe leaned over and picked up his marbles, leaving those he had won. "I do not play keeps," he said pleasantly. Sid returned all but the ones he started with, too.

They left in silence. Before they were out of earshot, Connie said, "Dirty Jew!"

"I do not wish to again play with those boys," said Abe.

"Me neither," said Sid.

"Connie is *der Tyrann.*"

"Der tyrann?"

"Somebody who pushes people around."

"A bully," said Sid, suddenly lighthearted.

"*Der Tyrann.*"

13.

PAWNEE ROCK

"Ready for Pawnee Rock?" Mr. Reid asked as they waited for the signal to yoke up one early morning. "We'll be there before night."

When wagons got to Pawnee Rock, they could say they were halfway to Santa Fe. Excitement swept the company when it first appeared as a purple bump on the horizon breaking the monotony of the endless plains. Long before wagon trains it was a favorite camping ground of native people. Countless pioneers spoke of leaving their names carved on the rock and of the sheer, breathtaking beauty of the view from its top.

For days, Pawnee Rock remained a bump teasing them. Now it steadily rose, a massive mound standing nearly 150 feet tall. Mrs. Payne told her students it was the site of Indian councils in olden times. "There's some dispute as to how it got its name. One tradition is that when Kit Carson was an inexperienced young man, he shot his mule in the night, thinking it was a Pawnee Indian creeping up on him. Others think it's named for a treaty with the Pawnee, Apache, and Osage Tribes. What do you think?"

Most of the children wanted the story about Kit Carson to be true. Ethel wanted to know what the Indians called it. Mrs. Payne didn't know.

The treaty hadn't lasted. What was said about it depended

on who was talking. Outside Sid's family circle, which included Mrs. Payne, most people seemed to think American Indians were nomads who lived in tepees, raided wagon trains, and could not be trusted. There were exceptions—Mr. Wood, Mr. Reid, the Joiners, the Sinclairs, Jeremy Sawyer, and maybe others he didn't know about.

Conversation often turned to politics around the campfire. Sometimes there were heated discussions. Ever since they entered Plains Indian territory, men had been edgy. Some of them seemed to think every wagon train was a target for Indian attack even though Mr. Wood constantly reassured them that attacks were seldom and usually provoked.

One night the topic came up again. "Look at it from their eyes," said Pa. "They have every reason to see us as the aggressors. Every wagon train coming this way is a threat to their way of life. We're using up the land they've always depended on. The game, every buffalo we kill means less for them."

"Plenty of buffalo up north, from what I hear," said Mr. Sawyer, Jeremy's father. "The way I figure, if they was smart, they'd settle down and build regular houses, plant crops."

"I don't know as it's fair to say the way Indians live is good or bad," said Mr. Reid, knocking ashes out of his pipe. "I reckon it depends on what you're used to. Fact is, tribes aren't all the same."

"I expect Indians are pretty much like other folk," said Jeremy. "You have your good and you have your bad."

"If we have a problem with Indians, it's a problem we made," said Pa. "I don't know what the answer is, but it can't be gobbling up their homeland and their livelihood without any thought as to how they're supposed to live."

Mr. Reid nodded. "Take the Kaw. Do you know what those treaties have done to them? They had their own ways, maybe not our way, but ways that worked for them. Their women planted corn, beans, all kinds of vegetables. Still try to. They took to teepees durin' the huntin' season, other times they lived in houses that the women built and owned—"

"Where's Joiner?" Mr. Sawyer called. "He's always going on about giving women the vote. He'd oughta hear this." Laughter went around the small circle of men.

Mr. Reid nodded. "Then here we come bringin' diseases that killed nearly half the Kaw and treaties that are worthless. We promise payments for what we've taken, then don't even give 'em a fraction of what we owe. They signed a treaty giving us use of land for the Santa Fe Trail. But look at those stores and all the houses cropping up in Council Grove. Do you think any of 'em are paying rent to the Kaw for use of their land? And who stands up for 'em when people start farming it? Couple of years ago when Andrew Rieder was governor, he was up to Council Grove looking it over as a place to locate the capital when Kansas becomes a state. You can't blame 'em if they don't trust us." He let out a long slow breath. "Well, I reckon you all will be telling Preacher Jones I'm tryin' to replace him."

Uneasy laughter broke out. The discussion left Sid's stomach in knots. One look around and he could see that Mr. Reid hadn't convinced anybody. He couldn't figure it out. They were still in Kansas Territory. Kansas was named for the Kanza people. *It's like they don't have any right to live here anymore.* Seemed like some people didn't think they had the right to live at all.

Mr. Wood sent out scouts every day and kept a watchful eye. He would have been the first to say Indians were not the only reason to keep a lookout.

The sun was starting to drop when they arrived at Pawnee Rock well past their usual stopping time. Pawnee Rock was massive. One side was sheer sandstone. Sid looked forward to seeing the face of the sandstone, where mountain men, teamsters, adventurers, and immigrants had carved their names. Jimmy and Matthew wanted to add their names. Ma said, "Fools names like fools faces are often seen in public places."

They reverse-yoked the oxen, leaving each yoke, or pair, facing in opposite directions. They could graze without straying too far. Sid looked up from his work to see Dale.

"I was looking for you. Reckon you oughta know Billy's gonna try and jump you up on Pawnee Rock. Best be on the lookout. Connie's got it in for you and Abe."

"Thanks," gulped Sid. "I don't think Abe's gonna be able to climb, but I was hopin' to get up to the top before dark."

"I'd wait till morning, give 'em less chance. They won't jump you if anybody's around. They'll try to catch you off guard. Billy'll do Connie's dirty work."

"You gonna climb?"

"Yeah, me and Eli. He's the one told me about Billy. We're waiting till morning. Pa said it's getting dark too fast. I'd ask you to come with us, but Eli's too scared of Connie. If they see him being too friendly, he'll catch it."

"What?"

"Can't explain it." Dale hurriedly looked around. "Their folk all work for Mr. Ryckman. Connie lords it over 'em. Back in Council Grove Billy beat up on one kid Connie had it in for—so bad his folk pulled outta the train. He'll do anything Connie says."

"I can't believe Mr. Wood would allow—"

"He didn't know. They was all too scared to tell. I'm glad to be away from 'em. I been telling Eli he better get out. Squeaker wants out, but he's in over his head. Don't know about Frog. Can't ever tell what he's thinking. Look,

I gotta go. Don't let them catch you alone." With that, Dale vanished among the men.

Across the way, Billy helped his Pa and older brother. Something Dale said clicked. There was a reason he thought he'd seen Billy before. Back in Council Grove Mr. Stokes had stopped a fight between two boys. It was Billy, beating up on a smaller boy.

Mr. Wood posted a double watch. People thought it was out of fear for the horses. Sid figured it was to protect Cora. But the night passed peacefully. The bugle sounded a little earlier than usual to give folk a chance to climb up Pawnee Rock to see the sunrise a little after six o'clock without delaying the train too much. Ma said Abe's ankle was much improved, but she was afraid for him to make the climb. He didn't argue.

Half asleep, Jimmy whined, "Who wants to see a stupid old sunrise?"

Sid could see Dale and Eli set out, wishing he could go along but he felt uneasy about leaving Abe alone after what Dale said. "Let's go look at the names on the sandstone wall, Abe."

People were crowded around reading names and trying to find a place to add theirs. Sid couldn't see anywhere to put his name if he wanted to. Every bit of the surface was covered. Some names were so high, he wondered how people had been able to carve them.

"This one says 1826," said Abe. They were so busy reading out names, they didn't realize others were leaving until they were alone. Suddenly, hands grabbed them from behind. Frog had Abe's arms pinned behind his back and Squeaker had Sid. Squeaker was a lot stronger than he looked.

Billy punched Abe in the stomach. "Take that, Jew-boy!" Connie said. Abe doubled over, falling to the ground as Frog released him. Before Sid could cry out, Billy whirled around, landing a blow in his stomach that knocked the wind out of him. Pain shot through his whole body as he crumpled to the ground. Connie called him something crude about being friends with Abe and the Payne family.

The boys vanished as quickly as they'd come. Sid pulled himself up and gave Abe a hand.

"Cowards," panted Abe, still trying to catch his breath.

"Dale tried to warn me," panted Sid. "Didn't expect 'em here. Thought they'd try to jump me on the way up the rock."

As they made their way back to the wagon, Jimmy and Matthew came running. "Hurry, Sid. You can see everything from up there," called Matthew.

"Pa says there's still time to go back if you'll come with us. Please?" begged Jimmy.

"Go Sid," said Abe. "I would go if could."

"Reckon you ought to see it too, Abe," said Pa. Jeremy Sawyer was right behind. "Jeremy and I are gonna help you up to the top now that we've seen what the climb's like. Come on. We have just enough time. We'll make a 'pack saddle' with our arms to carry you once we get to the climb."

They met Ethel coming down. Mr. Sinclair and another man carried her. "I have my own palanquin, too, Abe." She waved as they passed.

When they reached the top, Sid was glad Abe could be there, too. The sun was a bright yellow disk sitting just above the edge of the horizon against a golden-pink sky. They could see the Arkansas River winding its way toward the hills on the western horizon. To the east lay the vast prairie they had crossed. In the distance, herds of antelope and buffalo grazed, patches of tan and brown on the gray-green grass. When they returned to the bottom and set Abe down, Pa raced Matthew and Jimmy back to the wagon.

They met Billy and Connie. "Mornin' Jeremy," said Connie acting as if Sid and Abe weren't even there. He was the picture of innocence. "Great view from the top!"

Jeremy nodded, handing Abe his crutch. "Worth the trip," he said, "Right Abe?"

Abe leaned on his crutch. Looking straight at Connie and Billy, he spoke slowly and clearly. "In my country, there is a word for people who hit somebody who cannot fight back. It is *feigling*. It means coward. If you want a fight, Connie, I will fight you. It will not be necessary for someone to hold you while I hit you."

Billy scowled.

"Don't know what you're talkin' about," Connie lied.

"You heard what I said," said Abe.

"Get ready to yoke up," the call was repeated and passed along like an echo through the company. Billy and Connie vanished.

"What's this about?" asked Jeremy. "If Red Elston's little brother is fightin' again, Red's gonna have his hide."

Sid kept his mouth shut.

Abe let out a slow breath. "Sank you for helping me up to the top."

Jeremy looked at them thoughtfully. "It's fine by me if you don't want to talk about it, but if you decide to fight Billy Elston, let me know first. Red and I will be there to make sure it's a fair fight. You don't have to worry about Connie. You're right, Abe. He's a coward. Billy's pa works for Mr. Ryckman. Connie thinks it gives him the right to tell Billy what to do. Guess Billy's stupid enough to go along with it."

"What does Billy's Pa do?" Sid asked. Billy seemed to think he was better than the other boys whose parents worked for Ryckman.

"He managed his stables back in New York where they're from. Red works for 'em, too. He's a trainer. Learned it from his pa from the time he was about Jimmy's age. Has a way with horses like their dad. Funny, isn't it, how people in the same family can be so different? Red worries about Billy. See, their ma died when Billy was about two years old. Miz Ryckman has been awful good to 'em. But it isn't the same, not having your own ma."

Sid had a lot to think about as the train left Pawnee Rock. Knowing what he did might explain why Billy had such blind loyalty to Connie. *But it doesn't make it right.* Abe didn't have a mother either. It hadn't turned him into a bully.

14.

Sibley's Camp

They stopped for the night at Sibley's Camp. At lessons, Mrs. Payne explained that it was named for George Sibley, who camped there when he led a government survey of the Santa Fe Trail in 1825.

Sometime in the night, Sid heard Ma. "Ben, wake up. Miz Goodall's arm. If we act now, we may be able to save it above the elbow."

"What do the Goodalls have to say about it?" whispered Pa. "Does she understand the risk?

"Mrs. Goodall doesn't really have a choice, does she? I had Dale run over and get Mr. Wood and the Sinclairs. Mr. Reid's already there. Mr. Wood agrees. He thinks we should do it now. I know it's risky but the longer we wait, the more dangerous. We may need an extra pair of hands. And I need you for moral support. God love her, she's known since the fever shot up. We talked it through. It's what Doc Short woulda done. I wish he was here now, Ben. Lord knows I wish he was here. Mr. Wood says he can do it, but he's gonna need some strong arms to help."

"What can I do, Sadie?" Mrs. Payne looked out of her tent.

"If you'll watch over the children. There could be some screamin'. They might wake up."

Sid was already on his feet. He'd never seen an amputation

and didn't want to. Once Pa had told about having to do one back when he was younger. It would be a grim business.

"Sid, I'll need you to help Dale."

"I can help," Abe sat up. He had been helping Ma. She said he had a real knack for doctoring, and he wasn't squeamish.

"Come along then. Both of you."

As they hurried to the Goodall wagon, Ma gave directions. "The girls are asleep. Ethel's gonna watch over 'em. Sid, you help Dale carry 'em over there. I don't want Dale watchin'. He'll need somebody. Abe, you can help me get things set out and see there's a kettle of boilin' water. The men will do the heavy work. You 'n me will be there to stop the bleedin' and do the bandages."

Mrs. Goodall was lying up on a bed made with wooden planks on top of two barrels. Her eyes were wide with fright, but her mouth was set in a determined line. Mr. Goodall was at her side.

It was a puzzle to Sid how he could pick up Jimmy or Cora when they were wide awake, but let them go to sleep, and it was like trying to carry a sack of bricks. It was the same thing with Dale's sisters.

Ethel was wide-awake, her face drawn and pale when they brought Emma. "I'm sorry, Dale. Mamma says there isn't any other way," she whispered.

When they returned with Molly, Sid said, "Don't go tryin' to lift 'em, Ethel. Come get me if you need me. I'll be with Dale."

"I'm fine." She turned away.

Dale wanted to see his ma before the surgery. Sid felt useless. He desperately hoped to get away before the operation began. Reverend Jones was there. Mr. Goodall stood beside his wife, his good arm cradled under her neck, holding her head up so she could drink the whiskey Ethel's mother offered to blunt the pain.

Mrs. Goodall took a sip and sputtered. "There, there, Mamma," said Mr. Goodall. "Drink it all. You'll need it. Preacher Jones is here, just like you wanted. The Good Lord's gonna take care of you."

Reverend Jones placed his hand on Mrs. Goodall's head "It says in Psalm 91, 'He shall cover thee with his feathers, and under his wings shalt thou trust: his truth shall be thy shield and buckler.'" He said a short prayer.

Ma handed her a rolled-up cloth. "Miz Goodall, you put this in your mouth. You're gonna need to bite down on it when it starts to hurt."

"Boys, time for you to take a walk around the circle," said Pa. This isn't something to see."

"I'd like to stay," said Abe.

"I can't look," gasped Dale. "I— I'm not brave enough."

"I can't either," said Sid, stomach churning at the thought. He put his arm around Dale's shoulders. They walked behind the Goodall's tent.

"I wish I could tell you it won't hurt, Miz Goodall." They could hear Mr. Wood. "We'll be quick about it."

Sid wanted to be strong for Dale but the thought of what was going to happen made him lightheaded. Suddenly, Mrs. Jones was there, standing between them, an arm around each.

"Let's take a walk. It'll be over soon, Dale. Don't let anyone ever say you're lacking courage because aren't at her side. You're doin' exactly the right thing by bein' out of the way. I promise."

"I should be there." A sob escaped him.

"I know you want to be with her, like your Pa. But your mother asked me not to let you. It's what she wants. They'll fetch us when they're ready. Then you can see her. There's no shame in knowing your limits. Say it with me. Focus your mind on it: 'The Lord is my Shepherd'. . ." She began reciting the 23rd Psalm.

Sid wasn't sure how many times they repeated the psalm or when Mrs. Goodall's cries ended before Mr. Sinclair came.

"Dale, your ma is a brave woman. She's through the worst. Now we have to let Mother Nature do the work. She's resting. You can see her if you like. She'll know you're there even if she can't say anything."

All evidence of the gruesome surgery was gone. Abe was putting things back in Ma's bag. He looked white as a sheet. So did Ma and Pa.

"Your mamma's going to have some big adjustments to make once that arm heals," said Mrs. Jones, "but we're all here to help."

Tears rolled down Dale's face as he looked at his mother all covered with blankets. Sid realized the front of his shirt was wet, too. Tears streamed down his face. They were for Mrs. Goodall, for Dale, for all the hurt and loss he'd seen.

"Mr. Goodall, you try and get some rest," said Ma. "I'll sit with her till mornin'. Mrs. Sinclair is keeping the girls until Miz Goodall's well enough to see 'em. All we can do now is watch and pray."

Mr. Goodall shook his head. "I need to be here."

"Me, too," said Dale.

As he left, Mr. Wood said, "I'm calling for a hunt tomorrow. It's time and it will give Miz Goodall a few days to heal."

15.

Short Grass Prairie

When asked about hunting buffalo, Mr. Wood's reaction was, "Not until needs must as the devil drives." Pa said that meant not until driven by necessity.

However, as they neared short-grass country he began preparing the men for a hunt. Everyone would need plenty of meat for the trip through the desert once the company left Santa Fe. Now losses from the tornado made hunting urgent.

The glory of hunting buffalo was one of the myths that grew up around traveling west. Even boys Sid's age talked about "Getting my buffalo." Mr. Wood downplayed the glory of the hunt. He said it was dangerous work. People needed to know exactly what to do because they might have very little advance notice before a hunt. It required a team effort; only eight of the men would shoot buffalo with a dozen others providing support. Connie stormed around for days after the first meeting, complaining. "Been huntin' since I could carry a gun. Me 'n Billy have just as much right to hunt as anybody."

Some of the men thought they should shoot as many buffalo as they could bring down. Mr. Wood disagreed. "Worst possible message we could leave for Comanche and Arapaho is a bunch of dead buffalo."

"Reckon the wolves can clean 'em up," said one of the men. "Keep 'em from botherin' us."

"Don't think our plains brothers wouldn't know. It would be one more way to show disrespect. Plus, it's downright wrong to waste Mother Nature's bounty. This company takes what it needs. No more."

They'd seen plenty of buffalo bones along the way, piles of them bleached white from years in the sun. Once, just about nooning, they came upon what looked like hundreds of dead buffalo littering the prairie, bodies left to rot. Mr. Wood had directed the wagons to go on for almost another hour to get away from the terrible stench.

When Sid asked about the dead buffalo, Mr. Reid frowned. "Hunters kill off buffalo for their tongue. Rich folk back East think buffalo tongue's a delicacy. They pay a good price for it. All those poor animals had to die so somebody could have a fine meal. It's a sin against God and nature."

"Couldn't they sell the rest of the meat?"

"Butchering a buffalo slows 'em down. They don't get near as good a price for the meat. A lot of 'em take the hide, too. But that takes time, so some of 'em don't bother. They can get near 25 cents a tongue. Tongues don't take the space hides take. They can travel faster."

When they butchered beef back home, Ma always made a cold supper with the tongue. The very idea that anybody would kill a big animal for one little meal was beyond imagining.

"You haveta understand, Sid, buffalo aren't just animals to our native brothers. They believe God gave them the buffalo as . . . I guess we'd say as a sacred gift for their support and comfort. They respect the buffalo. When we shoot a buffalo without need, well, the closest I can come to describing it is if somebody came up to your farm and shot your cattle and left them to rot. Isaiah Wood is right. We only take what we need. Folk seem to think they'll last forever. And there's some that think getting rid of the buffalo is a good way to get rid of Indians. There's talk of putting a bounty on buffalo for that very reason."

When the bugle sounded just before dawn, the morning after Mrs. Goodall's surgery, word went out. Mr. Wood was calling for a hunt. The camp snapped into action with the last notes of the bugle call. People knew what was expected. Twenty men, counting Mr. Wood, were riding out to the hunt. Mr. Wood referred to the eight who were to shoot buffalo as the hunters. Every hunter needed a backup rider whose job was to rescue him if he got in trouble, spot where his buffalo went down, help him butcher the downed buffalo, and take meat back to camp. Three other men, the hunt supervisors, would follow the hunt as a whole and keep Mr. Wood informed. That way he would know when to call off the hunt or about any problems the minute they happened.

Back in camp, others would guard the livestock. The sound of the hunt would put them on edge. When fresh meat started coming in, the smell would be a magnet for wolves and coyotes. That would be enough to send the animals on another stampede.

Other men would divide the large chunks of meat as it came in and distribute it throughout the company. Most of it would be cut into thin strips to dry into buffalo jerky.

Excitement crackled in the air. Despite late hours, Pa was dressed and eating a hasty breakfast when Ma returned from the Goodall tent.

"She's made it so far," Ma sighed, taking the cup of coffee Mrs. Payne handed her. "Mrs. Ryckman came over to spell me off before she starts the noon mess. Mr. Wood wants everybody free to support the hunt, so she's organizin' all the cookin' again like she did after the storm. I finally convinced Mr. Goodall to get some rest. God love him."

"What about Dale?" Sid asked.

"Poor boy fell asleep about an hour ago, right where he was sittin'. We put a blanket over him. He was up at bugle, but I ordered him to bed." Ma sighed. "The next few hours will tell all."

Pa saddled Sandy and grabbed his gun. He was riding backup to Red Elston, Billy Elston's older brother. The men would get as close to the herd as possible without alarming them. As the herd took flight, hunters were to ride alongside, picking off slower animals or stragglers. It was a dangerous business. The herd could switch direction and surround a hunter before he could steer his horse clear. Sometimes a horse panicked and ran with the herd. Or a hunter could be thrown from a horse. A buffalo might turn unexpectedly and charge. That's why the backup riders were as important as the hunters.

Sid wished he didn't have to stay behind and set up for the meat to come in. Still, it was a relief. He'd looked a buffalo stampede in the eye. Once was enough. He was glad to hear Pa was assigned to be a backup rider, too. It sounded safer.

With Mr. Reid joining the hunt, Ma was the only one doing the doctoring. "Abe, we'd best see how our patients are doing," she said as Pa left with Sandy. "And we'd better be ready for some new injuries."

Sid took Jimmy, Matthew, Cora, and Lydia to see the men off. "Ready men?" Mr. Wood called. "Keep your distance until you have a good shot. Some of the professional hunters go into the herd, but they've been doing it for years. Their horses know what they're doing. No buffalo is worth the price of one of our men."

"Where's the buffalo?" asked Matthew.

"There up behind those thickets." Jimmy pointed to plum thickets that stood along a steep gully not far from camp.

"They'll be out there," said Sid, "but not so close to camp. Jeremy Sawyer was one of the scouts lookin' for 'em way before you two woke up."

Nobody lingered. There was too much work to do.

Sid's first job was to help get the livestock moved from the circle so the space could be set up to receive the meat as it came in. As soon as the circle was clear, they set up a place near the Ryckman wagons for the mess. Then barrels and planks were set up to serve as tables for dividing the meat. Campfires outside the circle were extinguished and new ones built inside. Willow branches gathered and prepared when wood was in good supply were transformed into drying racks near each campfire. By the time the meat arrived, the campfires had to be down to coals.

Even the younger children had jobs to do. "You youngsters get your gloves and baskets so you can help collect buffalo chips," Mrs. Payne said. "Fires have to be fed all day." Some of the children in the Wood Company didn't wear gloves when they collected. Sid wondered if they ever washed their hands. It didn't bear thinking about.

"Oh no," Jimmy groaned. "Not buffalo chips!"

"Come on," said Matthew. "We gotta do it. Let's get it over with."

Sid built the fire by their wagons. When it burned down to his satisfaction, he banked it and helped Mrs. Payne get their wagon tailgate set up to serve as a chopping table.

Shots rang out in the distance. The terrifying sound of a buffalo stampede signaled the hunt was on. It wasn't long after when the first meat arrived. It would be coming in for several hours as men butchered the downed buffalo where they fell. "Remember, no more than half an inch thick." Mr. Davies handed Sid a slab of meat. "Isaiah Wood says it takes about five days to dry for every inch of thickness."

Sid helped Mrs. Payne cut the meat into thin strips and hang them on the willow branches by their fire.

Feeding the fire was Jimmy's and Matthew's job. Sid kept a close watch on them, so the fire was kept alive but not in flames. Cora and Lydia got to play under Mrs. Reid's watchful eye—she took care of Anna and baby Clarence. When the boys objected, Mrs. Payne said it was harder to stay out of the way than to have a job. "You're older. Besides, you can make just about any job fun if you use your imagination."

"Nobody has enough imagination to make this fun," Jimmy complained.

"My baba shot a buffalo and cut up the whole thing all by himself," said Matthew.

"And there wasn't anybody to help him feed the fire," said Mrs. Payne.

Mrs. Ryckman said they'd cook the buffalo tongues at mess so everybody in the company could have a taste. As the rich meat from buffalo humps came in, she had men set it up on spits to roast over the fire. Mr. Wood had already cautioned, "Buffalo meat is tasty, but mighty rich for ordinary fare. Go easy on the fresh meat, or you'll spend tomorrow looking for a bush."

"Huh?" Jimmy hadn't understood.

"He means finding a private place to go to the toilet," Sid had told him. Jimmy was off to the next thing before he could explain that buffalo meat is fatty and over-eating meant the risk of diarrhea.

Meat kept coming in. Most of the processed meat would eventually go to those who lost the most supplies, but everyone worked together to preserve it, and everyone would get plenty. Sid cut strips of meat until he was covered with blood. If it hadn't been for smoky fires all around the camp, he'd have been covered with flies, too.

Ma and Abe came and went. She said Mrs. Goodall was in pain, but it was to be expected. She brought Molly and Emma along with the orphaned Isla and Mazie to play with the girls so Ethel could get some rest. She wasn't happy with the way Ethel's arm looked.

Sid figured Ethel would be frightened, despite the brave face she put on things. She sure wouldn't like being unable to help. Maybe there was a way to cheer her up.

Ma had one last patient to check on, but she made Abe stay behind and put his foot up. "Al Joiner's healing better than most," she said when she returned. "Havin' a fit over missin' the hunt, though."

"Anybody who could shoot the eyelashes off a flea would, now wouldn't they?" laughed Mrs. Payne, as she cut fat and gristle off a large piece of meat.

"I agreed to lettin' him help guard the livestock. I hope he doesn't have to shoot the eyelashes off anything."

"One thing for certain," said Sid. "I don't ever want to be a butcher." That's when he decided what he could do to make Ethel laugh. He had Lydia bring him a piece of paper. He put his hand down on it, leaving a bloody handprint. "Lydia, how about you write, 'See what you're missin'? Your friends.' You can get everybody to sign it and take it to Ethel." Lydia happily collected signatures. Cora, who had learned to write, added Serena's name, too. The other little girls wanted to add their names. Lydia wrote for them. She wrote "Sid" next to the handprint and drew an arrow to it.

By afternoon, row upon row of buffalo meat was drying all around camp. More came. Men brought buffalo hides, too. These were laid out for curing. It took a lot of time to properly cure a buffalo hide. Mr. Wood said it wasn't the best time of year for curing hides, but he wanted them for trade at New Fort Bent. It was another way to help people who lost all their supplies in the storm.

Mrs. Payne saved out a buffalo roast and some nice big chunks for stew. "This will give us fresh meat for several days."

It was well after noon when Mr. Wood and the last of the men returned to camp. Pa wasn't among them. Sid's heart sank as he stood with Ma, scanning the horizon for Pa riding Sandy.

But they didn't come.

The hunters thought he had taken meat back to camp.

Nobody in camp missed him because they thought he was on the hunt.

Mr. Wood had group captains check to see that everyone was accounted for. It turned out that Connie Ryckman and Billy Elston were missing, too, and they weren't even part of the hunt.

Nobody had seen Pa since after the second buffalo went down. No one had seen Connie or Billy since the men set off at dawn. They were supposed to be helping with the fires and scaffolding. No one could account for either boy. And their horses were missing.

*****

Sid was with Mr. Wood at the Ryckman wagons when Mr. Ryckman questioned Patsy O'Connell, their maid. Patsy burst into tears. "It was himself and Billy, Sir, and Miz Ryckman with Miz Goodall gone to stay—"

"Connie and Billy?" Mr. Wood asked gently.

Patsy nodded, "Himself told me the fire and scaffold to make, didn't he? Sure he's gone after his gun. Didn't he run off, sir. So, I look it. I do be working, too, sir."

"You should have told me immediately, Patsy!" said Mrs. Ryckman, anger edging her controlled voice.

"Yes, Miss. Em—"

"Em what?" Mr. Ryckman's face was red.

"Himself said he would hurt us, sir." Sobbing, Patsy put her face in her hands.

"Silly girl, of course he wouldn't hurt you." The anger drained from Mrs. Ryckman's voice.

It sounded exactly like something Connie would do.

"Girl deserves a good thrashing," said Mr. Ryckman, clenching his fists.

Mrs. Clark was questioned. "Bitsy 'n me was too busy to notice anything, what with helping Mrs. Ryckman and looking after our young 'ens."

"You should have been keeping an eye on the boys." Mr. Ryckman frowned.

"No sense wasting time trying to fix blame," said Mr. Wood. "Let's get out there and find those boys and Ben Johnson before it gets dark on us. I need ten volunteers. Rest of you help take care of the meat. It won't wait." Hands sprang up across the crowd gathered around Mr. Wood. "Ryckman, Elston, you got boys out there. Red Elston, you come, too. Reid, I need you. Jeremy, you and Preacher Jones—"

Someone in the crowd gasped. "Preacher Jones?"

"Don't go jumping to conclusions. Preacher's a good tracker. Better than most and we're missing Al Joiner."

Surprised mumbling erupted from the crowd.

"What, you think a man's a pantywaist 'cause he's a preacher?" somebody called out.

"Then you ain't read what the Good Book says about the prophets!" somebody else called.

"Get Sid a horse," said Mr. Wood. "Boy's got a right to help find his Pa. Don't you worry, Mrs. Johnson, I'll keep him with me."

"Take Mr. Payne's horse, Sid," Mrs. Payne waved her

hand above the crowd.

By the time Sid had Freedom saddled, Mr. Reid and Preacher Jones were busy studying the ground at the start of the hunt.

"Reid," Mr. Wood asked, "what's your best guess?"

"Hard to tell with all the coming and going, but looks to us like two horses left after the others from that gully with the plum thickets. If the boys set out right after we did, they'd wanna avoid being seen. Must have followed close on, not expecting anybody to be looking back, but close enough to the hunters so as nobody in camp would think anything of it if they happened to notice."

"Over here," called Reverend Jones from the thicket. "Tracks everywhere. It's deep enough to hide a horse. Tracks of two horses start from here. I expect it's the boys."

Mr. Reid shook his head, "Reckon they split off toward the hunt somewhere up ahead allowing there wouldn't be time to send 'em back if they was spotted."

Mr. Wood nodded. "Sound like your boys, Ryckman? Elston?"

"Connie's smart," said Mr. Ryckman. "Too smart for his own damned good. Had his heart set on getting a buffalo."

"Yeah, and my little brother would follow Connie if it led him off a cliff," said Red Elston.

Mr. Wood frowned. "Johnson wouldn't leave his post unless there was a mighty good reason. Must have spotted 'em once the hunt started."

After they started out, a lone, riderless horse seemed to appear out of nowhere. The prairie air played tricks sometimes. As they got closer, Sid gasped. "It's Sandy!" *Pa!* What had happened to Pa?

Mr. Wood halted the party. He nodded to Billy's father. "Elston, have a look. Sid, you, too. Horse knows you."

Sid dismounted, calling to Sandy. "Good girl." He took her reins, patting her on the muzzle. It felt like she was trying to tell him something. Could Bayless Sly and J.J. Gordon have waylaid Pa in the confusion of the hunt? It was nonsensical, and he knew it, but still . . .

"Hold her while I have a look, son." Mr. Elston talked to Sandy as he walked around her. Afraid to look, Sid leaned his head into her neck, feeling her relax under Mr. Elston's expert touch.

"Bad gouge on her right rump. Looks like a buffalo took a swipe. Somebody needs to take her back and treat that wound. I'd go—"

"You need to be here for your boy." Mr. Wood sent one of the men back with Sandy. "Speak to Miz Johnson first," he said.

Reverend Jones and Mr. Reid were on ahead of the party, studying Sandy's tracks.

"Don't worry about what you don't know, Sid. We'll find your Pa," said Mr. Wood. He divided the search party into groups. Reverend Jones took a group to follow Sandy's tracks. Mr. Reid took others to track the boys. It wouldn't be easy to follow them. Tracks left by men taking meat to camp crossed over earlier tracks. "Two shots in the air for finding 'em or for help. Red Elston and Sid Johnson, come with me. We'll start at the top of the hunt."

Ahead, the flattened grass where the buffalo had slept blended into the churned earth of the stampede. Carcasses dotted the near side of the path cut by the buffalo. Gray shapes shifted around them. Wolves.

"Johnson backed you up, Red. Which one is your buffalo?"

Dismounting, they led their horses, searching the ground around them as Red led them to where he downed a buffalo.

Wolves bristled and snarled as they approached. Sid had never been close to wolves before, except the wolf that Ta Lezhé killed. A cold chill ran up his spine. He wanted to jump back on Freedom and run. Fortunately, Freedom wasn't spooked by them.

"Spread your arms out and look big," said Mr. Wood. They'll back off. If they don't, we'll give them a shot to remember us by." The wolves bared their teeth. Snarling, they slithered away vying for room at nearby carcasses. Clouds of flies settled on the carcass, though the wolves had nearly picked it clean.

Tracks crisscrossed where horses wheeled as they followed buffalo separated from the herd. "Mr. Ryckman downed the first buffalo," said Red. "Reid took the second. Dad was back up for him. I spotted a cow a bit slower than the rest and picked her off right away. One clean shot. Dad saw my buffalo go down and came up to congratulate me. I guess we were both so excited we didn't think about Mr. Johnson. Next thing we were skinning buffalo—Reid's an expert and our two buffalo fell so close we all just worked together. I'm sorry, Sid, I didn't notice anything else."

It was hard for Sid to focus with wolves snarling and tearing at the buffalo carcass behind them. Mr. Wood didn't seem bothered. "Did you ever see Johnson?"

"He was right behind me. He called out, 'Good shot, you got him, Red.' I sorta remember him riding up, but we were too busy to think about it."

Mr. Wood nodded. "Something must have distracted him. Could have been the boys cutting in further down the hunt."

Sid had tracked with Pa along the creek in Illinois. This was different. The short praire grass was a tangle of turf torn by the stampede. Mr. Wood squatted down, examining the ground around the carcass of Red's buffalo. Sid couldn't make any sense of it.

"Here's where I dismounted." Red pointed to his boot track, dug into the turf. There was a maze of boot prints around the carcass left from butchering and collecting the meat.

"Wolves haven't made this any easier," said Mr. Wood, pointing to where they had torn and scattered the carcass, leaving their tracks. He led them from the carcass in a widening circle. "Looks like somebody started to dismount here, then changed his mind."

Mr. Wood read hoof, paw, and boot prints like a code written between the lines in a book. "See here Sid? Horse tracks come in a steady line back from that rise where the men riding backup waited. They've crossed the hunters. They're crossed over by the men riding back and forth for the meat. Then you have the wolves. It's hard to tell if this horse was Sandy, but these deeper boot impressions are from where somebody started to dismount, maybe your Pa. Your foot 'bout the size of his?"

"Just about," said Sid, choking back panic. "He says I'll be wearin' his boots soon."

"I'd say this was your Pa. You can see where he stepped down. But he didn't leave any other tracks. See how the boot mark slides around? He turned back. You can tell by the way the print's tilted. There's more dirt on this side. Wolves haven't done us any favors here either." Sid looked at the faint blur, noticing for the first time.

"Horse turned in a hurry, heading toward the hunt." Mr. Wood walked a few paces ahead. "He must have spotted trouble."

This much, Sid could see for himself. Once the footprints around the carcass left off, the tracks of a horse lengthening into a gallop were clearly imprinted over the buffalo tracks.

"It's Sandy," Sid wasn't sure he'd have recognized her unique hoofprint if Reverend Jones hadn't called it to his attention. "Her back right shoe is different." Sandy was headed toward the middle of the path made by the stampeding buffalo, and at an angle, well away from the downed carcasses.

The wolves closed in on what remained of Red's buffalo as they hurriedly followed Sandy's tracks, leading their horses, scanning the ground on either side.

"Here," Red called from ahead, near the middle of the swath cut by the buffalo. "More horses."

"Some of the hunters moving in to follow behind. Stay even with us, Red. Can't risk having your horse wipe out anything we need to see."

"There's buffalo tracks going over where these horses passed," said Red. "Looks like somebody cut into the herd."

"Or didn't wait for stragglers to pass," said Mr. Wood.

They walked on, searching the ground. Red kept to Mr. Wood's right, closest to the far side of the hunt, Sid to the left. A mass of prints showed where the last buffalo had been singled out. A cluster of wolves marked where it fell. Sid kept his distance, trying to convince himself they were too busy to bother him.

It seemed hopeless. They went on in silence, Sid nearly choking with panic. "Here's where the boys cut into the hunt," Mr. Wood said at last. "Reid's already been here and moved on. Your Pa musta spotted the boys early on, but Sandy's tracks are gone. Judging by what we've seen, I reckon the boys cut in after the last buffalo was downed, but before the last of the stragglers. Something happened further on down. Let's spread out again. We might pick up something Reid missed."

All Sid could see was pulverized earth and buffalo hoofprints. His heart sank. Suddenly Red yelled, "Tracks over here."

"Horse cut through the back before all the buffalo passed," said Mr. Wood, studying the prints. "Your Pa and one of the boys, Sid. No sign of the other boy. A seasoned hunter keeps his eye on the whole herd so as not to get caught out by the stragglers. It's one of the reasons I didn't want boys on the hunt." Standing, he surveyed the wide prairie ahead. There was nothing as far as they could see, not even the horses of the other men who were searching.

Let us find him, please let us find him. Sid breathed one continuous prayer, unable to bear the thought of anything happening to Pa.

After a while, Mr. Wood stopped, flicked aside some dirt, and pulled up a strip of red cloth. "Your Pa wearin' a red kerchief, Sid?"

"No. It was blue." Like all the men, Pa left with a big kerchief tied around his neck, ready to pull up to protect himself from dust.

"Reckon it's from one of the boys?" said Red.

"You can be danged sure it wasn't a buffalo wearing it." Mr. Wood signaled for them to keep going.

Sid fought to keep from giving up hope. Prints left by the search parties and their horses, endless buffalo tracks, on and on—suddenly, new tracks appeared in the buffalo-plowed dirt. "Over here. Two horses!" he called.

Mr. Wood examined the prints. "This one's a younger mount. Your Pa's horse intersects. Just what I thought. Spread back out."

It was like having pieces of a puzzle, where you know something goes in the middle, but you haven't found the pieces that fit on either side. They came back together every time somebody found a piece of their puzzle.

"Younger horse reared and wheeled," called Mr. Wood. Sid hurried over to have a look. There was turned soil and a heavy impression where the horse's front legs had landed, but after that, there was no trace of the horse.

"Panicked and stampeded with the herd," said Mr. Wood, grimly. "Rider stayed in the saddle or we'd have seen . . . " He didn't finish.

"Can't see anything of the other two horses," said Red, his voice catching.

Suddenly Sid realized Red was afraid, too. Afraid for Billy. In his fear for Pa, he hadn't thought of anyone else.

Mr. Wood, stood upright, stretching his back. "Thing is, with a stampede, you'll get two or three waves of buffalo coming along after the main part of the herd. If anybody fell on the trail, Reid woulda found 'em up ahead and we'd have heard from him. Our best bet is to keep on."

"Gunpowder," Red called a bit later.

"Over here," Sid yelled, spotting what looked like blood among the tracks. Before Mr. Wood could reach him, a shot split the air, followed by another.

*****

Mr. Wood was on his horse in a flash. Sid scrambled to mount Freedom. "Don't worry Sid, we'll catch up," said Red, waiting for him.

They rode toward the sound of the shots. The prairie reached on and on into nowhere in every direction. Cresting a low rise, they abruptly came upon the men gathered at the bottom of a dry ravine. A dead horse was all Sid could make out.

It felt as if time stopped. He couldn't think clearly. He must have dismounted, because he found himself standing among the men; Red's arm was across his shoulders. His eyes searched for Pa. It wasn't until he spotted him sitting near where Mr. Wood stood, that things came back into focus. Pa was stripped down to his waist. Billy lay stretched out with a makeshift splint on one arm, held with strips of Pa's shirt. Mr. Elston knelt beside him.

"Danged fool brother of mine. Can't keep himself out of trouble." Sid could hear the relief in Red's voice.

Pa was seated next to Connie, who lay stretched out, the dead horse's saddle blanket over him. He looked as pale as a waning moon. Mr. Ryckman knelt beside him. He held up one corner of the blanket, exposing Connie's bare right leg, trouser cut off high on his hip. A bloody tourniquet made from Pa's undershirt was wrapped around his thigh. Mr. Ryckman looked up at Sid, "Your Pa saved his life."

"He's not out of the woods yet," said Pa. "Need to get him back where we can wash out that wound proper. Got the bleeding stopped. Not sure the leg's set properly. It needs to be stretched. Takes more than one pair of hands." There was blood all over Pa.

"Here, put this on, Mr. Johnson." Reverend Jones handed him his own shirt. "You're gonna have a bad sunburn."

Sid fought tears of relief. He wanted to run grab and hold on to Pa, feel he was still alive. But he stayed out of the way, straining to hear.

"Boys are lucky to be alive, Johnson," said Mr. Wood. "I've seen more than one horse go down following buffalo. Sending your horse back was the smartest thing you coulda done. Risky, but smart. It gave Preacher and Jeremy a roadmap to find you."

Sid knew the risk. Sandy could have wandered off, been frightened by the sight of the wolves moving in on the carcasses and run off, or failed to find her way back to the train.

He tried to fight off the feeling that Billy got what was coming to him. Connie, too. He knew it wasn't right, but he couldn't help it.

"I fired a couple of times trying to get somebody's attention," said Pa, "but we're too far down. Wind was in the other direction. Had to save powder for the wolves."

"They wouldn't turn down a dead horse," said Mr. Reid. "Smell of blood will attract 'em. Lucky we left enough carcasses to occupy 'em."

Pa nodded. "Billy lost his powder somewhere in the stampede. Connie's gun is long gone with his horse. I had to try and stop the bleeding in Connie's leg first thing. He took a pretty mean gouge before I got him off his horse. Horse was terrified. I didn't have enough water to get the leg clean. Boys needed some to drink. Mighty hot out here without any shade. Then there was Billy's arm. Thank God it was just his arm."

"Dammed loss of fine horseflesh," said Mr. Ryckman bitterly. "Both of 'em Tennessee Thoroughbreds. If I weren't so relieved to find my son alive, I'd have his hide. We're headed to California to introduce Thoroughbred racing, not to hunt buffalo."

Sid longed to hear the whole story from Pa. It would have to wait.

Billy groaned and whined like a baby as Mr. Elston lifted him on to Red's horse. They put him in front, so Red could hold on to him. Pa got on Freedom behind Sid. "Miz Johnson will know what to do for the boy," said Mr. Wood.

"Preacher, you get on back with Johnson and the Elstons before you're burned, too. Speak to Miz Ryckman. Reid, you and your men stay with Ryckman and me. We'll have to walk Connie out of here on the blanket. We'll take it slow. We'll be pushing it to get back by dark."

It was a worried train that greeted their return. Ma, who could find something to fret about even when there wasn't anything to worry over, typically flew into action in a crisis. Without so much as a gasp of relief, she put Pa in the shade of the wagon and had him take off Reverend Jones' shirt. "Preacher, you sit down here, too where we can have a look at that sunburn. Good you had your waistcoat. At least it spared your back. I won't ask what happened to your waistcoat, Ben Johnson. Matthew, you and Jimmy run get Miz Jones. Tell her to bring him a shirt."

Mrs. Payne grabbed a basket, "Mr. Payne said the native people make a poultice for burns from cactus pods. Come along, girls. Sid, send the boys along to help when they get back. Sadie, we'll take care of things here. You see to the Elston boy."

Pa's arms, chest, and back were a bright shade of pink. "Sid, get them started drinkin' water," said Ma.

Mrs. Jones came on the run following Matthew and Jimmy. Ma promised to send her a poultice for his sunburn.

"Thank you, Mrs. Johnson, but not until I've talked with Mrs. Ryckman," Reverend Jones said, buttoning his shirt.

Pa grimaced when they were gone. "Get me some water so I can wash up, Son, and something to put on. I can't stand around here half naked."

"Ben Johnson, you're not puttin' anything on that back till you've had some doctorin'. Sit in the tent if you want some privacy." Ma left, giving Abe directions as they went. "We'll have a look at Billy. We'll probably have to get the men to help pull the Ryckman boy's leg . . ."

Pa grinned. "Your Ma is a force to be reckoned with, Sid."

He was eager to hear what had happened, but Sid could tell the sunburn was starting to hurt. He brought Pa a second cup of water and filled a pan with water so Pa could wash and change into clean clothes.

"Don't you go touchin' those, Jimmy." It was Cora. They

were returning with the cactus pads. "You get little pricklies in your fingers."

"You're the one who got cactus needles in your finger," said Matthew.

"She didn't listen to Miz Payne," Jimmy tattled.

"We all have to learn," said Mrs. Payne. "Now, gentlemen, I have work for you." She put Jimmy and Matthew to scraping the needles off the cactus pads, a job requiring great care. The large, wickedly sharp spines were obvious. But the prickly pear pads were full of fine hair-like needles. "Just because you can't see them doesn't mean they aren't there."

Lydia found Serena. The two girls settled just outside the tent where they could watch what was happening with the comfort of a cat.

"Did a prickly pear bite you?" Pa called from inside the tent.

"Here we go again," muttered Jimmy as Cora began a detailed report on the proper way to pick prickly pear pads. "You must be ever so very careful. Cactuses has teeny, te-e-e-ny, tiny little stickles that poke you and you can't see 'em."

"They can get in your fingers," said Lydia.

"And sometimes they don't ever, ever come out." Cora looked solemnly at her finger.

"I tried to tell her," said Matthew, vigorously scraping a cactus pad.

"You can't tell girls nothin'," said Jimmy.

Mrs. Payne inspected the cactus pads to make sure all traces of the hair-like needles were gone before slicing several of them in half. "Here, Sid. You gently rub these all over your Pa's burned skin. Make sure the juice gets on all the sunburn. And Matthew, run over to Mrs. Jones with these. You can tell her what to do." The remaining pads were blanched in hot water. "Come here Lydia, you can help

Jimmy mash these into a pulp."

Sid wiped cactus juice on Pa's shoulders and back, biting his tongue to keep from nagging him about what had happened. But Pa was ready to talk.

"Men got their buffalo right away. I happened to see the boys cut in up ahead after the last one went down. They were riding too close to the herd. I could tell they didn't see the second wave of buffalo coming up behind. I tried to get there in time to warn them. Connie fired into the herd before I could reach them. Hit a cow. Didn't kill her. Hurt her enough to make her mad. She turned on him and he took a swipe to the leg. By this time the second wave was on us. It distracted the cow. She ran on or we'd have lost Connie.

"Billy saw me. Got out in time. Connie's horse panicked and ran with the herd. I had to go in after him. Can't tell you how I did it. I guess the good Lord was riding with us. Sandy was a rock. Kept her head. If there's any credit due, it's hers. She cut into the herd and brought us up alongside Connie's horse. I was hoping we could save his horse, too, but I pulled him off and she was gone. It's a mercy she didn't throw him."

Mrs. Payne called, "Jimmy has cactus pulp for you, Mr. Johnson. You'll need to stretch out on your stomach so Sid can put a poultice on your back. You girls stay out of the tent. You can be the guards."

Jimmy said it was a boy's only tent, that he and Matthew were going in, and they didn't need any girl guards. Mrs. Payne put the boys back to work, squashing a threatening war before it could break out.

Pa chuckled, shaking his head. "Mrs. Payne is a force to be reckoned with, too."

He finished the story while Sid applied the cactus poultice. "Sandy managed to work our way out of the herd. She's a mighty fine horse. Always said so. Wouldn't be here now without her. She took a couple of gouges that would have sent another horse off with the stampede."

"What happened to Billy?"

"That second wave came in fast. Billy's got a strong arm. His horse was scared. He got her out, but by the time Sandy worked us out of the stampede, it was all Billy could do to stay in the saddle. Horse hit a hole at a full gallop coming down that ravine. Threw Billy forward. His arm took the brunt; that and the sagebrush where he landed saved his life. I thought sure his neck was broken. I had to shoot the horse." Pa shuddered. "Broken legs. Couldn't stand to see her in such pain. Poor thing."

That night, a somber mood hung over the train. Surrounded by drying meat and pride of hunt, everyone was aware of the cost of two headstrong boys disobeying orders. Ma was proud of Pa's work. She didn't have to reset Billy's arm, but he had a new, stronger splint. Connie's leg had to be pulled into place so Ma could set it properly. The bleeding started again. She and Abe managed to get it stopped. But Connie had lost so much blood his life hung by a thread.

Sid tried to feel sympathy for Connie, but he kept seeing him punch Squeaker in the stomach and watch while he and Abe took Billy's punches, unable to fight back. *He got what was comin' to him.*

*****

They didn't have lessons that night. The company met. Mr. Wood wanted everybody to have the same story about what happened. He didn't condemn anyone. He emphasized the way the men worked together. "Preacher will say a payer. Then Miz. Ryckman has asked for Bitsy Clark to sing a hymn."

Bitsy Clark? Sid couldn't believe it. *Mrs. Ryckman must be out of her mind.*

After the prayer, Bitsy stepped up. There was no simpering or eyelash batting. She closed her eyes, lifted her head, and her voice rose into the star-spattered sky, strong, clear, and sweet:

> Abide with me; fast falls the eventide;
> The darkness deepens; Lord, with me abide;
> When other helpers fail and comforts flee,
> Help of the helpless, oh, abide with me.

As she sang, images swept through Sid's mind: the Goodalls; little Ella Sue Davies, with Tobias still unable to comprehend her death; Isla and Mazie, orphaned; Mrs. Turney and her girls going on; Ethel, her arm still not healing properly; Squeaker's brother with broken ribs; Al Joiner—then, unexpectedly, he thought of home, of all he'd left behind, of the Stokes Company, of Jim Payne, and Grace Willis orphaned and kidnapped. Did he dare let his mind dwell on it? He'd hated Mr. Swathmore so long all he could feel was numbness.

Maybe it was the words to the hymn, the unexpected gift that Bitsy shared, or being too weary to hold onto bad feelings—whatever it was, Sid let go of something. Mrs. Payne's words came to mind as clearly as if she were looking him right in the eyes, "I felt so much hatred toward the Swathmores. But what good does that do? It just poisons me."

But he couldn't let go of his bad feelings about Connie and Billy.

*****

The children were asleep when Billy's father came over

to see how Pa was doing. He accepted a cup of hot coffee. "Sure appreciate what you did for my boy, Mr. Johnson. He's a handful, no doubt about it. I'm afraid I spoiled him after his Mamma died." He sipped his coffee, slowly, as if he were thinking what to say. "But he's my boy. Couldn't bear to lose him."

"I expect you've done your best," said Pa. "How's he feeling?"

"Arm's hurting him, but that's to be expected. Seems like he has to learn everything the hard way.

"I took another look at your horse. Wound is healing proper. She may not have a fine pedigree, but she's a good one. Well-balanced, sturdy structure, clear-eyed, even-tempered, smart. She must come from good stock. I gave her some extra oats for supper. Hope you don't mind."

Pa grinned. "Thank you kindly, Mr. Elston. I reckon she deserves oats and the credit that's been heaped on me. Don't rightly know her background, bought her as a colt off a man in Alton, Illinois who said she was Kentucky bred. I didn't put much stock in what he said, figured it was an excuse to hike up the price. Means a lot to have the best horseman in the company say that about her."

"Well, I don't know about that," said Mr. Elston. Finishing his coffee, he declined another. "Connie isn't out of the woods yet, but he wouldn't have had a fighting chance if you hadn't been there—Billy either, for that matter. The Ryckmans are good people. They've seen me through thick and thin—Mrs. Ryckman has been like a mother to Billy. I'm praying Connie will make it. He's their only child. I'm glad Mrs. Johnson is with them. She knows what she's doing."

Pa went to bed shortly after Mr. Elston left. Sid, Mrs. Payne, and Abe lingered around the campfire waiting for Ma's return.

"Abe, I'm wondering if you have considered studying medicine," said Mrs. Payne.

Sid nodded. "Ma says Abe's been more than another pair of hands. He has good instincts about doctorin'."

"My grandpa in Germany was a doctor. He went to medical school. I think about it. But I don't think there's a medical school in Santa Fe."

"I have the makings of a medical school in my wagon. The Johnsons and I both started out in the same company as Dr. and Mrs. Willis—"

"And Grace Willis," Sid injected.

—"and Grace. Their dream was to start a medical school in California. They were killed"—a sad look swept across her face—"along with my husband. I decided to make sure Dr. Willis' things get to California. You're way beyond where I can teach you very much except English and you're starting to sound like a native speaker. Maybe you'd like to have a look at Dr. Willis's books. You could learn a lot by the time we reach Santa Fe. At the least, it may help you know if you want to study medicine."

Abe's face lit up. "Could we look now?"

They opened a crate of books. Mrs. Payne lifted out a thick volume. "*C. Hering's Domestic Physician: Revised*"— she didn't read the whole impossibly long title—"it was published in 1851and revised from the 7th German edition. Maybe your grandfather studied from an earlier edition."

"What about this one?" Sid lifted out a smaller book about chemistry.

"Maybe I'll start with the German. If I survive, I shall go on to the others."

"If you survive that big book, we'll call you Doctor Abe."

After that, when Mrs. Payne wasn't drilling him on spoken English, Abe spent almost every spare minute with his nose in the big medical book. But almost every night, unless he was tending to somebody's injuries with Ma, the two boys sat propped up against a wagon wheel, talking. Sometimes Pa had to remind them, "Boys, sun comes up same time as usual in the morning."

They talked about all kinds of things: what it was like in Germany and in Brooklyn, life on the farm in Illinois, how Sid felt when he learned Ma and Pa were part of the Underground Railroad, why girls are so silly—like Bitsy, then completely surprise you being able to sing like she did, and Ethel, who wasn't silly but defied human understanding.

"When we get to Santa Fe, my brothers will help you restock," Abe said one night. "Then nobody will cheat you. Nathan says there are some merchants who will take every penny."

Another night he confided, "I hope they won't try to make me part of the business. I will be very bad at it. I want to be a doctor."

"But they won't, will they? Your grandpa was a doctor."

"If it had been up to me, I would be Germany with Papa. I could go to medical school in Germany. It is my home. I didn't want to leave. . ." He sighed. "Papa said there is no future for me in Germany. Brothers should stay together. But then I had to stay behind when my brothers leave Brooklyn. My uncle makes all the decisions. Ach! I am a coward. I would not go anywhere if I did not have to."

"I wouldn't say that. Think about it: by yourself on a steamer? Your money stolen. Nobody waitin' in Kansas. No money for a hotel. And you set out on foot? I don't think I coulda done it. You got nearly halfway to Santa Fe on your own before that storm."

"Hmmm," was all Abe said.

"Seems to me courage isn't thinkin' you can do somethin'

and doin' it because you aren't afraid. Seems like courage is thinkin' you *can't* do somethin', but you have to, so you just get up and go on, shakin' in your boots."

"I was shaking in my boots."

From the direction of the hunt, the howl of wolves split the night.

16.

ALONG THE ARKANSAS RIVER

It was four days before the company moved on—four days of smokey fires, fine eating on fresh buffalo meat, and healing for Mrs. Goodall, Connie, and Billy. Ma wasn't so worried about her other patients. Billy was healing rapidly. Ethel's arm looked better, too.

Ma said Ethel had the note with his handprint pinned up in the tent. "Miz Sinclair said she hadn't seen her laugh like that since before the storm."

Women cooked as much fresh meat as would keep. It was too early for berries to make pemmican, the mixture of pounded buffalo meat, berries, and fat common to the native people. All over camp, pots of bones and meat scraps simmered in water. Mrs. Payne put Matthew and Jimmy to work watching their pot. "You can take turns. Keep a low, steady fire going. You have to skim the grease off the top when it starts to collect."

"Is this what I'm afraid it is?" asked Matthew.

"It's pocket soup." said Mrs. Payne cheerfully.

Matthew groaned. "We're in for it, Jimmy. We gotta let this cook down to jelly. Then it has to dry out. Then we have to cut it into pieces and flour it so they won't stick together. Then we have to pack it up."

"Yoicks!"

"All that work and it isn't that good." Matthew rolled his eyes.

"If it was good enough for Lewis and Clark, it's good enough for us." Mrs. Payne offered no sympathy.

Sid didn't like pocket soup either, but it was an important addition to their reserves. It could be softened over a fire by adding hot water and drunk as broth or added to dried beans, dried vegetables, onion, or wild greens. And it could be carried in a pocket if it came to it.

"Makin' soup is women's work, anyway," Jimmy scowled as he skimmed fat from the broth.

"Better not let Ma hear you." said Sid. "A man has to know how to cook. You think the Roman army took women along to do their cookin' for 'em? Every Roman soldier had to do his own cooking—and they ground their own grain to make bread."

Jimmy made a face.

Mr. Wood posted extra guards around their camp day and night. Wolves, drawn by the smell of meat, were a constant danger. Bones and unusable scraps had to be carried far away from camp and dumped.

For children, it was a grand holiday with hide and seek, tag, and exploration of the prairie dog town close by. Older brothers and sisters supervised, keeping them away from the smoldering fires, out from underfoot, and close enough to camp to be safe from the wolves. Sid thought of how he and Grace Willis organized games for children in the Stokes Company. It felt like years had passed since then. He tugged at his hat.

He checked horse and oxen shoes, and harness gear. Pa repaired boots and shoes. Cora had outgrown hers. Lydia's outgrown shoes fit Cora, but their soles needed repair. Pa worked on new shoes for Jimmy and Lydia and replaced the soles on Matthew's boots. His sunburn was healing, but he wasn't comfortable wearing a shirt. He wore one, though.

"Connie's getting' his color back"—Sid couldn't help overhearing Ma talking with Mrs. Payne—"Mrs. Ryckman's a good nurse, but she protects the boy too much. Had to convince her to let him sit up some to get his strength back. I want him to start tryin' to walk on that leg. It's what Doc Short used to say. 'The longer you stay under the covers, the longer it's gonna take to get up.'"

Mrs. Payne shook her head. "That probably explains a lot. She overprotects him."

"Mrs. Ryckman's good as gold in some things. She's constantly doin' for other folk. She'd sit up all night with Abe if he was to fall sick. She doesn't complain about him helpin' me. But she wouldn't want Connie to be friends because he's a Jew. Now doesn't that beat all?"

"I hope he can apprentice himself to a good doctor in Santa Fe."

"Then there's Patsy. Mrs. Ryckman treats her nice as can be, but make no mistake. Patsy O'Connell is her servant."

"Patsy hasn't been in this country for long. Immigrants are coming in from Ireland in droves. I expect Mrs. Ryckman will take good care of her, but Patsy will always have to come in the back door. She's a right smart girl, too. I wish she could learn to read. She could make something of herself."

"I worry about Connie," said Ma. "It isn't just the wrong ideas, its—I don't know how to describe it. They keep tellin' him about the family name, how important he is, how special, and talented, praising him for every little thing."

Mrs. Payne nodded. "It puts a lot of pressure on him to live up to their expectations."

They never ran out of things to discuss. Sometimes, they fell into fits of giggling like schoolgirls. Mrs. Payne would say, "What would my dear Mamma think?" Or Ma would say, "We'd set the world right if it was up to us two."

He hadn't ever thought about it. But maybe you never quit needing friends.

Billy strutted about camp, sporting his splint and bragging. "Connie nearly brought down a cow. She charged him. I went straight for that buffalo. Cut her off. Saved his life."

"You didn't save anybody's life," Red seemed to appear from nowhere. "You're lucky to be alive after a stunt like you two pulled. What Billy and Connie did was stupid, plain *stupid*. I don't want to see any of you acting like that. But then, I expect you have better sense than my little brother."

With Billy's arm out of commission, and Connie still barely able to move, the gang was broken apart. Eli spent his free time with Dale. Squeaker and Frog disappeared from sight. Billy didn't have a hold over the boys without Connie.

17.

CHOUTEAU'S ISLAND

Jimmy and Matthew wanted to explore every landmark along the trail. Their main interest was finding treasure, especially robber's gold.

Mrs. Payne, on the other hand, used landmarks as an opportunity for history lessons. There weren't many landmarks. The trail now followed along the Arkansas River, but the only real change was trees along the near bank and sandhills across the river where vast desert plains reached to the south. The near side of the river opened to infinite plains dotted with herds of grazing buffalo and antelope.

Chouteau's Island appeared in the distance. Jimmy and Matthew were sure they could find gold buried there. Sid didn't tease them. Back in Illinois, he'd spent hours thinking about finding treasure. Besides, it looked like the sort of place you'd bury treasure.

"It is a sad place," Mrs. Payne told her students. "It's named for a hunting party led by a man named Auguste Chouteau. They were returning with furs collected during the winter and took sanctuary on the island to escape an attack by the Pawnee. It was a turning point for the Pawnee Nation. They'd never been exposed to gunfire. Even though they vastly outnumbered Chouteau's hunting party, they lost more men. They must have realized things never would be the same."

It was a turning point of another kind when Squeaker stopped at their campfire one day at nooning. Ma offered him some cornbread. He ate hungrily, licking his fingers. "Don't reckon the boy's not gettin' enough to eat," Ma said later. "He's still growin' and his family's short on supplies."

"Now Squeaker is an interesting nickname," Mrs. Payne handed him a chunk of pan bread sprinkled with sugar when he appeared again. "I'd like to know your name."

Squeaker's eyes darted about the camp. "Name's Winston. Winston Horace Warwick." He took a big bite of bread.

"That is a very distinguished name," said Mrs. Payne. "Why don't you come to lessons with Sid and Abe, Winston?"

Squeaker looked around again, talking with his mouth full. "Pa don't want me having nothing to do with—" He stopped abruptly.

"I see. Do you think your Pa would object to Sid as your teacher?"

Squeaker shrugged his shoulders.

"Sid's in charge of the library, Winston. He'll help you pick out a book to get started."

"Can't read," said Squeaker, looking hungrily at the rest of the pan bread.

"You can learn. I'll save a nice big piece of this bread for you to enjoy after Sid gets you started reading."

Squeaker shrugged his shoulders, sat down with his back against a wagon wheel, and waited as if he expected to start immediately. "Sid, get him the primer and first reader. Find out what he knows first."

Sid was appalled to learn Squeaker really couldn't read. He couldn't even write his own name. "Didn't you go to school?"

"Went for a week." Squeaker snickered. "Teacher threw me out. Said it was a waste of his time and mine if I couldn't sit still."

"Well, how about I show you how to write your name?" Sid wrote "Winston Horace Warwick" on a scrap of paper. Squeaker seemed fascinated to see it in writing. Then he showed Squeaker how to make the letters in the dirt by the wagon and had him practice until he could do it by himself. He gave Squeaker the paper and a stub of pencil. Squeaker wrote Winston Horace Warwick under where Sid had written it. He was so proud of himself, he danced with glee, then tucked it in his waistcoat. Sid figured he'd more than earned the sugared pan bread.

Later Mrs. Payne said, "If Mr. Warwick doesn't want Squeaker studying with a black woman, he still needs to learn to read. If it takes a bit of sugar to get him here, it's worth it. You're perfectly capable of teaching him. Learning to read may not change Winston's attitude. I suppose most of us hang on to what we've been taught growing up, even if it's wrong. But there's always the chance."

Ethel and Bitsy arrived for school with younger children in tow. "I've been practicing my Latin, Abe," Bitsy giggled. Abe coached Ethel and Bitsy in Latin, though Sid figured Bitsy was mostly batting her eyelashes at him. He couldn't get over how anybody so silly could have such a beautiful singing voice. It threw him off guard, so much so that sometimes he found himself thinking about her. It was unnerving.

He was hitching up the next morning when he noticed Squeaker looking both ways before pulling something from his waistcoat. He looked at it mouthing "Winston Horace Warwick." From then on, Sid took time every day before lessons to sit with Squeaker and read. There was always something extra for him to eat after they finished. Winston Horace Warwick couldn't sit still, but he could learn, and so quickly it astonished Sid.

Frog Barton was left at loose ends, too. He didn't wander about the way Squeaker did. Sid couldn't figure him out. He'd never heard Frog say more than a few grunts. Frog's Pa was a hard worker and did more than his share of work for the train. Sid didn't think he treated Frog very well, though. It wasn't that he beat him, or anything like that. It was the way he talked about him. "Boy ain't got good sense. Good for nothing but hard labor."

"He has to be smart, though, doesn't he?" Sid asked Pa one day. "He couldn't be so good at marbles if he didn't have good sense."

"I've heard of folk like that," said Pa. "Can't say as I know what causes it. Sometimes folk who are different take a real beating in life."

"His Pa doesn't think he can do anything." Sid worried about Frog. He talked it over with Abe and Mrs. Payne. "Reckon he could learn to read?"

"You'd have to get him here first," said Abe.

"We could loan him a book, like Squeaker. Squeaker's already through the second reader. I don't think he even needs me, just for the odd word. I started him on arithmetic, but he already knows numbers and how to do sums in his head. He's a whiz at it. All I had to do was show him how to write it down."

Mrs. Payne sighed. "I think Abe's right. I can't imagine anybody in young Mr. Barton's family encouraging him along those lines. There are lots of things that keep people from talking. Sometimes they're born with it. Sometimes they have a terrible experience and just quit talking. I've seen children who have escaped slavery who couldn't talk. I wonder how it must feel, to have everything locked up inside. That doesn't mean your friend will have a bad life.

He'll be a good farmer. I wish we could help him." A sad look passed over her face, leaving a furrowed brow. "Sid, we can't fix everything that's wrong in the world. We can only do our part every day to make it right. I honestly don't know how to help him, not if we can't get him here. Even then, I'm not sure."

"You sound like my Mama," said Abe. "Nathan—my eldest brother—Nathan would get angry about the way people treated Papa at our store. They wouldn't pay their bill. They call Papa a dirty Jew and say he cheats them. I was too young to understand. But Nathan understood."

****

One evening Squeaker brought Frog along. Frog looked at Sid with his big, bulging eyes, "Read." It was the first word Sid had ever heard him say.

"I been reading to him," Squeaker had a sheepish expression on his face like he was confessing to a crime. "Showed him I could write my name."

"Come with me." Sid took Frog to Mrs. Payne. Frog didn't seem to have any objection to studying with her. At least he sat down when she asked. Squeaker hung about on the periphery doing a nervous dance like it was a game of marbles.

"Sid, get me the alphabet book. We'll start there. Mr. Barton, I'd like to know your name. Frog is fine for a nickname, but I want to call you by your given name."

"Don't know it," Squeaker shrugged his shoulders.

Frog didn't say. All he did was stare at them without any expression on his face. But he looked at the pictures in the alphabet book with Mrs. Payne. She read each letter to him. As the younger children came for lessons, she said, "I hope you will come tomorrow, Mr. Barton. Take the book with you."

Frog looked at her blankly. He didn't take the book.

The next evening, Frog and Squeaker returned. "Name's Earl," said Squeaker. "Earl Barton. I asked his folk."

After that, Mrs. Payne worked with Earl before lessons, while Sid worked with Winston. She insisted on calling Frog and Squeaker by their given names. It was hard to remember.

Earl never said anything. His expression never changed. But Mrs. Payne felt sure he was learning in his own way. He could write the letters of the alphabet when she named them, and he could write Earl Barton. Sid wasn't so sure Mrs. Payne was thrilled to discover that he could write Frog Barton, too. Squeaker taught him. "There's more to both of those young men than meets the eye," was all she said.

Squeaker began to linger on the edge during lessons. Mrs. Payne left him alone. "Winston's hungry to learn. That's a good thing. You don't have to sit down or sit still to learn."

18.

BENT'S NEW FORT

It was near evening when they spotted Bent's New Fort standing on a bluff overlooking the Arkansas River. It was in an ideal location between a limestone cliff to the east and a rock bluff to the south. Made of native rock, its walls were reported to be sixteen feet high. A cannon atop each corner was a grim reminder of its defenses. Tepees stood outside the walls housing some of the men who worked for Mr. Bent, others belonged to native people who were there to trade.

The fort was a major stopping place for traders and travelers taking the Mountain Route to Santa Fe. Part of a flourishing trade network, it connected to forts to the north and south as well as other company stores. Bent's men bartered with the Arapaho, Cheyenne, Kiowa, and Comanche people for buffalo robes. They offered guns, gunpowder, knives, calico, beads from Europe, clay pipes, tea, coffee, Mexican chocolate, and other goods such as kettles, barrel hoops—in demand for metal arrow points—coffee grinders, axes, tin pans, tin cups, and skillets. Bent could buy a buffalo robe for a few cents in goods and sell it for five dollars in Missouri. Alcohol was available for trade, too. One buffalo robe bought a pint of watered-down whiskey. "Don't get me talking about that," said Mr. Reid. "They water down $10 worth of whisky and get $8000 worth of goods for it. It's criminal."

After wagons were circled with the livestock inside, Mr.

Wood called a meeting. "Stick to the train tonight. Folk wanting to pick up supplies before Santa Fe, this is where you can trade tomorrow. If we can hold out till Fort Union or Santa Fe, we'll find better prices. I'll see what we can get for our buffalo robes to fill in supplies. Best keep the youngins away from the tepees. Nobody wants a bunch of folk gawking at them. You'll see plenty from inside the Fort. And men, stay away from the whiskey. The last thing we need is half our company getting drunk and picking fights.

"Anybody asks about our company and who's in it, your best answer is no answer. We're a big company. You don't have to lie, but you don't have to tell them all there is to know. And don't let the youngins run wild. There's folk passing through who'd be glad to add our youngsters to their workforce. We're a company. We look out for each other."

The next morning Pa had guard duty. Mr. Wood was going to ask the Army doctor at the fort to come around and have a look at Mrs. Goodall and Connie. The Ryckmans wanted an expert opinion on Connie. Ma was willing to miss going to the fort to learn what she could from the doctor. Abe stayed, too, saying he'd see enough trade in Santa Fe. "

Mrs. Payne and Sid took the children into the trading post. Pa said Cora couldn't go unless she promised to keep her sunbonnet on. Her bottom lip went out.

"You, too, Lydia," said Mrs. Payne. "Otherwise, folk will want to pat your hair—yours because it's brown and curly and Cora's because it's yellow and curly. That would be a whole lot more annoying than wearing a sunbonnet. Besides, I'm wearing my bonnet."

"Don't forget what happened in Council Grove" Sid was worried about Cora, but he also knew firsthand that Lydia and Matthew were never out of danger. When his family left Illinois, he had hoped they were leaving slavery behind.

He'd learned differently. Men had tried to kidnap Lydia and Matthew back in Council Grove.

"Come along, you two mischiefs." It was Al Joiner. "You don't mind company, do you? These old ribs are mighty stiff, but I wanna see the fort. Pearly's afraid I'll spend too much money if I'm left to myself. Reckon these girls can keep an eye on me, Jimmy?"

"Sure, Mr. Joiner," said Jimmy, eying the revolver conspicuously tucked behind Joiner's belt. Sid was relieved to see it.

The fort was teeming with activity. Some of the men who worked there were American Indian or married to Indians. Many had been trappers or traders. It seemed like a continuous auction inside as people with things for sale asked for bids. Kiowa Indians bargained over blankets in one corner. Mountain men had pelts to trade. Mexican traders, Arapaho, Cheyenne, Kiowa, and Comanche Indians—all bought and sold.

"What is this?" a wizened old man looked at Sid. "Have you come to trade these two fine young women for a buffalo robe?"

Cora, who prided herself on having grown so much in their weeks on the trail, suddenly grabbed Sid's hand and leaned into him.

"Well, I reckon that depends"—Mr. Joiner winked at Lydia—"These two are just about priceless."

The man cackled, "No? The girls are not for trade then? Such a pity. My little girl would love to have such fine playmates. Here's something for you to remember Old John by." He gave them each a small leather cord strung with colored beads and feathers. "You boys have need of a piece of genuine flint rock?" He reached into his waistcoat pocket. "It's the very rock Arapaho warriors use to make arrows.

You can see where it's been worked."

Al Joiner bought moccasins for Pearl. Everybody else got moccasins, too. Just as Sid was paying for theirs, Mr. Wood came over to shake hands with Old John. "I hope you haven't cheated my friends too badly, John."

"It's my soft French-Canadian heart," Old John grinned. "I only charged them double the price instead of triple."

"So, John, I'm looking for a couple of rough customers who stopped by our wagon train a few days back. One of them is tall and thin. Looks tough as buffalo jerky. Wore black, hair slicked back, clean shaved. Calls himself Bayless Sly. The other is a bit taller than me. Big guy, red beard, curly red hair. Goes by J.J. Gordon. Seen them in here?"

Old John nodded. "Yep. They wasn't together, though. Gordon's been through before. Used to work with William Gallagher out of Santa Fe. Doubt he'd give you any trouble. Bought himself some gear and left; said he was on his way to Santa Fe. Never seen the other fellow before. He hung around a few days. Took up with a real weasel name of Norbert Greenbriar who was around here all winter. Didn't ever hear what they're up to, but I'll warrant it's no good. Left a couple of days ago with teamsters headed down toward the Old Spanish Trail. Glad to see the backside of both of 'em, to tell the truth."

Mrs. Payne collected letters, one was from her family in New York, another addressed to Ma from Mrs. Harold, their neighbor in Illinois. And one was addressed to 'Master Sid Johnson and friends, care of Ben Johnson, William Stokes Company.' Sid couldn't wait to read it.

Abe was bursting with news when they retured. "The Army doctor told Mr. and Mrs. Ryckman they were lucky to have Mrs. Johnson in the company. Without her help, he would have lost his leg. He looked at Mrs. Goodall's arm and said it was healing nicely. He said Mrs. Johnson saved her life by acting quickly. Also, he said he could probably learn a thing or two—"

"No need to go on and on," Ma protested, blushing.

"I reckon I won't need to apprentice myself to a doctor after working with your Ma."

"Oh go on! He had a compliment for Abe. He said Abe is gonna make a fine doctor, and he should keep readin' those medical books. If he ever decides to apprentice to an Army doctor, to look him up."

When he finally had a chance, Sid looked at the letter addressed to him.

Dear Sid, Grace, Matthew, Jimmy, Lydia, Cora, Serena, Myrtle, and Otis—

Sid had to laugh. Someone didn't know Serena was a cat.

I found your letter in the Post Office Oak at Council Grove. You are right. It is nice to be in a wagon train.

My brothers and sisters and I are going to Oregon on the Oregon Trail. We are from Indiana. I hope you have a safe trip, too. I am glad I found your letter. If this finds you at New Fort Bent, you can write to me at Fort Vancouver.

Yours most sincerely,
Lucia Smith, 14 years old
c/o Alfred L. Smith,
Culpert Company, Morris Culpert, Wagon Master

P.S. I'm sending another letter to Santa Fe in case you don't stop at the fort.

Sadness nearly choked him as he thought of how Grace had written the letter they left at the Post Office Oak. *She would have loved this*. He hoped she had been rescued. But what would happen to Otis and Myrtle Swathmore—no older than Cora and Jimmy—growing up in such a family?

That night Mrs. Payne had everyone tell what they had seen at the fort. Sid read the letter.

"And Serena signed it, too," said Cora.

Jimmy rolled his eyes, elbowing Matthew.

After lessons Ethel said, "I'll write to Lucía Smith, too, if you like, Sid. We can mail the letter at Ft. Union." Then she blushed.

Sid hardly knew what to say. "Sure," he stammered. Why did she always catch him off guard? "She'd probably like hearing from a girl."

"*We*?" Bitsy Clark giggled.

Ethel gave Bitsy a look to kill and tossed her head.

19.

TO THE ROCKY MOUNTAINS

Another letter was on Sid's mind all the time they were at the Fort. He hadn't checked on it lately. Maybe he should see if it was safe. Serena rubbed up against his face, blocking his vision as he groped for his box of soldiers under the cradle.

It wasn't there.

No!

Choking back panic, he pulled everything from under the cradle. Then from under the wagon seat where he had originally kept it. *Jimmy*. He was always digging into things.

Jimmy and Matthew were playing under the Payne wagon with a toad they had captured. Jimmy didn't sit up and look guilty. And Matthew vouched for him.

Cora? But she was already fast asleep in the tent.

He told Mrs. Payne.

"Oh dear, Sid. The girls may have moved things around in their play. Lydia's already asleep or you could ask. Surely it will turn up. There hasn't been anybody outside the company hanging about. Things have a way of settling inside these wagons."

Pa agreed with Mrs. Payne. "Likely you'll find it when we shift the load in Santa Fe. If the letter's gone, it's gone. You've done your best. That's all anybody can do. We've had a tight watch on the train and Mr. Wood says we won't

199

be letting down our guard."

The letter was more than something Mr. Gallagher and his wife valued. It was a matter of trust. He vowed to search every cranny in the wagon before they reached Santa Fe.

The trail continued along the Arkansas River, leaving the monotonous sand dunes behind as it reached the long tree-lined canyon cut by the Purgatory River as it joined the Arkansas. Near the burned-out ruins of Bent's Old Fort, they crossed the Arkansas. It felt anticlimactic after the stories they'd heard of quicksand and broken wagon axles. Mr. Wood didn't take any chances. All the wagons were triple-teamed. He said the key was to go fast. The minute a wagon stopped it could sink. Thankfully, the company crossed with no major accidents. Mr. Reid said they were more than lucky.

"We were due for some luck," said Pa.

Long, flat-topped mesas loomed in the distance. They were in high plains country now. Short grass was interrupted by shallow creeks and riverbeds that ran fast and wide after rain.

In spare moments, Sid searched for the letter. He carried his worry silently, a constant burden. *Gallagher trusted me. I let him down.* He felt like a failure. The threat to Cora was his fault. In a recurrent nightmare, Cora was kidnapped while he stood frozen, watching in horror.

They entered piñon country. Mr. Reid said by late summer the pinecones would be full of piñons. "Pine nuts are mighty tasty if you can beat the wild animals to 'em."

Cedar trees were a regular part of the landscape now, too, their dark green branches contrasting with the scruffy, yellow-green branches of the piñons, and vast stretches of gray-green grass reaching to the far horizon.

They had their first sighting of the Rocky Mountains, two unmistakable, dusty blue mounds in the south: the Spanish

Peaks. Day after day they seemed no closer until clouds hovering over the southwest horizon came into sharper focus. They turned out to be the snow-topped peaks of the Sangre de Cristos. Just before they turned south toward the Spanish Peaks, they could see the tall, deep violet silhouette of Pike's Peak to the north.

They talked about the mountains at lessons. "Pike's Peak was named for Lieutenant Zebulon Pike in 1806 as he explored the boundaries of the Louisiana Purchase," Mrs. Payne explained. "The Ute people, who lived in that region, called it Sun Mountain Sitting Big. They called themselves Tabeguache, or People of Sun Mountain."

"So why was it renamed?" asked Ethel, "It wasn't actually discovered by Lieutenant Pike if it was already there."

"Interesting question. Anybody have a thought?"

"But Indians aren't civilized." Bitsy Clark looked at Sid.

"I suppose that depends on what you mean by civilized," said Mrs. Payne. "I daresay they don't feel uncivilized. In fact, they probably think we are the uncivilized ones. What we think of as civilized depends on what we've been taught about what is proper and how to act responsibly."

"It's kind of arrogant, isn't it," said Ethel, "to think we're the only ones who can name things?"

"Did those peaks have another name?" asked Abe. "

Mrs. Payne sent Jimmy and Matthew to find Mr. Wood, who said the Spanish also called them Twin Mountains. "Those peaks are very important to native people. They named them Wahatoya, the breasts of our mother earth. We forget that even the Spanish were newcomers."

20.

Iron Springs

At sunrise and sunset, the Sangre de Cristo mountains were tinged with red-gold. The twin peaks appeared and disappeared as the trail made its way across the high plains. They climbed steadily through rocky, ragged hills, some bare and others covered with piñon, cedar, scrub oak, and mesquite. Narrow valleys cut through the hills. Sometimes Sid could have sworn they were going downhill, but the oxen strained. When he looked behind, he could see they were still climbing. He shouldn't have been surprised. Mr. Wood had warned the company that they would climb nearly 3,000 feet in the 32 miles from the Purgatoire River to the summit of Raton Pass. On the plains, they usually made 12, sometimes even 18 miles in a day. But it was slow going up the steep climb. By the end of the day, people and oxen were covered with gray-brown dirt.

"This is just our introduction," said Mr. Reid. "When we come to the end of the high plains, it'll be slower still. Time was when this was only used by pack animals. We can thank Kearney's Army for opening it up to supply trains during the Mexican War. Wagons can make it now, but we'll have to go slow and steady."

Sid had learned about Colonel Stephen Kearney and how he marched 2500 troops across Kansas, taking the rough trail through the mountains to invade New Mexico. He had no idea what that meant when he was in school in Illinois. Now he'd walked across Kansas, too.

One evening they camped at Iron Springs. A teamster train from Fort Union headed to New Ft. Bent was already there. Mr. Wood talked with the teamsters about what they had found on the pass. They had to clear fallen rock and trees, but they'd made it through. It was encouraging.

The rocky foothills gave way to mountain slopes lined with magnificent pine trees, much taller than the piñons. Far above, Raton Mesa hovered like a castle standing between the high plains and the mountains. It marked the beginning of the pass. Ahead, a chain of mesas reached like an arm toward the Sangre de Cristos. Small herds of sheep and cattle grazed near what remained of a small trading settlement. They camped one night at Hole in the Rock, named for a watering hole in a creek that was usually dry.

While the climb up to the Raton Pass was challenging, it was a glorious time. Lush green grass carpeted high meadows where they camped at night. Above, huge outcroppings of white rock and lofty pine trees opened to a crisp, blue sky with ever-changing cloud formations that lifted to reveal magnificent views of the Spanish Peaks, and breathtaking glimpses into little valleys below. Sometimes they awoke, surrounded by clouds.

There were more songbirds than Sid could keep track of. His favorite were the bluebirds that fluttered among the trees. Wild turkey and prairie chicken were plentiful. They spotted black-footed ferrets laying claim to prairie dog holes. There was talk of bears. Sid wasn't sure how he felt about eating bear. *Maybe, if I was hungry enough.*

One evening something amazing happened. Squeaker had a strange expression on his face when he and Frog came for lessons. Frog said, "Give."

Sid was so startled; he didn't know what to say. The only other thing he'd ever heard Frog say was, "Read."

Squeaker began one of his shuffling dances, looking down. "Give." Frog said it again.

Squeaker handed Sid his box of toy soldiers. "Connie wanted it," he whispered, looking around furtively. "I stole it for him."

"Stole it for Connie?"

"When Connie seen something he wanted, I stole it for him. But I done stole it back. Me 'n Frog, Earl"—he glanced in Mrs. Payne's direction—"we been stealing back stuff from Connie while he's been laid up. He don't even know he has half the stuff. He just likes havin' it. Me 'n Forg's been sneakin' it back. Most times, folk don't know they lost it." He snickered.

Sid opened the box. He thought his heart would stop. The soldiers were all there. But no letter.

"What happened to the letter?"

Squeaker looked at Frog, then back at Sid, a puzzled look on his face. "Don't know nothing about a letter. Wasn't one when I gave it to Connie, cause"—Squeaker looked down at his feet—"cause he opened it and Billy said you was a mamma's boy still playing with your little soldiers."

"My grandpa made these. That's why I kept 'em." Billy didn't have to be there to get his goat.

Now, he was really worried. Was someone else in the wagon train a thief?

THE RATON PASS

The Raton Pass was not overrated. It was so narrow in places there was barely room for a wagon; the climb so steep that sometimes wagons were double-teamed and men helped the wheel oxen by pushing behind each wagon. In other places, brakes and wheel locks alone were not enough to prevent wagons from plunging headlong off the trail and down into valleys below. Men held ropes tied to the end of wagons to counterbalance them. Sometimes they unhitched teams, putting ropes across trees on either side to create a wench. Oxen walked back along the trail, pulling the ropes to bring a wagon up to the next spot. It was move and stop and wait—mostly wait.

Axles and wheels took a beating. Oxen needed new shoes. Even so, those who knew said the trail was wider and less difficult than in its early days. Sid found this hard to believe.

The train often came to a standstill. Mr. Reid encouraged people to climb to the highest point they could reach while they waited. "It's a view you'll never forget. But mind, young 'ens need plenty of supervision. There's bears, wolverines, and panthers all through these woods, not to mention wolves. Make plenty of noise. Wild animals want outa the way. You just haveta give 'em fair warnin'."

Nearly everybody made the climb at one time or another.

Ma and Mrs. Payne took the children on a climb. "Mr. Payne always said he didn't have words to describe it," said Mrs. Payne. "Now I know what he meant."

"It was like standin' on top of the world," said Ma.

Sid spent most of the waiting time helping the men check wagons and make repairs. But after lessons one evening Ethel said, "Sid, Dale says he'd like to climb up to the high point tomorrow. Maybe you and Matthew and Jimmy and everybody would like to come along. My daddy says the more noise we make, the better. And Dale's got a gun."

"Thought Dale was takin' care of their wagon." Sid wasn't sure why he was irritated.

"Can we go, Sid? Can we go?" Cora danced up and down.

"*May* we go. Sure, if Pa says it's all right and I don't have work to do."

It turned out to be more fun than he expected. Just about everybody in Mrs. Payne's wagon school went along, including Squeaker and Frog. It was good to see both Ethel and Abe making the climb, though Ethel still used a stick.

Sid started to take his gun, but Jeremy Sawyer said he was going and would have a gun. *Anyway, no self-respectin' bear would let himself be found near all this racket.* He was glad Jeremy was there. Jimmy and Matthew ran circles around each other whooping it up. They didn't fuss with Jeremy when he asked them to slow it down.

When they got as high up as they could go, they looked down into a deep valley where clouds clung to the trees below. Far ahead were the snow-capped Sangre de Cristos with the Spanish Peaks looming large.

"This is when I wish I were an artist," said Ethel. "I wish I could capture all of this beauty."

"It's so romantic," giggled Bitsy. Then she made as if she were falling so that Dale had to catch her. "Oh Dale"—like she didn't know exactly what she was doing—"I don't know what I'd have done if you weren't here." She looked at Sid as if he was supposed to care.

Grace Willis was the only girl he'd ever cared about that much. He always figured he'd marry her when they grew up. But Grace wasn't giggling all the time and fluttering her eyelashes. He tugged at his hat, refusing to let himself think about what had happened to Grace.

Cora and Lydia delighted in picking wildflowers and chasing butterflies that seemed to be everywhere. They were about halfway across a meadow when Jeremy had them stop and stand perfectly still. A bear and her cubs were across the meadow near the trees. "She's headed over to the other side," Jeremy said. "We don't want to alarm her. Jimmy, Matthew, you stand here with me like proper scouts." Even Jimmy and Matthew watched in silence as the bear and her cubs disappeared.

"If I had me a gun, I'd shoot that bear," said Jimmy.

"Oh, I hope not," said Ethel. "What would happen to her cubs? I hope she stays on the other side of the mountain and never comes back where she's in danger."

"I don't know, Ethel," said Jeremy, an amused look on his face. "She'd make a mighty fine bear rug in front of somebody's fireplace."

Ethel gave him one of her stormy looks.

An afternoon shower left the trail so wet and slippery they had to stop early. It was hard enough to make good time without having the wagons slip and slide. Sometimes it felt as if they were barely creeping along. Sid felt sorry for the oxen. They were giving it their all. He was proud of Buttercup. She worked all day and gave them milk morning and evening. But she wasn't giving as much milk. He hoped she wouldn't dry up. Butter and cream were one of the few luxuries they had left.

They were almost to the summit the next morning when a wagon skidded and turned over. As accidents go, it was fortunate. The wagon didn't crash down the side of the mountain along with oxen pulling it. But it was damaged. It brought the company to a complete halt.

There wasn't much to do while men worked to repair the wagon and save what they could of its contents. Sid wanted to help, but Pa said sometimes the best thing you can do is stay out of the way. Ethel and Dale came by with a gaggle of the younger children. "We're going to climb to the top of the ridge," Ethel said. "Come along. It's just up to those white boulders. Dale thinks we'll be able to see the summit from there."

Dale thinks. It wasn't that he didn't like Dale. But he was getting tired of Ethel yammering on about Dale all the time. He should have told Ma. He should have grabbed his gun. But Matthew, Jimmy, Lydia, and Cora clamored to go, and Dale had already started up with Ethel. Sid looked at Abe. Abe shrugged his shoulders. They were between jobs. It would be a help to Ma and Mrs. Payne to have the children out of the way and the great white boulders at the top were in clear view of the train.

Ethel and Dale reached them first. "Sid, Abe, come on up," called Ethel. "This is just the halfway point!"

Cora found it hard to get a firm footing on the scree. "There's too many little rocks, Sid." She held out her hand. Lydia and the boys scampered ahead like mountain goats.

Abe took her other hand, "You don't like scree?"

"No. I don't like little rocks." She gleefully joined the others as soon as she had her footing.

"Let's go on up to the top!" Ethel called.

"I'm going to need a strong arm, Dale," said Bitsy, looking back at Sid and giggling.

"Spare me," Sid muttered.

"Don't take it to the heart." Abe grinned. "She's a—what is the word, flirt?"

"Yoicks!" yelled Jimmy, already at the top. "It's a long way down there."

"No horsing around," called Matthew.

Ethel was right. The climb was worth it. They were higher than they'd climbed before. Ahead, the trail reached the summit and started down. Clouds hovered along a winding canyon cutting its way through mountains to the south. A village nestled in the valley far below. Cows grazed in a meadow. Sadness welled up as Sid thought of the farm in Illinois. He'd never see it again.

"It's too beautiful for words," said Ethel. They stood quietly—even the little ones. Even Bitsy. Then, marking the spot where the Wood Company was stalled, they began their climb down. The little girls began picking wildflowers in the meadow as they passed the white boulders. Suddenly Cora darted back through the meadow after a butterfly, past Sid who brought up the rear, and disappeared behind the boulders.

"Cora! Come back." He started after her.

The others were laughing and calling out as they always did on their climbs, scaring away the bears. They didn't hear Cora's muffled cry. But Sid heard. "I'm comin', Cora," he rounded the boulder straight into the steel grip of Bayless Sly.

"One sound and Norbert here's gonna hurt that pretty little girl," snarled Sly. "You understand, boy?"

Sid understood. Cora was pinned down with a red handkerchief clamped over her mouth, eyes wide with fright, still clinging to a bunch of wildflowers.

"You kick me again and I'll break yer little arm,

sweetheart," said Greenbriar. If such a thing were possible, he looked even more sleazy than Bayless Sly. Stringy iron-gray hair flew in all directions from under a brown felt hat. He was dressed in buckskins and wore moccasins.

Sly smiled a chilling, heartless smile. "Tell Johnson if he wants to see his little girl alive, he'll meet me up at the summit tomorrow at sunrise. He can bring a certain letter he's been hidin' and two of those fine horses. And he better be alone. Tell 'em I don't have no patience with those that can't follow directions."

Sid gulped. "Let her go. Please. If you need a hostage, take me. I'm his son. She's just a little girl. I won't give you any trouble. I promise."

"Got us a little hero here," Greenbriar leered at him. But he didn't let go of Cora. "Maybe we oughta take 'em both."

A buffalo robe closed over Sid. Everything went black.

The next thing he knew, Abe and Dale were untying him. Bayless Sly, Norbert Greenbriar, and Cora had vanished. A bouquet of crushed wildflowers lay on the ground nearby.

"Ethel's gone for help," said Dale, taking out his pocketknife. "They made these knots to stay. I'm gonna cut this rope."

Sid was barely on his feet when Mr. Reid appeared, rifle in hand, reaching out to steady him. "Good thinking, boys. Sid coulda suffocated if you hadn't got that robe off."

Mr. Wood, Reverend Jones, and Al Joiner were already searching the ground for clues. Sid breathlessly explained what happened as Pa arrived on the scene.

"I can only make out one accomplice," said Reverend Jones.

"Norbert Greenbriar," said Mr. Wood. "How many of them, Sid?"

"Two, I think." He couldn't say for sure. It happened

so quickly.

"Preacher you and Reid follow them. Joiner, stay behind out of sight. Don't use a gun unless you have to. Give 'em plenty of space. Find out where they're taking her. They won't go too far if they're planning to meet Johnson at the summit. They won't hurt her. She's their ticket to something else. Johnson, your heart's in going but right now everything depends on their skill. I'm good, but they're better. Joiner's our best shot. He knows how to hold his fire, too. That's just as important."

Abe and Dale helped Sid back to the wagon where Ma put a cold wet cloth on his forehead, her face drawn with worry. "What letter? What in heaven's name do they think we have?"

Mr. Wood called the men to a meeting. Sid went to explain about the letter. On the way, Pa said, "Honesty is the best policy Son, but you don't have to tell everything you know. Don't mention treasure. The very mention of treasure makes some people crazy. Tell about the history and how they think Mr. Gallagher will pay a lot of money for the letter."

The men listened in silence. "You mean to say he'd pay a small fortune to get it back, and that's all there is to it? Family history?" Mr. Davies sounded incredulous.

Sid nodded. "That's what they said. Mr. Gallagher paid a lot of money to some man in St. Louis. He told me it was worth more than gold to his family."

"First thing is to get your girl back, Johnson," said Mr. Ryckman. "If it takes two of my horses, so be it. We'll see about getting the horses back once she's safe. They may find Thoroughbreds aren't as easy to ride as they imagine. I'll give 'em two that aren't saddle broken."

"But we don't have the letter," said Pa.

It suddenly occurred to Sid. "What if we make a copy? Mrs. Payne translated for me. It was written in Spanish.

They never had their hands on it. Maybe they won't know the difference." It seemed like a good idea. In any case, nobody had a better one.

Shortly before supper, the men tracking Cora returned. "Trail left off right away. We was all over the summit, to the pass and downward. No sign of 'em, not even a broken leaf," said Mr. Reid.

Sid felt his heart sink.

Evening lessons were suspended. Sid came up with a very authentic-looking duplicate of the letter paper by pouring coffee on a piece of paper and letting it dry in a pan over the coals. Mrs. Payne did the writing. "We don't have an envelope," she said, "but they aren't interested in the envelope."

Ethel came as they were finishing. "I'm so sorry, Sid. It's my fault for suggesting we go climbing without waiting for an adult. If anything happens to Cora, I'll never forgive myself." Her nose was red, and her eyes brimmed with tears.

"I'm the one that shoulda known better, Ethel. They've probably been followin' us ever since we left the fort."

He couldn't sleep that night. Poor Cora must be terrified. *Why didn't they take me?*

Abe tossed and turned nearby. Jimmy bolted upright. "Will they kill her, Sid? Will those men kill Cora if they don't get what they want?"

He hadn't let himself think it. But it was there, in the back of his mind, haunting him. "Oh Jimmy, no. It can't come to that."

"Mr. Wood is working on a plan to trap them, Jimmy." Abe spoke up. "Our job may be hardest. We have to stay out of zee way and pray it will work."

Would it work? Even if they gave Sly the letter and the horses, would they release Cora? *What if they see the letter is a fake?*

22.

THE SUMMIT

It was the darkest moment before dawn when Sid heard Pa stirring. He scrambled to his feet, Abe right behind. Ma and Mrs. Payne were up. Had they even gone to bed?

"Mr. Wood went out in the night with Reid and Preacher," Pa told them. "They'll be hidden up at the summit, ready to step in if things go wrong. Joiner's been up there all night." Pa's hand trembled as he tucked the letter in his waistcoat. "Walk with me for a piece, Son."

Mr. Ryckman joined them, leading two horses. "I'll walk them until we get close to the summit, Ben. They're not saddle-broken but they're well-disciplined. They won't give you any trouble."

"There's no way to thank you for this."

"It's what we do. We're a company."

Sid longed to go, but Pa gave him strict orders to stay put.

Dawn broke with breathtaking beauty, a beauty Sid was unable to appreciate in his fear. It seemed like everybody in the company stood by their wagons looking toward the summit in pensive silence. Mrs. Jones called for a prayer meeting. Sid and Abe stayed behind so somebody would be there if Jimmy, Matthew, and Lydia woke up. Sid couldn't see how praying was going to do much good anyway.

It felt like the longest morning of his life. He tugged at his hat.

The sun had been up about an hour when Pa returned with the horses. Mr. Wood was with him.

But not Cora.

"They weren't there," Pa's voice broke. "No trace of 'em anywhere."

"Something's gone wrong." Mr. Wood's face was a map of worry lines. "Joiner hadn't seen any sign of them. They're searching the other side of the summit. We'll find 'em. I don't take Sly for a fool. He won't hurt Cora, Miz Johnson. She's his only bargaining tool."

Ma looked stricken, but she didn't cry. Sid almost wished she would. He dared not think of what might happen to Cora. *And it's my fault for not watching her.*

"Ben, Miz Johnson, I'm taking Jeremy," said Mr. Wood, putting his hand on Pa's shoulder. "We'll head back up where they took Cora and fan out through the Woods down this side. They may have doubled back on us—old Indian trick. Ground's rocky, but the light's better this morning. There'll be a rock out of place, a bent leaf, or a broken branch somewhere.

"You, stay put here in case anything new develops. Sly may send word. He won't give up so easy. Ryckman, you're Wagon Master in my stead. Jeremy, get yourself some jerky and water. We may be out a piece. Miz Johnson, don't you give up. We'll find her."

They hadn't been gone for long when the fearful silence hovering over the camp was broken. "Someone's comin!" Three figures made their way down the trail from the summit.

Ma let out a cry, gathered up her skirts, and ran, Pa behind her, Sid and Abe behind him.

Walking between Reverend Jones and Mr. Reid was a great big man with a bushy red beard. Red hair stuck out from under his hat. Sitting upright in his arms, sun dancing on her golden hair, was Cora, waving to Ma and Pa.

The camp broke into cheering, gathering around as Ma threw her arms around Cora and the man. Mr. Ryckman fired a shot, signaling Mr. Wood.

"We was making our way through the woods down past the summit when we heard voices coming our way," said Mr. Reid, grinning from ear to ear. "One of 'em was a little girl, laughing and chattering like she was on a Sunday School picnic. There was Cora, holding on J.J. Gordon's hand, walking up to the summit big as you please."

Cora, suddenly shy from the attention, threw herself into Ma's arms, burying her face.

"Couldn't let 'em hurt a little girl." J.J. Gordon looked at his feet.

Reverend Jones spoke for him. "This is J.J. Gordon. He was with Bayless Sly looking for the Johnsons back before we got to New Fort Bent. He split with Sly"—J.J. briefly looked up from his boots, red creeping up his neck and spreading over his face—"Mr. Gordon didn't want any part of kidnapping Cora. He aimed to put a stop to it. He caught Bayless and Greenbriar late last night. They're tied up in a lean-to just past the summit."

"I sent Joiner to put the fear of God in 'em," said Mr. Reid.

By this time Mr. Wood and Jeremy were back. Mr. Wood wasn't ordinarily one to give away his feelings, but his face was one big smile. "If they still have any vinegar left by the time we reach top this afternoon, we'll hold them prisoner till we get to Fort Union. Soldiers are back and forth between Bent and Union pretty regular. Might be able to hand them off before we reach Union."

Ma insisted that J.J. join them for breakfast. He sat down by the fire, big and awkward. Holding Serena, Cora climbed into Pa's lap while J.J. told what happened. It seemed to be easier for him to talk with a small group.

"I told Sly I was goin' back to Santa Fe when we was in Kansas. But I couldn't find a teamster train needin' hands. I stuck with 'em till we got to the new fort. We sat around a lot of campfires lookin' for you folk. Then he started talkin' about kidnappin' the youngin. I couldn't let that happen.

"Sly found his-self a new partner. Made a big fuss about goin' on to Mexico. I didn't believe him. So, I made like I was going on, doin' some trappin'. I doubled back and followed 'em. They was waitin' fer the right time to get the little 'en, God bless her. I figured it'd be somewheres near the summit so as they could light out to Santa Fe soon as they had their hands on that letter—Sly figures you have a letter he wants."

"Except I don't," said Pa.

"They caught me off guard," said J.J. "Sure am sorry."

Suddenly Cora sat up wide-eyed. "They rolled me up in a buffalo hide! It was hot." She burrowed her face against Pa.

"I cursed myself fer lettin' 'em get her. They built a lean-to down the other side. Ya haveta know it's there to find it. I stayed close, waitin for the right time so as the little one wouldn't get hurt. Poor little darlin' was cryin' for her Mamma."

"And J.J. got 'em." Cora sat up again, her eyes blazing.

"Mr. Gordon," Ma corrected her.

"Mr. Gordon grabbed 'em by the collar and hit their heads together. Bam! Bam!"

Wide-eyed, Matthew and Jimmy followed every word.

"And he said I could go to sleep, 'cause he was gonna find my Ma and Pa in the mornin'. And he told me a story."

J.J. flushed and shook his head, though a smile spread across his face. "It wasn't quite like that. Sly was standin' guard. I know his ways pretty good. Reckon I did knock their heads together, when they needed remindin'. I'd of brought her home in the night except I didn't want to risk getting' shot."

"Mr. Gordon, there's no way we can thank you," said Ma.

"This here fine breakfast is thanks enough, ma'am." His eyes widened as Ma handed him a plate. Mrs. Payne had made apple dumplings to celebrate. She explained that Abe taught her how to make them.

"Biermann? I know your brothers, Abe. Honest men. Run a fine business. You'll havta get 'em to start tradin' in apple dumplins. These is mighty good."

Abe grinned.

Mr. Wood joined them, sitting down by the fire and accepting a cup of coffee from Ma. "Gordon, I hear you're on your way back to Santa Fe."

"Yessir, I was hopin' to get my old job with Gallagher Tradin' back, if they'll have me."

"I figure we can make the summit today. It's a mighty steep grade. I could use a strong man like you. I'd be mighty grateful if you could help us at least till we get through the pass. Can't pay you, but I know of Mr. Gallagher. I'll be glad to put in a good word when we get to Santa Fe."

"That'd be real good of you, Mr. Wood."

"Know anything about driving oxen?"

"Yessir—oxen, mules, horses."

"We've got a widow with us. Husband was killed in a tornado that hit just above the Arkansas. She has two youngins and another on the way. She's no business trying to drive oxen. Folk have been taking turns helping, but I sure could use you driving that wagon as far as Santa Fe. She's gonna have to decide what to do once we get there."

"You ain't cuttin' off out of Las Vegas over to Anton Chico

and the Pecos River? Road's a lot harder through Santa Fe."

"That was our plan till the tornado hit," said Mr. Wood. "Some of our folk are gonna have to durn near start over. I'm not counting on bein able to supply at Fort Union."

"You got that store Sam Watrous put up on the other side of Union at La Junta," said J.J., "though I reckon it ain't the best place to stretch a penny."

"Samuel Watrous has made a good place for himself—"

"But he ain't made such a good place for the Jicarilla Apache," said J.J.

Mr. Wood nodded. "Time was you could see their tepees stretched all over that valley."

"Be glad to help the widow." J.J. stood. "My horse is picketed down on the other side of that lean-to. Reckon I'd better get 'em before the bears do."

"Check on those two rats while you're at it," said Mr. Wood. He stood without spilling his cup of coffee. "Tell Joiner he can come back."

"You're one heck of a scout, Gordon, I'll say that for you," said Mr. Reid, shaking his hand. "Couldn't find a trace of you anywhere along the ridge."

J.J. grinned. "I learned from the Comanche when I was a boy."

"Take my horse, Mr. Gordon," said Pa. "Be quicker and it will save Joiner having to walk back."

J.J. Gordon stayed with the company and helped with the crossing, adding his enormous strength and experience to getting the train over the summit and through the Raton Pass. Pa told J.J. there was a place for him around their campfire at mealtime.

"The food and the company is mighty temptin,' but Miz Turney says if I'm drivin' her team, the least she can do is feed me. I reckon it gives her somethin' to take her mind off her troubles." J.J. was big and fierce looking, but he had a soft heart.

Bayless and Greenbriar were none the happier for going without breakfast or dinner. Ma gave them some supper. Sid wouldn't have done it. They had to walk; hands tied behind their backs. Greenbriar was tight-lipped, but Sly tried to convince everyone within hearing he'd been wronged.

"You ain't got nothing to complain about," said Mr. Reid. "Wagon master coulda had you shot and left you for the bears."

"Whining makes me nervous," said Al Joiner. "I get nervous, I could accidentally shoot somebody."

Leaving the summit and making the descent from the mountains was as treacherous as their ascent had been. Now wagons were turned around, their brakes locked. Oxen braced the wagons from behind. Men pulled against the wagons along with the oxen, easing their descent on the most treacherous stretches. It was a noisy business, too. Mrs. Payne's wagon rattled so much Sid thought it would break apart.

Ethel organized climbing parties. Abe went, but Sid made excuses. The missing letter weighed on him. He had to face it: he was not worthy of Mr. Gallagher's trust. Pa said he needed to quit worrying. Ma said, "All anybody can do is their best."

Mrs. Payne said no good could come from torturing himself. "Things happen that are beyond our control, Sid. You'll just have to tell Mrs. Gallagher what happened. You can give her the copy we made. At least she will have her family's history. It's the best we can do—and Sid, sometimes that is all we can give, even if it isn't enough." She turned away, but not before Sid saw the tears in her eyes.

All told, they passed through the 15 miles of Raton Pass in five and a half days. Axles, hitches, and wheels had to be replaced on many of the wagons. One wagon was nearly destroyed, but not a single animal was lost. Mr. Reid said it was nothing short of a miracle. But some oxen were so spent it didn't seem like they could go on. Mr. Wood called for a day of rest. They all needed it, especially the oxen. He said they'd be in Santa Fe in two weeks if their luck held out. It hardly seemed possible.

The soldiers Mr. Wood had been expecting didn't come, but a small party out of Fort Union stopped while the train was at rest. They had been following a group of Jicarilla Apache who had helped themselves to about 300 sheep belonging to a Mexican settler. They hadn't had any luck finding the sheep, but the soldiers took Sly and Greenbriar off the company's hands.

23.

NEW MEXICO TERRITORY

Ethel lingered as Sid and Abe helped Mrs. Payne put things away after school one evening. Bitsy wasn't there. Ethel usually had to get the orphaned girls, Isla and Maize, back to the wagon and to bed. "They were over at Miss Joiner's all day. They played so hard they were cranky so she put them to bed early. They're spending the night."

"When we get to Santa Fe, I'll introduce you all to my brothers." Abe talked about his family more now. "Nathan is married to an Apache woman. Her name is Nascha. They have two boys and a girl. They have our family names and Apache names.

"How nice," said Mrs. Payne. "It honors both families."

"My uncle made Kurt's match. He sent her with a family three years ago. Her name is Sarah. They have twin girls. The house will be full of children."

"That will keep you busy," laughed Ethel.

Sid didn't know what to say. Having Ethel there looking like she expected him to say something threw him off. It made him angry with himself, too, for being thrown off.

"What about Max?" asked Mrs. Payne.

"Max isn't married. He says he's waiting for the right girl."

"Your uncle doesn't have a girl for him?" Ethel raised her eyebrows.

"Hmmm. How to put it? My uncle had girls for Kurt and for Max as soon as he learned Nathan married an Apache. He thought it was like the Hebrews marrying a Canaanite. Max says he is waiting for the right girl. When he sees her, he will know her if she's from one of the lost tribes of Israel or from one of the Apache tribes."

"Why is it such a bad thing for somebody to marry an Apache?" Ethel's brow furrowed. "Where we lived back in Indiana a man married a Free Negro. Some people never spoke to him again. That's something I just don't understand."

"Don't expect to," said Sid, finding his voice. "Folk like that are blind. They don't want to see. If you want to know the truth of it, we have some folk in the Wood Company—"

"I know," sighed Ethel. "But still, you'd think—"

"You'd think, Ethel. That's the difference. You think. Lot of folk don't think. Their minds are closed shut, except to things that fit the way they already see 'em."

"Well, that's just wrong." Ethel sounded so much like an older edition of Grace Willis, it left Sid speechless.

"There is a lot that's just wrong," said Abe.

"But young folk like you are the ones who can help make it right," said Mrs. Payne. "I hate to end this discussion, but my young ones need to get washed up and ready for bed."

Ethel started to leave, hesitating. "Could I ask you something, Mrs. Payne?"

"Of course," Mrs. Payne smiled. "I can't promise an answer."

"How did you know you were in love with Mr. Payne?"

Abe rolled his eyes and mouthed, "Just like a girl."

"I didn't at first. You know, folk think the biggest barriers in getting married are across race, like your brother, Abe. But class barriers are hard to overcome, too. My people were free. They came to the U.S. free. Mr. Payne's people were slaves. He was separated from his parents when he was a young boy. My people are highly educated. Mr. Payne could neither read nor write when we met. I taught him to read. That's how we met."

"That's so romantic," said Ethel.

"He was a brilliant man. But my people were terribly opposed to the match. They felt Mr. Payne was inferior on every count. But we were determined. And I'm determined to move you three out of here so I can get my young ones to bed."

As they left, Ethel paused, "I guess it's hard to think about getting to Santa Fe, Sid. Abe will stay, but we'll go on." Her brow was slightly furrowed. "We'll miss you, Abe, but Sid will miss you the most."

Why did she have to go and say that? Sid felt for his hat. He wasn't sure he could stand to lose another friend.

Rayado and Ocate Creek Crossing

They were in grasslands again. Gone were the nearly empty plains that stretched from Council Grove to the Rocky Mountains. There were more and different kinds of cacti, some as tall as trees. And they passed mud houses here and there where rancheros stayed while looking after cattle and sheep. Mr. Wood said if anybody wanted to replace oxen lost in the tornado or that were exhausted from crossing the mountains, they could do business with the rancheros.

Pa said Buttercup was getting on fine as a team member. Mrs. Payne didn't need to replace her. Josiah seemed to be depressed, following along tethered to the wagon. They tried to give him some attention every day. But Pa said he'd wait until they got to Fort Union and see if he could find a teammate.

One day Mrs. Payne's wagon was in line following Mrs. Turney's wagon. Jimmy and Matthew ran alongside J.J. Gordon, who seemed to delight in watching them explore along the trail. He pointed out lizards standing erect on rocks as if inspecting the train as it passed. The boys tried catching one. It escaped with astonishing speed.

"See that bird with the gangly legs up ahead?" J.J. pointed to a large bird with a long beak and tail. "I have a penny for the first one to touch his tail feathers—don't worry, he won't hurt you. Walk up slow."

At first, the bird ambled ahead of the boys as if it didn't notice, but as they were almost close enough to reach out and touch it, the bird took off like a rock from a slingshot. "Woah!" said Jimmy. "Look at that thing go."

"I thought he'd fly off," said Matthew, wide-eyed.

J.J. laughed. "He's a chaparral—we call him a roadrunner. They can fly, but they usually run. Reckon a roadrunner could outrun a horse. Take a look at his tracks."

"Looks like he was walking in two directions at once," said Matthew.

"Yoicks!" said Jimmy, "He's writin' X with his feet."

A group of children began stamping on the ground just off the trail, yelling, "Tarantula, Tarantula, come out, come out! Tell us what it's all about!" Matthew and Jimmy ran to see and came racing back to report, "There's these big fuzzy spiders, and they're stomping on 'em when they come out of their holes," said Matthew.

"And squishin' em." Jimmy wrinkled his nose, grimacing.

Mr. Wood must have heard the commotion. He put a stop to it. "It's fun looking for tarantula holes. You youngins stamp and call all you want, but don't harm the tarantulas, just watch them. They're interesting creatures. There's a reason for all God's creatures."

"Even scorpions?" Jimmy asked.

"Even scorpions. They eat pests. And a lot of desert creatures like owls and lizards eat them."

"Ewww!" Jimmy made a face.

Several adobe houses and a postal stage stop marked the settlement of Rayado. They made camp nearby.

"Kit Carson has a house in Rayado," said Sid, "but don't get your hopes up, Jimmy, he doesn't live here."

Jimmy, who used to play Kit Carson before they left Illinois, and saw their whole purpose in going west as a chance to meet him, suddenly looked puzzled. "Is Kit Carson a good guy or a bad guy?"

"What do you mean?"

"Well, everybody says Kit Karson is the greatest scout there ever was, but Matthew says he owns slaves."

As clearly as if it were just now happening, Sid remembered. Shortly after he discovered their farm was a stop on the Underground Railroad, he was helping a freedom seeker get to Liam Robinson, a member of the Society of Friends. A slaveholder stopped him. Unlike the bounty hunters he had met, who looked like crooks, this man was well-dressed, polite, and spoke in a kind and respectful way. Baffled, he'd asked Liam Robinson, "How could he be a nice man and own slaves?"

"There's the rub," Liam Robinson had said. "There's a bit of God in everyone, Sid Johnson, but some things cannot be reconciled. An answer to thy question is beyond me."

"Jimmy, that's a question I can't answer. I expect Kit Carson has done lots of good things and maybe his share of bad. I don't know about the slaves part. Mr. Wood said he bought Indian children who were going to be traded or sold to protect 'em from slavery. I don't know what to tell you."

"Hmm," Jimmy looked thoughtful. "Maybe he's good and bad." He was off to the next thing before Sid could say any more.

The subject of slavery came up again at the Ocate Creek crossing. "Isaiah Wood says this is an ancient trading site," Mr. Reid said as they turned teams loose for nooning. "Comancheros bought wild ponies, meat, and buffalo from the Indians who wanted knives, blankets, and guns."

"That ain't all they traded," J.J. Gordon face clouded over. "They traded slaves—mostly Indian women and children. Kidnapped 'em and sold 'em to traders all up and down the

Santa Fe Trail. Been happenin' since before the Spanish ever came, Indians makin' slaves of people they defeated in war. Spanish tried to put a stop to it. Still goes on."

Was slavery a problem among native people, too? Seemed like there was no getting away from it. How could anybody think it was right to "own" another person?

"Indians call this the Valley of the Wind," J.J. said. It was easy to see why. Tall feathergrass and Indian wheat waved in the wind. It whipped gray, sandy trail soil into clouds of choking dust that hung in the air and found its way into the wagons. They could taste the dust.

*****

Some things didn't change. Sid worked with Squeaker who devoured books like he was starving, and somebody had set a table heaped with delicious things before him. He was rapidly going through Mrs. Payne's small library. She thought he was ready for *Julius Caesar*. Sid didn't think Squeaker was up to Shakespeare. He might get the words, but there was a lot in the play that would go way past his head. But Mrs. Payne was the teacher. Sid gave him her book and asked him to be ready to talk about Act 1.

He usually planned some questions to help Squeaker understand what he was reading, but he wasn't as well prepared as he should have been when Squeaker appeared with *Julius Caesar* in hand. Admittedly, he had been wasting time looking for the lost letter.

Squeaker dropped to the ground. Leaning against the front wheel of the Johnson wagon, he munched on cornbread—he didn't have to wait for a snack anymore. Sid eased himself down beside Squeaker. "So, *Julius Caesar*, Act 1: what do you think it's about?" He asked mechanically.

"They're out to get 'em. Cassius thinks Caesar has done

got too much power." Squeaker licked butter from his fingers. "But see, Cassius wants it for his-self and Brutus just tags along."

Sid was stunned. Maybe Squeaker *was* ready for *Julius Caesar*. "So what do you think about it?' He groped for what to say.

"Ain't nothing to *think*. It's like Connie with Billy running after 'em." Squeaker studied his fingers looking for a last bit of butter. "Me 'n Frog thinks it's how come Billy sticks to him like molasses. Billy wants to be a big shot like Connie. He's took to wanting us—me—to get stuff for him, too. That's how come me 'n Frog decided to return stuff I took. We've was fed up." He took a bite of cornbread, chewing it slowly. "Reckon it's like when Miz Brutus—"

"Portia," Sid offered, hardly knowing what to say.

"Yeah, her. Portia tells Brutus he can't go blaming the stars for stuff that happens—"

"'The fault, dear Brutus, is not in our stars, but in ourselves.' But that's in Act 2."

"We done read the whole thing." Squeaker snickered. "I been readin' it to Frog, and we both wanted to know what happened."

Sid was dumbfounded. Squeaker wasn't stupid even though he acted like it most of the time. But reading *Julius Caesar* to Frog? "I think you're gettin' way ahead of me, Squeaker," he confessed, giving Squeaker his full attention. "That's not a bad thing. When I was readin' it, Mrs. Payne asked me what I thought about how Shakespeare uses power in the play."

"Yeah. Well, me 'n Frog's was thinking about how stuff was gnawing at Brutus. It's like that missing letter gnawing at you. Something like that can bring you down. It brought Brutus down."

Sid was speechless.

"So we done decided to help you find it."

"Wait a minute, do you mean Frog actually *talks* to you?"

"Frog can talk. He just don't want to—don't you go blabbing it around."

"Come on, Sid. Come on Squea—Winston," Jimmy called, ending further discussion. "Me and Cora is goin' to lessons."

"Cora and I," called Ma.

"Is Miz Johnson goin' too?" asked Squeaker.

"No, she was correctin' Jimmy's grammar." Sid pulled himself up, frustrated for being so unprepared, for underestimating Squeaker, and completely baffled about Frog.

"Huh?"

"You're supposed to use I when it's the subject of a sentence." Sid didn't say any more. Now wasn't the time for a lesson on the finer points of grammar. Besides, after a few weeks of hanging around on the edge of things, moving closer and closer, Squeaker—Winston—had become part of the older group of students. He was learning so fast he was way ahead of everyone in mathematics, even Abe. He wasn't any good at Latin yet, but Mrs. Payne said to give it time. *Let her explain "I" and "me."*

Frog was already at Mrs. Payne's wagon reading aloud to her. "The dog . . . has a . . . black . . . spot . . . on . . . his back." Frog was well into *McGuffey's First Eclectic Reader*. He had a feeling Mrs. Payne was prouder of Frog than any of them. Frog sat with the older students during lessons. He never said anything. The same blank expression stayed on his face. But there was a lot going on inside Frog's head, something Squeaker seemed to understand better than anybody else.

Sid could hardly wait for lessons to be over so he could ask Squeaker what he meant about helping him find the letter. He didn't think Ethel and Bitsy would ever leave. He busied himself putting things away, hoping Squeaker and Frog would stick around. The opportunity finally came.

"What did you mean about helpin' me find the letter?"

"I 'n Frog been listening in on what folks is saying. We listen long enough, somebody's gonna say something about that letter."

"You mean you've been eavesdropping," said Ethel dryly, appearing out of nowhere. "I know what's going on. If you weren't so stubborn, you'd let us help you, Sid. I need to give this book back to Mrs. Payne. Meet me over at my campfire soon as you can. It's time for some serious planning. My mother and father are over at the Joiner campfire. We won't be disturbed." She tossed her head, returned the book to Mrs. Payne, and disappeared.

Frog stared at him. Squeaker snickered. Sid shrugged. "I guess I'll see you over there."

"Shall we tell your Ma and Pa where we are going?" Abe asked.

"You, too? Is this a conspiracy?"

"I do not know this word." Abe grinned.

Ma's smile lit up her face. "Just what you two boys need, some socializing with the others."

*****

Squeaker and Frog were there when they got to the Sinclair campfire. So was Dale, who never came to lessons. "What about Bitsy?" Sid asked.

"Can't keep a secret," said Squeaker, snickering.

"So, what's this about?"

"Thought you knew," said Dale.

"Here's what we know." Ethel took charge. "Ever since Cora was kidnapped, you have been out of sorts. You haven't had time for anything fun."

Squeaker snickered. "Been spending all his time looking for the letter."

"Winston's not saying anything we don't already know," said Ethel. "Everybody in the Company knows the kidnappers wanted a letter—"

"and we figure it hasta be more than a family history," said Dale, "nobody's family's that interesting."

"Yeah, maybe it's a treasure map," Squeaker said, pacing back and forth.

"None of our beeswax," said Dale.

"What is our business," Ethel said, "is that you're worrying about it."

Squeaker snickered—Sid felt like throttling him—"Yeah, like Brutus worrying over Caesar—"

"Except the analogy breaks down, Winston. Brutus betrayed Caesar. Sid's the one being betrayed. Sid, we're thinking that if we put our heads together maybe we can figure out a way to find the letter."

"We're pretty sure it's here," said Dale. "It has to be."

Ethel nodded. "I don't like to think somebody in the company stole it, but somebody else could think it's about more than family history."

"Why. . .why bother?" Sid stammered.

"You're our friend," said Ethel, then went all red.

"There hasn't been anybody else poking around in the Wood Company like those men who kidnapped Cora," said Dale. "Where else could it be?"

"We figure Connie done took it outa that box of soldiers," said Squeaker. "I never opened the box. I just stole it."

"How did—"

"That's beside the point," said Ethel. "We need to make some decisions before my parents get back."

"We learned about the letter that night we was spying on you and Miz Payne," said Dale.

"Yeah," snickered Squeaker, "Miz Payne said you'd done lost your sparkle. Then Joiner come along and shooed us away. But we came back."

"Connie said it was too good to miss," said Dale. "We didn't hear enough about the letter to notice. Connie never said nothing about it. He wanted the soldiers. It's not like he was gonna play with 'em. He just wanted 'em because they're yours. He wanted to bring you down."

"Yeah," snickered Squeaker, "like Cassius was jealous of Caesar."

"Of me? I thought I was Brutus," Sid snapped. He wished Squeaker would quit going on about Julius Caesar. *I swear I'll choke him if he doesn't stop that snickering.* Besides he was starting to feel like he was somebody's school project.

Ethel frowned. "Don't be silly, Winston. Mrs. Payne says we all have Cassius and Caesar and Brutus in us. Can we just stick to the point, everybody? Sid, we've narrowed it down to Connie."

"Has to be him unless you talked about it to somebody besides Mrs. Payne," said Dale.

"I told Pa and Mr. Wood when I heard about the plan to kidnap Cora. Didn't even tell Ma, didn't want to worry her."

"Connie musta found the letter when he opened the box of soldiers," said Dale. "Then when he heard about Cora getting kidnapped, he was either too scared or too spiteful to own up. We gotta get him away from their wagon and have a look. Ain't goina be easy. Since his injury, he's glued to that wagon."

"Then you will have to get Billy away," said Abe.

"What if we get Patsy O'Connell on our side?" Sid was beginning to warm to the idea despite himself.

"She wouldn't want to betray Mrs. Ryckman," said Ethel, "but she has every reason to hate Connie." Then she went all red again.

"Ain't no good sneaking around in the middle of the night." Squeaker danced around while he talked. "Miz Ryckman wakes up if you drop a feather."

"I will talk to Patsy," said Abe.

"You?" Dale raised his eyebrows.

"We are immigrants to New York. I am talking to her when I go with Mrs. Johnson to see Connie."

"Good," said Ethel. "I'll find out when the women are meeting again. We have to get Mrs. Ryckman away from the wagon, too."

"Huh?" Squeaker said, "The women?"

Sid had no idea what she was talking about either.

"You boys! Don't you pay any attention to what's going on around you? The women meet to talk about how to get by on short rations and repair clothing that's beyond repair and the thousands of things they have to deal with every day that men don't pay any attention to. They usually meet at nooning while you men are napping."

Before Ethel's parents returned, they had agreed to several things. Everybody was going to start paying more attention to things said around them. Frog and Squeaker would focus on people working for Ryckman. "I and Frog hear a lot. Folks thinks we're too dumb to know nothing. They don't even shut up when we're standing there lookin' at 'em."

They decided not to bring Eli into it. "Too risky," said Dale. "He wouldn't want to tell. But he would. Connie would pry it out of him. He still calls the shots with Billy and Eli."

"He thinks he calls the shots with I and Frog," Squeaker snickered. His attempts at correct grammar grated on Sid almost as much as the snickering and dancing around.

"What about you, Sid?" Ethel asked. "You need to do something positive, so you aren't going around in a cloud of gloom pulling that hat down over your eyes."

Ethel had a way of making him want to do the opposite. But he ate his feelings. "Al Joiner has an ear for what's goin' on. Reckon I can talk to Joiner."

"Tomorrow night after lessons?" said Ethel. "We can meet here."

Despite feeling like a project, it was the first time Sid had felt the least bit hopeful since the letter went missing.

*****

Villages became more frequent as the company moved south. J.J. Gordon said people lived in New Mexico Territory long before the Spanish began occupying Mexico. "Most of these folk are Spanish married to Mexican. Some of 'em Mexican."

Jimmy looked puzzled. "I thought they was all Mexican if they live in New Mexico."

"I reckon you're right, Jimmy. But I was thinkin' of folks who lived down in Mexico before the Spaniards. Some of 'em come on up this way and settled. Now all these 'newcomers' complain about so many folk settlin' in New Mexico Territory. They're all crowdin' out the Jicarilla Apache, the Ute, and the Comanche."

"What's a Jicarilla Apache?"

"They're one of the Apache tribes," J.J. said.

Freshly cooked tortillas with beans, onion, and chili peppers were for sale along the trail. They smelled delicious. Sid longed to try them, but Ma said there wasn't money for extras.

Young children watched from the shade of houses, counting the wagons just like Sid and Grace had counted wagons when they were camped at Westport before they set out on the trail. They saw women dressed in black and men wearing brightly colored shirts. Some members of the company were offended by what they saw. Ma always said, "Isn't it interestin' how different folk do things?" She took toddlers running naked in stride, but even Ma looked a bit put back when they passed a stream where some women stripped down to their camisoles and bloomers, in front of everyone, to go for a swim.

"Well I never!" said Mrs. Reid.

"Yes, well . . ." Ma was speechless for a moment. "It certainly is different."

"Let's just be glad they kept their camisoles and bloomers on." Mrs. Payne laughed. "Anyway, where's the harm in it?"

"Lawsey, mercy," said Mrs. Reid, "there's been some days I've longed to do the same thing myself. I expect there'll be more of them days before we're done."

*****

Abe was the only one with anything to report when the small group of conspirators met again. "Patsy O'Connell will help us. Connie has a trunk he keeps locked. She knows where the key is."

"So, it's a matter of finding the right time." Sid tried to take charge.

"That ain't gonna be easy," said Dale. "Mrs. Ryckman keeps Patsy pretty busy."

"Oh, but it is perfect!" said Ethel. "If Patsy O'Connell helps us with Connie, all we have to do is figure out the logistics—I knew she'd help. It's bound to work."

"What's bound to work?" Billy Elston demanded, stepping into the light of the campfire. Bitsy and Eli were right behind.

Sid thought his heart would stop.

"Caught you, Ethel!" Bitsy giggled. "What are you up to with all these boys?"

Ethel bit her lips, frowning. Dale's jaw dropped like he'd been caught standing over a dead body with a smoking gun. Squeaker stopped in his tracks and looked at the ground. Frog was Frog, unmoving. Abe had an unreadable expression on his face.

"*Julius Caesar*," said Sid—he could never explain how he came to say it—"*Julius Caesar*."

Billy scowled, "What the—"

"We're puttin' on a play of *Julius Caesar* for the whole Company. But we gotta convince Connie to play the part of Caesar—"

"—since Caesar is the king," Ethel jumped in without so much as a pause. "Patsy promised to see if Mrs. Ryckman will encourage him. There will be parts for everyone. You can play Calpurnia, Caesar's wife, Bitsy, since she's the queen, and I'll be Portia."

"Ohhh," Bitsy squealed. "I love a play!"

Dale looked straight at Billy. "We was hopin' you'd be in it, too."

"Humpf!" Billy grunted.

"Billy, it's about the most famous play ever written," said Ethel. "Ask anybody who's been to school. Everybody studies it in school. It won't be the same without you and Connie."

"Come on, Billy, don't be a spoilsport," Bitsy pleaded.

"We were hopin' you'd be Cassius," said Sid. "He's a general in the Roman army."

Arms folded across his chest, Billy scowled. "I ain't gonna learn a bunch of lines in some namby-pamby play."

"You won't have to," said Ethel. "See, we'll tell the story.

The actors just show what's happening. That way we don't have to have a bunch of rehearsals."

"Yeah," said Sid. They were improvising so fast his head was spinning. "We want to have the play before we get to Glorieta Pass. When we get to the pass, we'll be so close to Santa Fe everybody will be too busy."

"Be a whole lot easier while we're camping on flat ground," said Dale.

"Let's do it Billy," said Bitsy. "Please? You too Eli. Do say yes! It's our chance to be in a real play."

"Maybe," said Billy, his scowl relaxing. He'd probably have to ask Connie.

"I gotta get back, Billy," said Bitsy, "I promised. Ma will have my hide."

Sid let out a big sigh of relief as they left.

"Now you've really put us in the soup, Sid Johnson," said Ethel glaring at him. "We have to do a production of *Julius Caesar* in less than two weeks. How are we going to do that and find your letter."

Squeaker snickered.

"But it is brilliant," said Abe. "The whole company will watch, and we can get into Connie's trunk."

"There's a lot to figure out," said Sid, "but it could work. Let's talk with Mrs. Payne. Maybe I can catch her now. She and Ma like to gossip after the youngins are in bed."

"Then let's go ask her now," said Ethel. "Don't mention the trunk." Like he had to be told.

Ma and Mrs. Payne were deep in conversation. "Mrs. Sinclair says he's very good with the children," said Ma.

Mrs. Payne nodded. "Mrs. Turney was telling Lila Reid that Mr. Gordon told her his stepmother and little sister were taken by an Apache raiding party and sold as slaves. He never got over it. It drove his father to drink."

"That must have been a blow. She said his stepmother was Comanche"—Ma suddenly noticed them—"You three must be up to something."

"Keep it simple," Mrs. Payne said when they explained. "We can make it part of your lessons. But if you want to do it, it's up to you. Have Mr. Wood announce it to the Company so all the children who want can take part. There are plenty of crowd scenes for them. I wouldn't have a lot of rehearsals with them, though, maybe one before the performance. Don't try to follow Shakespeare exactly. Stick to the main plot points."

The next evening at lessons, Ethel had a rough draft of a script. It generated a heated discussion. Bitsy wanted to know who got what part and if there would be any kissing. Abe rolled his eyes and shook his head.

"It's not that kind of play, Bitsy," Ethel said.

Mrs. Payne had them share with everyone before lessons ended.

"And we're all in it?" Jimmy jumped up, waving an imaginary sword, "I get to stab the king." A look from Mrs. Payne disarmed him.

"When are you ever going to learn to keep your mouth shut?" Matthew muttered.

Cora was so excited that the minute school was over, she jumped up and down, hugged all her friends, and ran back to Ma yelling, "There's gonna be a play and we're in it and somebody gets stabbed, but Jimmy don't get to stab him."

"Doesn't, sweetheart," said Ma. "Jimmy doesn't get to stab him. And who is it Jimmy isn't stabbing?"

*****

"We've got to have our script perfect and know exactly what we're doing before we rehearse with our main actors," said Ethel when they met after lessons.

Sid agreed. "We have to know what's goin' on with the play and how that helps us. . ." he started to say 'get into the trunk' and caught himself. They couldn't talk about it with Bitsy there.

"With timing." Dale rescued him. "We have to get the timing right."

Sid reported that Mr. Wood liked the idea. "He thinks we should try and stage it after we leave Fort Union, somewhere before Las Vegas."

"Word's all over camp," said Squeaker, dancing around and snickering as usual.

Dale nodded. "Eli says Connie's bragging about it. Thinks he's a big star."

"Mrs. Ryckman is excited, too," said Bitsy. "She said she will be happy to help us with costumes. My mother says Mrs. Ryckman hopes it will get Connie involved without demanding too much while he's in such a delicate condition."

"Delicate as a rattlesnake," Dale muttered.

Sid was afraid that in the excitement they'd forget about the letter since they couldn't keep Bitsy from coming to meetings without arousing suspicion. But they never wavered from their dual mission. Ethel became more reasonable the more they worked together, though they almost came to blows over who would narrate the performance. They might have, too, if Ethel hadn't been a girl. They had it out after everyone except Abe left.

"Everything depends on somebody holdin' the audience's attention," Sid insisted.

"Mrs. Payne agrees. Winston can do it. You keep underestimating him."

"He can't say three words without snickerin'. And he twirls around like some kind of ballerina. How's he gonna get through an entire play?"

Abe wouldn't side with either of them. In the end, Sid figured Ethel was better at directing anyway. Even if she wasn't, she was determined to do it. If Squeaker made fools of them, at least he'd create a diversion for getting into the trunk. Besides, his job was to think things through, like what he'd say if he were caught getting into Connie's trunk.

He had learned a lot from Ma and Pa when the farm was part of the Underground Railroad. Without attention to the smallest detail, lives could have been lost and the brave freedom seekers who came their way would have been taken back into slavery. He began to study how the guards moved around the camp at night and how long it took to get from one side of the campground to another.

25.

FORT UNION

One afternoon Mr. Wood called from the top of a rise in the trail, "There she is: Fort Union." The first row of wagons pulled to the top and cheering broke out, repeated like waves breaking on the shore as each row topped the rise and started down across the wide sweep of prairie that gradually descended into the valley where the fort stood, its back to a long mesa.

To their left, the late afternoon light poured on the Turkey Hills, sacred to the Jicarilla Apache. To Sid, they looked more like low mountains than hills.

Fort Union was not what he expected. Tiny dots in the shadow of the mesa, its scattered buildings looked less like an orderly military fort than like a giant child had been playing with blocks and failed to put them away. Even so, it was a welcome site. Sid cheered as the lead oxen, Hope and Buttercup, crested the rise.

Situated at a point between the mountains and desert plains, the fort was built to house the Ninth Military Department of the U.S. Army and serve as a supply depot for garrisons throughout the region. It was located strategically to protect the mountain and desert branches of the Santa Fe Trail, standing as an unspoken warning to native people, primarily the Jicarilla Apache.

The company made camp outside the open gate of the

fort. Teamster trains were camped nearby; others arrived from the east. There was plenty of prairie grass and water for the animals. Mr. Wood said they would take a day's rest, giving the oxen another chance to regain their strength. The road ahead wasn't so demanding, but Glorieta Pass waited.

With the date set for the performance—the first campsite after they passed through Las Vegas—and the script in place, Ethel thought it was time for a rehearsal with the principal characters. They talked it over in a rare moment without Bitsy. "I dread it," said Dale. "You watch. Connie will try to take over."

"First, we should set up an imaginary stage, so we get a pretty good idea of the action," said Sid. "Mrs. Payne said she'll excuse us from school." The way he figured, there were two major tasks: deciding where to place the characters and getting to the trunk without being missed. Ethel agreed without a fight.

Frog ignored them, squatting on the ground nearby playing with rocks.

"We'll need the stage to be opposite"—Ethel halted, looking around.

Dale nodded. "But it's goina depend on where the wagons are when we make camp."

"Meaning we can't be certain," said Sid.

"Where will the actors be when they are not on the stage?" asked Abe.

Frog sat back, looking at them. Suddenly Sid realized what he'd been doing. "Look, Frog's worked it out. Here's the circle of wagons and this is the stage—"

"Oh, well done, Earl!" said Ethel. "Where we put up the stage will depend on where—"

"Front of the wagon directly opposite, you know, the *main wagon*," said Dale. "One of our wagons is bound to end up close enough."

"So,"—Sid pointed to Frog's mockup—"behind this wagon is where we put all the props and where the actors—"

"Except if Caesar and Brutus wait back there," said Dale, "they'll know when . . ." He didn't have to say the rest.

"Well, for one thing, we'll have to wait for dark," said Ethel.

Squeaker, snickered. "How's anybody goina see it?"

"Guess we're goina have to borrow a whole bunch of lanterns," said Dale.

Sid nodded. "We have to plan it so everybody thinks I'm there when—"

"Thought that was Squeaker's job," Dale interrupted. "He'd be better at it. No offense. He's been doin' it."

"That's a good reason for him not to," Ethel said, lowering her voice. "He'd be more likely to be a suspect if Connie sees the trunk has been touched. Besides, he can't do that and be narrator."

Abe volunteered, but Dale pointed out that some people don't trust Jews. He might be a target. "Besides, if Mrs. Johnson needs you at the last minute, we'd be up a creek."

"It has to look like everybody's there all the time," said Ethel.

Sid ended the argument. "It's my responsibility and I have an about idea how we can do it. We haveta make some small changes in our script. And we keep Connie and Billy on stage for the whole play, you know, to protect his delicate constitution. We shift 'em slightly to the left of the stage center when they don't have lines."

Dale snorted, "Then we'd better keep Billy and Eli there, too."

The conspiracy was taking shape.

*****

The next morning while some of the men hunted antelope Sid and Abe explored Fort Union. Decaying bark was scattered around the pine log buildings. In some buildings logs were horizontal, in others upright, leaving the impression there had been no master plan for the fort.

Soldiers and teamsters—Anglo, Black, Indian, Mexican—unloaded teamster wagons and loaded wagons waiting to be sent to supply garrisons throughout New Mexico Territory.

Abe was eager to visit the hospital, a separate building with a dirt roof. The Assistant Surgeon, Jonathon Letterman, was busy. "If something's ailing you, come in. If not, there's nothing to see here. All I could show you is bed bugs. This peeling bark is a haven for bed bugs." He frowned, pointing to the decaying door frame around him. "The place is falling apart, not a dry room in the building. They threw the fort together. Soldiers built it without the help of anybody who knows anything about building. Good luck if you want to be a doctor. Pray you don't get assigned to a hole like this one. Now I have patients to attend to."

Abe was crushed. But they collected the mail. A letter from his brothers put him in a better frame of mind.

Children from the wagon train had a glorious day playing in sand along the sides of the fort. "See all that sand, Jimmy?" Matthew asked. "If it was a windy day, it'd be in our wagon."

"Yoicks! We already got enough sand."

Women took advantage of nearby water and the dry air to do laundry and cook food to eat on the trail. The men brought in fresh antelope meat.

Taking Jimmy and Matthew with him, Pa went into the fort to see if he could find an ox to replace Gregg. Sid was left to grease the wagon wheels, check for damage on both wagons, and examine ox shoes. He had plenty to do. Even so, he felt abandoned by Abe, who spent the rest of the day with his nose in a medical book. Once they reached Santa Fe, it would be the end of the journey for Abe. It was one more thing to worry about. He adjusted his hat.

Mrs. Payne's wagon had survived the Raton Pass without serious damage. A spoke on one wagon wheel needed to be replaced. The oxen's feet were in remarkably good shape. He was pretty sure they'd need new shoes by the time they reached Santa Fe. He was worried about Buttercup. She pulled like a real trooper, but the stretch over the Raton Pass had worn her down. Samson and Star, the Johnson wheel yoke, needed new shoes. They'd had a heavier load without Josiah and Gregg.

Between jobs, he looked for the lost letter on the off chance it might not be in Connie's trunk. How could he face Mr. Gallagher? Everyone was excited about getting to Santa Fe. He dreaded it. His failure weighed on him like a heavy yoke across his shoulders.

Pa returned leading an ox. Jimmy and Matthew outpaced him, bursting with excitement. "It's Gregg! It's Gregg!" Sure enough, it was their Gregg looking worse for wear. He'd been found wandering on the other side of the Arkansas. "Now what were the chances of that happening?" said Pa. "I had to buy him back. But he's worth every penny." Gregg knew his yokemate, and Josiah rubbed his face against Gregg, the happiest he had looked since Gregg disappeared.

That evening the conspirators met outside the wagon circle in the area where they had marked out a stage. Bitsy arrived early with Ethel. Billy came with Connie, who limped on a cane. Things went much better than Sid had feared. It was a stroke of genius to let Ethel direct. Connie didn't have a chance to take over. She squelched Billy's sarcasm before it even started. "That girl could run a wagon train," he confided to Abe. Things were falling into place.

26.

La Junta

The Wood Company made good time the next morning, passing through lush plains where scattered herds of antelope grazed in the distance. They were about an hour out from La Junta when they stopped for nooning. The trail was busy with traffic making its way toward Fort Union from the south. After he released the oxen to graze, Sid stood looking ahead where a wagon train turned toward the north. Another passed it, coming from the south. "You're looking over to the Cimarron branch of the trail, Sid," said Mr. Reid.

"Trails come together up ahead," said J.J. Gordon. "La Junta is 'junction' in Spanish. You get a lot of places named La Junta. The Indians liked to say the Sapello and Mora Rivers meet up here in the valley so as to share gossip about goin's-on in the mountains. I expect the people was sharin' gossip, too." He swept his hand out toward the tree-lined riverbanks ahead. "Samuel Watrous owns most of the land in this valley. Planted all these cottonwood and willow trees."

"Heard he has his own wagon trains bringing in supplies," said Al Joiner. "They say the place is run with Indian and Mexican youngins he's bought. Supposedly he got 'em out of slavery and put 'em to work here so they can make something of themselves."

"You mean make 'em like us?" asked J.J. Sid felt the edge in his voice.

Mr. Reid shook his head. "You probably know more about this than I do, J.J., but they was saying back at the fort that Watrous got the land about ten years ago and the Apache are supposed to be sent off to a reservation. I heard he's trying to help the Apache by feeding 'em."

J.J. nodded. "I reckon he means it for good. Indians wouldn't need him to be feedin' 'em if he weren't sittin' on their land. The Ute and Comanche used to hunt here, too. Hardly ever see 'em now."

"Yeah, but where are people gonna live?" said Jeremy's dad. "When we get to California, we're gonna be taken up land. Is there gonna be some Indian saying it belongs to him? If the government buys up the land and offers it for settlement, what have they got to complain about? You can put a tepee up just about anywhere if that's how you want to live. But if you're gonna farm, you gotta have land."

"I don't think we solve the problem by cheating people out of their land," said Mr. Reid. "There has to be a better way. There's plenty of land for all if we use it right."

Sid mulled it over later. It seemed like there ought to be a fair way to do things. *Did our land in Illinois belong to Indians? What happened to them?* He hadn't thought about it before. It was a troubling thought.

They passed La Junta and the long tree-shaded adobe building that was home, store, and storerooms for Samuel Watrous and his family. It was set at the juncture of the Mora and Sapello Rivers.

After they made camp for the night. and Sid was free of chores, he and Abe met up with Dale, Squeaker, and Frog to set up a place for rehearsal. Ethel said they had to bring in all the children who were going to be citizens and soldiers. Sid hadn't realized how many children were in the company until they swarmed to the rehearsal. They'd always been there, playing underfoot, sharing secrets in little groups. He hadn't made friends with those closer to his age. He had to admit that after he met Connie, he hadn't tried making friends with anyone else.

Ethel started by asking all those who wanted to be soldiers to stand on her left and all those who wanted to be citizens to stand on her right. The boys all clamored to be soldiers, leaving the girls as citizens, except for a few hardy girls who elected to be soldiers. "Ain't got girls in the army." Jimmy protested loudly.

"No girls allowed!" yelled Matthew.

Ethel threatened to expel Jimmy and Matthew from the play and asked everyone to count off with odd numbers being citizens and even numbers soldiers. That didn't work. Some of the children hadn't been in school and couldn't count. Desperation crept into her voice. "Everybody eight-years-old and younger will be citizens. Everybody else, including girls, will be soldiers, unless they prefer to be a citizen."

Sid wasn't sure it was a good idea.

"Maybe it isn't historically accurate, but we aren't exactly following the script word for word either."

It was no good arguing with Ethel when she dug her heels in. Most of the girls joined the citizens anyway.

Not everybody was happy. Cora wanted a part in the play for Serena. Jimmy was furious because he ended up a citizen while Matthew got to be a soldier. "Nobody's goina see nothin' in the dark anyways," he grumbled.

Sid thought the rehearsal went very well, despite nearly thirty overly excited children. Ethel looked like she was about to burst into tears. "It will never work. We must have been mad as hatters to even think it."

"It will work, Ethel," said Abe. "They also want to see the play. And their parents will expect them to behave."

"And if they aren't good," Dale added, "it means more distraction for Sid."

"Yes," said Ethel, unconvinced, "but if we're going to all this trouble, it ought to be done right."

"Me and Frog's done figured out the lighting." Squeaker nodded to where Frog was on his knees between two dollhouse-sized campfires placing rocks in different positions. There were burned spots marking their experiments. "See, we build a campfire on either side of the stage, but they have to be the right distance. Then we hang lanterns—"

If Frog had figured it out, Sid knew they didn't have to worry. He had to admit it was a stroke of brilliance when Ethel asked him to be stage manager.

27.

LAS VEGAS

The Trail led through the plaza at the center of Las Vegas. Mr. Wood said it was founded in 1835 after trains first started traveling the Santa Fe Trail. Now Vegas was a thriving city, the largest in New Mexico Territory. Row upon row of faded pinkish-red adobe houses fanned out from the busy plaza. People came and went, stepping aside for the wagon train as it passed. They laughed and called to each other in Spanish. Dogs barked. Sheep and goats bleated. Hundreds of other unidentifiable noises added to the sounds of life. Strings of red chilies hung from doorways. Smoke rose from cooking fires. The smell of people, animals, and road dust was accompanied by scents completely new to Sid.

Mrs. Payne walked with him, carrying baby Anna, who seemed transfixed by all the new sights and sounds. "Brigadier General Kearny claimed New Mexico Territory for the United States from the top one of these buildings in the plaza."

They camped well past Las Vegas. The minute wagons began pulling off the trail, Sid started mentally calculating where their stage would be. Unfortunately, it didn't look like any of their wagons would be in a very good position. Suddenly Mr. Wood held up the wagons forming the circle, motioning a wagon aside to let others pass. After a while, he motioned it to move forward. It was the Sinclair wagon. It stopped directly across the circle from the Ryckman wagons.

"How'd you make that happen?" Sid asked as they marked off the stage in front of the Sinclair wagon.

"I asked." Ethel gave him a know-it-all look. "I told Mr. Wood I needed our wagon to be the stage and I needed to see how the circle looked before I decided on the best location." Sometimes Ethel was infuriating, especially when she was right.

Campfires on either side of the stage were banked and ready. Props were laid out behind the Sinclair wagon. Frog and Squeaker set up two poles, stretched a rope between and draped them with bed sheets. It gave them a curtain almost large enough to hide the stage. Lanterns stood all around the front of the stage, their candles waiting to be lit. A place slightly off-stage to the right of the audience was marked for the main actors to wait when they weren't in a scene. There was even a trunk bed for Caesar to recline on.

"It belongs to the Ryckmans," said Eli as he and Dale set it down, "they got two of 'em."

"When Connie's scenes end, all we have to do is slide it over so there's a place for that bunch to sit when they aren't acting," said Dale.

Excitement fairly crackled in the air as twilight settled on the train. The audience began gathering as soon as supper was cleared away and campfires around the outside of the circle were banked. People sat on camping chairs, stools, and on the ground facing the Sinclair wagon.

Children chattered in anticipation as they took their places for the performance. Citizens sat to the left facing the stage. They were dressed with all the imagination and ingenuity families could muster with a good bit of help from Mrs. Ryckman. Some wore shawls over their clothing, some were wrapped in bed covers.

Roman soldiers sat opposite the citizens, with a space

between them. They dressed in a similar manner but carried pot lid shields and stick swords; some wore cooking pot or colander 'helmets."

As twilight faded Mr. Wood called for order. Everybody was there except for the unlucky ones on guard duty. Those guarding the horses would be too far from the Ryckman wagons to worry about. But Sid's heart sank when he learned the two guards posted to watch over the circle: Al Joiner and Jeremy Sawyer. "Only thing worse would be if it was Reid and the preacher."

"Timing," said Dale. "They'll make rounds. It's all in timing."

Easy for him to say.

Mr. Wood smiled out over the company. "Our young people have quite a show in store for us. They've written it themselves and produced it. We're right proud of them. Miss Ethel, the stage is yours."

Frog and Abe put wood on the coals of the two campfires that waited, teasing them into flame while Dale and Sid lit candles in the lanterns. Wrapped in a bedsheet over her dress, Ethel stepped out from behind the curtain. "We are happy to present our adaptation of *Julius Caesar* by William Shakespeare. Thank you to all who have helped us with costumes and props, especially Mrs. Cornelius Ryckman. Tonight, Julius Caesar is played by Cornelius Jauncey Ryckman IV. Caesar's wife, Calpurnia is played by Elizabeth Alice Clark—"

"Who?" a woman in the audience asked.

"Bitsy Clark," somebody called. "Keep your voice down."

"—Cassius is played by Billy Elston. Brutus by Eli Mason, Portia by Ethel Marie Sinclair, Mark Antony by Sidney Benjamin Johnson. Senators are Dale Goodall and Abraham Biermann. The narrator is Winston Horace Warwick—"

"Squeaker? They can't mean it," somebody said. It was still light enough to see the flush creeping up Squeaker's neck.

"Citizens and soldiers are played by Wood Company children. Many thanks to Mrs. Clarence Reid and Miss Pearl Joiner who are supervising them. The production is directed by Ethel Marie Sinclair. Earl Barton is stage manager assisted by Dale Goodman and Abraham Biermann."

Applause for Ethel died as she stepped behind the curtain to take her place for the opening scene. Squeaker walked out from behind the curtain to face the audience wearing a shawl tied at his neck. He carried a long stick. Matthew stooped over and clutching a blanket around his shoulders, held a lantern high, scattering light over the audience as he made his way from behind them crying, "Beware the Ides of March! Beware the Ides of March!" When he reached the stage, he set the lantern down in front and helped Squeaker pull back the sheets. Caesar reclined on the camp bed at center stage, propped up on one elbow. Calpurnia (Bitsy) sat at his feet. Cassius (Billy) stood near Caesar's head. Eli and Ethel, who were playing Brutus and Portia, sat on camp stools near Bitsy at the end of the camp bed.

Behind the Sinclair wagon, Abe nodded to Sid and Dale as he left to meet Patsy and get the key to Connie's trunk. Sid tried to calm himself by letting out a long, slow breath as Abe disappeared into the shadows outside the circle.

Squeaker began. Gone was the high-pitched squeaky voice. He sounded as if he were born to the stage. He didn't twirl or snicker once. "Julius Caesar has returned home from war, victorious." He paused while the citizens and soldiers stood to yell, "Hail Caesar!" a couple of times. They were so enthusiastic that Mrs. Reid and Pearl Joiner had to hush them before Squeaker could be heard.

"Caesar and his wife Calpurnia are going to celebrate by

watching games in honor of his victorious return. Senators Cassius and"—Billy began snickering. "Shut up," Connie said from the side of his mouth. A titter swept through the front rows of the audience. Ethel gave giggling citizens and soldiers a severe look.

"Brutus and his wife Portia are with Caesar and Calpurnia. Mark Antony"— Sid's cue to step on stage—"Caesar's cousin and trusted friend is going to take part in the games. He kneels before Caesar. Caesar asks him if he will touch his wife Calpurnia's robe during the races. It will bring her luck in having children. Mark Antony says he will."

Billy snickered again, trying to stop himself. "I said shut up," whispered Connie. It made things worse. Billy sputtered, fighting for control. Eli began snickering.

The only thing to do was to keep going. "Hail mighty Caesar," Sid cried, trying to drown out snickering among the citizens and soldiers. "You would make a good emperor."

Squeaker carried on. "The crowd agrees with Mark Antony. They want to make Caesar their emperor."

The citizens and soldiers stood on cue, yelling in unison, "Hail Caesar! Hail Caesar! We want you for our emperor." Jimmy stepped to the stage and held up a crown made of leaves. Connie shook his head, holding up his hand as if to stop the crowd as Sid made his exit. He could hear the citizens and soldiers yelling, "Hail Caesar! Hail Caesar! We want you for our emperor," a second time.

Mark Antony would not need to appear again until his famous speech at the end, not unless he was back in time to stand behind the senators when they murdered Caesar. There was no time to dawdle. As one of the senators, Abe had to be back in time to stab Caesar. But he wasn't back yet. Sid nervously took off his shawl and laid it down with the props. He was torn between setting out to find Abe and waiting. Precious minutes ticked away. "Hail Caesr! Hail Caesar! We want you for our emperor!" rang out for the third time as Abe came running.

"Here. . ." he puffed, "too many people close to the Ryckman wagons. . .had to wait. . . trunk in middle wagon, right in front. It's not that big."

Taking the key, Sid headed for the Ryckman wagons, slipping into the shadows between wagons when he spotted Al Joiner coming his way. With Joiner out of the way, there was little else to worry him. The company was riveted on the play.

Applause told him the first scene was ending. Squeaker's voice boomed out as he described the plotting between Cassius and Brutus.

The coast was clear at the Ryckman wagons. Even Patsy had been excused from her duties to watch the play. In his haste, Sid tripped as he climbed into the middle wagon, nearly lost his balance, and dropped the key.

It bounced on the wagon's tongue and hit the ground.

No! It couldn't be happening.

He hadn't thought to bring a candle. He could only guess where it had fallen. Dropping to his hands and knees, he patted the ground around him, panic gripping him like a cold fist.

Applause signaled the end of Act I.

"What happened?"

He looked up banging his head on the wagon tongue. *Ethel.* "What are you doing here?" he hissed. "You nearly scared the daylights out of me."

Without saying anything, she dropped down beside him and began patting the ground.

"Looking for something?" It was Jeremy Fischer.

"I...we...," Sid stammered.

For once, even Ethel was speechless.

"Don't tell me. I don't want to know." Jeremy handed them a lantern that appeared to be unlit. "It's shuttered. You won't have to disturb the audience." Opening it a crack, he sent a shaft of light to the ground. "Leave it with your props. I'll pick it up on my way around." With that he was gone.

They found the key almost instantly. "Take the lantern and get back," Sid whispered. Cold sweat made its way down his forehead. "You shouldn't be here."

"I wrote it into the script. This is not a one-person job," she whispered between her teeth. "How are you going to see in the trunk?" There wasn't time to argue. Besides, she was right.

Squeaker's commanding voice reached them as Act II began. "Jealous of Caesar's power, Cassius and his friends have gathered support. They try to pressure Brutus into joining them."

"He's getting too powerful, Brutus." Billy apparently controlled himself long enough to deliver his line. Eli's "Caesar is ambitious," was barely audible.

Ethel perched on the wagon tongue keeping watch and holding the lantern. Its shaft of light shone on the trunk. The key turned once. Sid held his breath, turning it again.

It clicked.

Handing the key to Ethel, he began digging in the small trunk. Baby blanket, an odd collection of toys, marbles, some books—he dug all the way to the bottom, before his fingers touched the smooth, cool surface of paper: an envelope. "Got it," he whispered, holding the envelope to the light.

"It says, 'Master Cornelius Jauncey Ryckman IV, Sartoga Springs, New York,'" whispered Ethel.

He wanted to burst into tears.

"Let me look." Ethel handed him the lantern and began rummaging. She looked at everything in turn and went through the books. "It's just not here, Sid. There's not another scrap of paper. We'd better get back." She carefully locked the trunk, handing him the key.

All his hopes rested on the letter being in Connie's trunk. "It has to be here." He took the lamp from Ethel, shining the slice of light into the depths of the wagon.

Hearty applause, cheering, and Ethel tugging at his arm, brought him back to his senses. "Come on. They're starting Act III. *Go!* You have to be there after they kill Caesar."

The senators were stabbing Caesar as they reached backstage behind the wagon. Sid set down the lantern. Ethel threw him his shawl. Tossing it over his shoulder, he slipped on stage as Eli, Dale, and Abe "stabbed" Connie. Squeaker read, "In his last gasp of breath, the noble Caesar looked at his friend Brutus and cried out."

"Et tu, Brute?" Connie delivered his one line with a melodramatic gasp and fell to the ground. His writhing death agony looked like it might go on forever, but Squeaker read on, "The conspirators bathe their arms and hands in Caesar's blood."

The senators lifted Caesar to the camp bed, nearly dropping him, and sending Billy into another fit of snickering.

Undeterred, Squeaker read, "Mark Antony asks if he may be allowed to speak at Caesar's funeral. Cassius thinks it is a very bad idea. But Mark Antony promises loyalty to Brutus, so Brutus decides to let him speak."

Kneeling in front of Brutus, Sid waited for him to deliver his line. Billy snorted, nearly choking himself. Caesar's dead body—stretched out on the camp bed—muttered, "I'm goina kill you, Billy."

Eli managed to keep his composure, calling out, "'You may speak, Antony, but I'll go first."

Squeaker read, "Brutus imagines that he can help the

citizens who love Caesar to understand why they had to kill him before Mark Antony can do any damage to their cause."

The soldiers stood, yelling in unison, "Our noble Caesar has been murdered!"

The citizens stood, echoing the soldiers, "Our noble Caeser has been murdered!" The citizens let out such a storm of wailing and crying that it took a great deal of shushing from Ethel, Mrs. Reid, Pearl Joiner and three attempts by Squeaker before he could be heard. "Brutus steps before the people as the noble Caesar's body lies before them."

Sid stood by Caesar's body. Eli, ignoring Billy—who looked as if he was being strangled—stepped forward and delivered the famous lines spoken by Brutus.

> If there be any in this assembly, any dear
> friend of Caesar's, to him I say that Brutus' love
> to Caesar was no less than his. If then that friend
> demand why Brutus rose against Caesar, this is my
> answer: not that I loved Caesar less, but that I loved
> Rome more.

There was an outbreak of applause for Eli before Squeaker carried on: "Brutus tells the people that Caesar had to die because he was ambitious. The Roman Republic had to be preserved. But Mark Antony hopes he can turn the people of Rome against the conspirators."

It was Sid's big moment, second only to getting into the trunk. He stepped forward. Numbed by disappointment, he faced the audience.

He couldn't open his mouth.

Their eyes were fixed on him.

It was silent. Dead silent.

Not a sound from the soldiers and citizens.

Suddenly Ethel and Abe were at Squeaker's side. Ethel

spoke, "We invite all of you who learned this famous speech in your school days to join Mark Antony." They began, "Friends, Romans, countrymen, lend me your ears." Mrs. Payne, Ma, Pa and a few other voices joined in, "I come to bury Caesar, not to praise him."

By the third line, Sid had his voice back. And he felt it. Putting aside his disappointment, he joined in. He was Mark Antony stirring the Roman citizens to action.

The evil that men do lives after them;
The good is oft interred with their bones.

The audience became Mark Antony, too. As they reached the end of the speech, Sid was fully in command though his voice was drowned by the audience. Ethel motioned for the audience to be silent. Sid said the last lines alone.

You all did love him once, not without cause.
What cause withholds you, then, to mourn for him?—
O judgment, thou art fled to brutish beasts,
And men have lost their reason!—Bear with me;
My heart is in the coffin there with Caesar,
And I must pause till it come back to me.

Wild applause broke out along with cries of "Bravo!" He could see Mrs. Payne, tears running down her cheeks. Ma wiped her eyes. It took a while before Squeaker could go on.

The young children burst into squeals and giggles as Connie stood to hover over Eli, who gave a very convincing 'Brutus in terror' look upon seeing the ghost of Caesar. Squeaker brought the play to an end. All of the actors took bows to a cheering, whistling, stamping, clapping audience.

It was over. A roaring success.

But Sid felt like a failure.

28.

CAMP TELOCOTE

As Sid rounded up the team, Jeremy's dad called out, "Congratulations, Sid. I thought for a minute there last night you'd forgot your lines. Lordy, it's been years since I learned Mark Antony's address. Wouldn't of thought it was still with me."

"Me neither," said Mr. Sinclair. "We're right proud of all of you."

Mr. Reid shook his hand. Men slapped him on the back. Somebody called, "Friends, Romans, Countrymen, lend me your ears." Somebody else yelled, "I grew up with the Bible and Shakespeare sitting on the same shelf." "Missez said she wasn't going to California without 'em." "Well done!" Sid couldn't keep up with everything being said. It would have felt good if he hadn't pinned his hopes on finding the letter in Connie's trunk. It was hard to think of anything else.

Abe walked with him as the train set out. Then Ethel. She'd never done that before. He figured they'd planned it. They said about the same thing, "Don't give up. We'll keep trying." He knew they cared but they were both preoccupied with the success of the play, especially Ethel. It was hard to talk with her anyway. He never knew what to say.

Jimmy rescued him. "It's them little doors!"

"You mean the hills Mrs. Payne told us to watch for?" Ethel asked.

"Yeah," said Matthew, "where General Stephen Watts Kearny passed on his way to Santa Fe with the Army of the West. My baba knew a lot about the Mexican-American War."

As they reached the crest of the hills, Jimmy complained, "Where's the little doors? I can't see no doors."

"Not real doors, nincompoop," said Matthew. "It's a pass, like the Raton Pass."

"Wasn't no doors there neither." Jimmy grinned.

Matthew made a face.

"Look ahead," Ethel pointed toward snow-capped mountains that seemed to appear out of nowhere. "We're back to the Sangre de Cristo Mountains. My father says we'll cross them again at Glorieta Pass."

"Yoicks!" said Jimmy. "Not again? How many times do we cross the same mountains?"

Despite his friends trying to cheer him, a cloud of gloom hung over Sid. Dale was waiting when it was time to hitch up the animals again after nooning. The boys rarely spoke. It was a tacit agreement not to look on good terms, their way of protecting Eli from Connie and Billy. "We're meetin' again tonight, Sid. Ethel says we have to get to the bottom of this letter business."

Ethel says! He swallowed a sarcastic comment. "She didn't tell *me*."

Dale looked puzzled. "I just saw her, Emma and Molly was over at nooning to play with Isla and Maize—" the call to hitch up ended further conversation.

Sid couldn't shake his gloomy feelings or the sour feeling he harbored toward Dale. Dale might have been a friend, but he had Eli. Besides, Dale was too busy finding excuses to be with Ethel. He didn't need to; they were in the same wagon group. With Squeaker and Frog, he never knew. They didn't need him anymore anyway. The play proved that. Abe was preoccupied with medical books, consulting with Ma about patients in the train, and talking about how excited he was to see his brothers again—like it didn't matter that he would stay in Santa Fe and they'd go on. Like they weren't friends. He didn't have any true friends except the ones he'd left back home in Illinois. The letter was still missing. He was too tired to care anymore. The train plodded along, every step bringing him closer to Santa Fe. He clawed at his hat.

"Anna was out of sorts all morning." Mrs. Payne came to walk with him. "She's refusing to nap. I'm hoping the animals will distract her and get her to sleep."

They passed herds of sheep and little farmsteads. In the distance a tall mound stood alone, looking as if somebody had snipped off its peak leaving it flat. "That must be Starvation Peak. There's a story that Spaniards were trapped at the top by native people and starved to death, but I imagine it's one of those tales that grew in the telling."

Sid didn't know what to say.

"You know, Sid, Mr. Payne saw a lot of grief and loss in his life. He saw unspeakable things when he was a slave. He was sold at auction along with every member of his family. He never saw them again. He didn't even get to tell them goodbye."

Sid had no idea why she was telling him this. It made him uncomfortable.

"I asked him once how he bore so much pain. He laughed and said it was his name. He never told me everything. I didn't ask. There were things that happened while he was in the army, too. He always said not to be afraid of troubles because they're always with us, we carry them like a sack. Sometimes when his sack started to feel too heavy to carry, he'd have a look inside. He imagined taking everything out and looking at it. 'Is that something I need to think about today?' he'd ask. He'd pick one thing to think on, like his mother and father. He'd let himself feel the sadness and pain of losing them all over again. But he'd feel the happiness, too, when they were together as a family. He said when he let himself think on it and feel it, the pain was never quite so great, and the sack was always lighter.

"Everybody in the Wood Company is carrying a sack. I don't know everything you have in yours, Sid. But you aren't alone. Mr. Payne would say that if you keep stuffing things in your sack without looking at them, the sack will be too hard to carry. Don't be afraid to think about what's there. The sadness won't overcome you. And don't be afraid to reach out for help. You are surrounded by people who care."

Anna was fast asleep.

The words from Mark Antony's speech came to him, "My heart is in the coffin there with Caesar, And I must pause till it come back to me." *I reckon Mrs. Payne's heart is in the coffin with Mr. Payne. But she keeps on.*

*****

That night the train camped near Camp Telocote, an army post on the banks of Telocote Creek. Patches of winter wheat were destined for Fort Union to be distributed to other Army Posts. Villagers from nearby Telocote village sold some of their wheat and corn crops to wagon trains, too. Dotting the meadows were flocks of sheep, goats, and cattle—most of them also destined for Fort Union.

After lessons the group met at Ethel's wagon. Abe was helping Ma with somebody who had done something to themselves. Sid didn't much care. Squeaker was so excited about all the attention he was getting after the performance that he danced around, completely useless. Ethel thought they should try and remember all the strangers who had camped with them about the time the letter went missing, but Sid wasn't even sure when it had gone missing.

"There aren't any more places to look," said Dale, "we can't go looking through everything in every wagon."

"I done looked in most of 'em anyway," said Squeaker.

It was a dismal waste of time. Bitsy, Eli, and Billy found them, ending the discussion before it could get anywhere. They were all excited about the performance. Billy strutted around like he hadn't been a complete jackass.

They reached San Miguel the next morning, another lively community. At the edge of its busy plaza they crossed the Pecos River. Lush green fields we watered by irrigation ditches flowing from the river."

They had been steadily climbing since Las Vegas. Now even the illusion of flat plains was gone. Houses and farms nestled between tree-covered foothills, another reminder that this was a busy part of the world long before Westerners arrived in the 1500s.

Sid didn't go to Ethel's wagon after lessons. Abe was busy and the last thing he needed was for Ethel to feel sorry for him.

Traffic on the trail had been heavier since they left Fort Union. As they drew closer to Glorieta Pass, it felt as if they were part of a long parade of mule-drawn teamster trains, government supply trains, and ox-drawn wagons. The closer they got, the heavier Sid's heart felt. He tried imagining he was carrying a sack, like Mr. Payne. It didn't do any good. The only thing he could think about was letting Mr. Gallagher down.

29.

PECOS PUEBLO

The camp buzzed with excitement, when they stopped for the night at Pecos Pueblo, near Glorieta Pass. Sid wouldn't have said the climb was easy, but the trail was broader between the red wall of Glorieta Mesa and the Sangre de Cristo Mountains than it had been through the mountains to Raton Pass. Once they were over the pass, their next camp would be in Santa Fe.

Instead of lessons, Mrs. Payne had children meet right after the teams were unhitched to visit the large adobe building that could be seen from their campsite while it was still daylight. It was the last remaining building of the Pecos Pueblo. Jeremy Fischer and Red Elston went with them, carrying guns. Mr. Wood said rattlesnakes were a danger now that it was starting to get warmer. Other children came, too, with older brothers and sisters. "Pueblo means village in Spanish," Mrs. Payne explained. "Long before the Spanish came, this was a trade center for Pueblo farmers and the hunting tribes of the plains. It was a thriving city before the Pilgrims landed at Plymouth Rock."

"Where'd all the people go?" asked Jimmy.

"The Spanish and the Pueblo Indians had different ideas about how they should live. This church was built so Spanish missionaries could convert the native people to Catholicism. Some people did convert. Some didn't. But they were all

265

expected to live like the Spanish people. I suppose there came a time when the Pueblo Indians decided they'd rather live somewhere else where they were free to live the way they wanted to."

J.J. Gordon came over to their campfire after dinner. He looked almost sheepish. "Wanted to say somethin' before we get to Santa Fe," he began.

It was a crisp, cold evening. Pa moved over to give him a place near the fire.

J.J. sat down awkwardly, taking the coffee Ma offered. Moving the tin cup around in his hands, he began. "I done asked Miz Turney if she'd marry me. She said she would."

"Congratulations!" Pa reached over to shake hands. Ma and Mrs. Payne said how happy they were for him.

"Preacher Jones is gonna marry us at noonin' tomorrow. I'd be right proud if you'd stand with me, Mr. Johnson. You 'n Mr. Wood showin' confidence in me and all."

"I'd be honored," said Pa.

"I've seen the way you get on with those youngins," said Ma, "you'll be a fine father to 'em."

"Thank you kindly." Red crept from J.J.'s neck to the top of his head. "There's somethin' more." He took a deep breath as if he dreaded saying what he was about to say.

"I ain't made much of my life. Spent too much of it livin' on the edge of the law, shootin' it out over some fool thing or other. William Gallagher gave me a chance. Helped me turn things around. Then Bayless Sly came along. I let him sweet talk me into believin' Mr. Gallagher was cheatin' us of pay every week. He showed me the figures. I was disappointed in Gallagher, and fool enough to believe Sly. He said he knew a way to get our money back without hurtin' anybody. Bout the time we got to Kansas City, I figured I'd been hoodwinked. Sly was takin all my money the way he'd been skimmin' off Gallagher.

"We seen you at the Gillis Hotel in Westport, Miz Johnson. Sly was sure you all had that letter he was after. You can't reason with somebody like Sly. I figured I'd better keep an eye on 'em. Thought maybe I could get it before he did and draw him off. Then I could give it back to Gallagher and maybe get my old job back." J.J. let out an enormous sigh. "I reckon you been lookin' for this." Reaching inside his shirt, J.J. produced the lost letter. Sid was stunned.

"Mr. Gallagher musta had his reasons for givin' it to you, Sid. I can't keep it now. Wouldn't be honest. Miz Turney says I have to face Mr. Gallagher like the prodigal son in the Bible, confess what I done was wrong, and ask him to have me back. Reckon I need to ask your forgiveness. She's right. I done caused you all a lota anguish.

"Mr. Wood's gonna put in a good word for me. If Gallagher won't have me back, I'll sign on with somebody else. Me 'n Miz Turney is determined. I ain't getting' off the path again. Don't know why I trusted Sly when Mr. and Miz Gallagher was so good to me."

Sid struggled to find his voice. "How did you know—"

"Didn't"— a slight smile flashed across J.J.'s face—"not till I seen you was listenin' in on us that night."

Sid's jaw dropped.

"I took to my bedroll so as you'd leave. Then I told Bayless I couldn't sleep. Said I wanted to have a look around yer wagons. He didn't care, long as it didn't put him out. I seen you get that box. That's when I knew for sure."

"How did you know I was watching you?—and Al Joiner, nobody gets past Al Joiner."

"Grew up Comanche. Pa married again after my mama died bringin me into the world. My pia was Comanche."

"Pia?" Curiosity overcame Jimmy, who had been listening

from under the wagon.

J.J. grinned. "Means 'Ma' in Commanche." He stood. "I hope this don't change your mind about standin' up with me, Mr. Johnson."

"You're a good man, J.J." Pa stood. Giving him a pat on the back he walked J.J. back to the Turney wagon.

That evening Mrs. Payne's older students gathered at her wagon out of habit.

Bitsy was all worked up over the wedding. "Miz Jones and I are going to sing. I think it's so romantic!"

"Well, I don't!" said Ethel, face like a storm cloud. "They haven't known each other that long."

"No." Mrs. Payne sat down with them. "But that doesn't mean it isn't a good match. There are many reasons to marry that don't sound romantic, but they're good reasons. Mr. Gordon is kind to her. The children are foolish about him. It isn't easy for a woman on her own. Mr. Gordon has been alone for a long time. I think he is glad to find a family. I believe they'll be good for each other."

"Well, I'll never, ever marry except for love."

"Me neither," sighed Bitsy, "unless he's rich."

"Beyond belief," Sid muttered to Abe.

Mrs. Payne said they wouldn't have lessons again until the train left Santa Fe. "I want you to get as much as you can from being in Santa Fe. The oldest church in the U.S. is there, San Miguel Chapel. It was built in the 1600s. You'll find people selling their wares in the shade of the Palace of the Governors. Mr. Payne always said the plaza is like a history lesson in itself."

They went from there to Ethel's wagon. Sid wanted to tell them the letter had been found, but Bitsy came along. Dale and Eli were already there waiting. Ethel apologized that there wasn't any more cocoa for hot chocolate. "When we get to Santa Fe we will have chocolate," said Abe. "It is for sale by my brothers. They will give us some."

"Chocolate first came from South America," Squeaker said, snickering.

Dale gave him a look.

"It's in the book I'm readin'. It's made from cacao beans. Hernán Cortés took it to Spain. The king and queen thought it was the best thing they ever tasted. At first, the Aztecs thought it was medicine—"

"That's more than I wanted to know," said Dale.

We've created a monster. Sid didn't want to hurt Squeaker's feelings, but now that he was reading, he had an annoying way of dumping facts on everyone around him.

He was about to give up and leave when Bitsy said she had to go and asked Eli to walk her back. "Guess I oughta turn in," said Dale. "Mr. Wood said we'd have a long day tomorrow."

"Wait, Dale." Sid told them about the letter.

"But it wasn't for nothing," said Ethel, "us working together to do the play. We've all become friends now."

It was a nice thought, but what good are friends if you have to leave them? Sid didn't have much to say as he and Abe walked back to the wagon. That night he thought about Mr. Payne's sack. Why didn't his sack feel lighter now that he had the letter?

The next morning, they crossed over Glorieta Pass and through the high, towering walls of Apache Canyon. Jimmy and Matthew were convinced there were bandits waiting to ambush them. Fortunately, they were disappointed.

At nooning, Mr. Wood called the company together. "As everyone knows by now, Miz Turney and J.J. Gordon are getting married. They will live in Santa Fe. We'll miss them, but we wish them well. After Preacher pronounces them man and wife, Miz Ryckman has organized some refreshments. We'll celebrate together."

Pa stood with J.J. and Reverend Jones as Mrs. Jones and Bitsy sang "How Can I Leave Thee!" Sid looked at Ethel. Her face looked like it would curdle milk.

Mrs. Turney carried a bouquet of wildflowers and wore a pretty straw hat. Mrs. Sinclair stood with her. Reverend Jones read from the Bible, said some words about family and responsibility, and pronounced them man and wife.

People clapped. "Ain't ya gonna kiss her?" somebody yelled. J.J., whose face was already a bright pink, leaned down and gave his bride a peck on the cheek. Cheering and whistling broke out. Some of the men struck up lively music on guitar and fiddle as people congratulated the couple.

Word went around that Mr. Ryckman was paying for a room for Mr. and Mrs. Gordon at the hotel on the Plaza. Mrs. Sinclair was keeping the children overnight. "Must be mighty glad he didn't have to give up those Thoroughbreds," somebody muttered. Pa said it was an ungracious remark. "We may not agree with Ryckman on some important matters, but that doesn't mean he is without goodness. I'll never forget how he offered those horses when Cora was kidnapped."

Sid figured it was another example of what Liam Robinson had said. Some things cannot be reconciled.

30.

SANTA FE

It was a short celebration. When group captains called, "Hitch up!" nobody argued. Santa Fe was the next stop. Sid caught his breath as the oxen crested a hill and Santa Fe lay before them. Sun danced on the Rio Grande River as it stretched toward snowcapped mountains in the distance. Far to the south, a vast open land was dotted with mesas. Down the hill they went, crossing over a water ditch, through a wooden gateway arching above them, and into a long narrow street, barely wide enough for the wagons. Strings of chili peppers hung from adobe houses with iron-barred windows. Barking dogs, goats, chickens, little children with wide eyes, women dressed in black with shawls wrapped around them—all milled in the streets. The train made its way through to the plaza, where Mr. Wood consulted with a man who oversaw arriving trains.

The long porch of the Palace of the Governors lined one side of the Plaza. The twin towers of the old church rose beyond. "Look, Sid. 'Biermann Brothers Specializing in Dry Goods and Native Curios.' That's their store!" Abe pointed to a sprawling store along the Plaza.

"I wrote from Fort Union to say to expect me soon. I guess I will walk in and see if they know me." As he lifted his pack from the wagon and began hitching it on, two men approached Mr. Wood and the overseer. "Come on, Sid, it's them! Nathan and Max."

Sid hesitated but Mrs. Payne called, "Go! I'll watch the team."

"Abe! I declare you're near as tall as Max," said Nathan, slapping Abe on the back. He extended his hand to Sid. "Sid Johnson? Can't thank you enough for taking care of our boy."

"You ain't gonna pass for a boy much longer, little brother," said Max, giving Abe a kind of side-ways hug and shaking hands with Sid.

They were talking so fast among themselves Sid couldn't have slipped a word in edgewise even if he'd understood German. The realization that he and Abe would part company hit again, hard.

"We'll take him off your hands, Sid," said Nathan. Sid couldn't help liking Nathan. He had an easy way about him that made Sid feel as if he'd always known him. "We'll let you get settled and be over to meet your family and Mrs. Payne. It would be our pleasure to have all of you join us for supper tonight."

It was already late, close to sunset. "Tell your Mama and Mrs. Payne not to mind about trail dust. We're used to it. Our business depends on it." Nathan seemed to know about everyone.

"Abe, we're gonna have to get you some clothes." said Max. "You look like you're fresh off the boat from Germany."

Abe blushed.

"He's lucky to have any clothes, after what he's been through." Sid rushed to Abe's defense. "When my Pa found him, he'd nearly been blown away by a tornado."

"Sure enough?" Max surveyed Sid with merry eyes. "You didn't tell us about that, little brother."

Pa stepped over to shake hands with Nathan and Max.

"Can't stay. Have a team to mind, but I wanted to meet you. We sure enjoyed having Abe with us."

Nathan repeated his invitation, inviting Mr. Wood, and promising to send Abe and Max to get them.

Mr. Wood said the train had been directed to make camp southwest of town where there was pasture and room to stretch. Abe waved as they moved out of the plaza. Sid swallowed hard and felt for his hat.

As he unyoked and watered the oxen, he wondered how he would find Mrs. Gallagher. He couldn't rest easy until he'd given her the letter.

Ma and Mrs. Payne were all in a flutter about people washing up and changing clothes when he returned to the wagon. Jimmy squalled about washing behind his ears. "Come on, Jimmy, us men have to make a good impression. You got enough dirt behind your ears to plant petunias. Or should I say cacti?"

"Ain't either," said Jimmy.

"Don't either," corrected Ma.

*****

Max and Abe came for them in a horse-drawn buggy. Abe looked like a real Westerner. He wore a round top, broad-brimmed hat, trousers, shirt, and waistcoat like Max. He was full of news as they made their way through fading light in winding streets. Abe's brother Kurt was on his way to Mexico to strike up a trade agreement. There was a new baby. They were waiting to decide on the baby's Apache name.

Sid was glad for him. But he felt hollow.

The Biermann home was a sprawling, pink adobe house with geraniums blooming in large pots on the doorstep. They could have been entering a parlor in Alton, Illinois, except for a colorful mixture of furnishings from back East and

New Mexico Territory.

The evening didn't seem real when Sid thought about it later. For reasons he couldn't explain, it felt strange to eat on fine china and drink from crystal glasses. They'd never had anything so grand back in Illinois. *So, what did I expect—to eat in a tepee because Nathan's wife is Apache?*

Mr. Wood seemed to enjoy himself, too. And Sid found the answer to a question he'd wanted to ask for a long time. They were talking about the different Jewish and Apache customs that Nathan and Nascha Biermann had to get used to once they got married. "I know what that's like," Mr. Wood said. "I'd spent years trading with the Kaw. Thought I knew all there was to know about them when I married into the tribe. I sure had that wrong!"

They left with an invitation to dine again the following evening. It was more like a command. "But you must allow us to offer you hospitality," said Nascha Biermann. "You have cared for our brother. Perhaps you would like to try traditional Santa Fe food?" It was agreed.

On the way back to the wagon, Jimmy and Matthew told Sid about how Mr. Biermann talks to his boys in German and Mrs. Biermann talks to them in the Apache language while their auntie and everybody else talks to them in English or Spanish, and how their father wants them to learn Hebrew, and how they got to spend most of every summer with their grandparents in an Apache village, and learning to shoot with bows and arrows, and weren't they luckier than anybody—until both boys were out of breath and Sid's head was swimming. Cora and Lydia were delighted with corn husk dolls they'd been given, pelting him with information about Spanish dresses, and what Apache girls wear in the village, and a dollhouse almost as tall as Cora. He felt like he was watching himself listen in on two different conversations without being present to either. There had been little time to talk with Abe. He had already lost him.

When they returned to camp, Mr. Reid said a man was waiting for him.

"Sid Johnson?" The man stood. "I am Juan Vargas Rodriguez a servant in the house of Señora Catalina Lucía Esteban-Valdéz Gallagher. She has asked me to deliver this to you and to wait for your reply." He handed Sid a letter addressed to Master Sid Johnson. It read:

Welcome to Santa Fe. I would like to request the pleasure of the company of you and your family on Thursday evening for an early supper at 6:00 PM

Yours sincerely,
Catalina Lucía Esteban-Valdéz Gallagher

P.S. My husband tells me I should mention Esteban's cross so that you know the letter is from me. CG

Sid looked at Pa and Ma. "Yes, of course," said Pa. "We must accept her hospitality."

"What about the children?" Ma asked pensively.

"Jimmy and Cora can stay with me," said Mrs. Payne.

"You should go, too, Mrs. Payne," said Sid. "You're. . . family." He started to say, "translated the letter," but thought better of it. He wasn't sure what, if anything, Mr. Rodriguez knew. Besides, Mrs. Payne, Matthew, and Lydia were family.

"The household is a happy place with many children. Señora, you are all most welcome," said Mr. Rodriguez.

"Well," said Pa, after Mr. Rodriguez left, "More than one set of eyes waited for the Wood Company."

That night Sid tossed and turned. He pulled his hat down over his face, trying not to think. Then it came to him. Being in Santa Fe was a bit like getting off the Loulabelle at

Westport Landing. He didn't know there was a Grace Willis then, or a Willis family, or Mr. and Mrs. Payne. Everything was changing again. It didn't matter how hard he tried, he couldn't make it come out right. *Mr. Payne would say my sack is too full.* He stifled the lump welling up inside.

The next thing he knew it was morning. Jimmy was laughing at him. "Whatcha wearin' your hat to bed for, Sid?"

The camp hummed with activity all day as people reassessed their supplies and shopped. Ma and Mrs. Payne had lists. The Biermann brothers were more than generous. When Ma asked about trousers for Sid, Nathan said, "Max was about his size when we came out here. I'll have my wife set some of his things out for Sid to try on tonight. She was saving them for Abe, but they don't fit him. He's a bit taller than Sid. We may have some things for the others, too. Our children come in all sizes."

Ma and Mrs. Payne looked wistfully at calico and lace. Ma fingered the colorful embroidery along the borders of a rebozo, the shawl worn by local women. "This wouldn't take up any room at all—"

"And if we bought rebozos, they'd freshen us up a bit," added Mrs. Payne.

In free moments, Max, who seemed more like a big kid than a grown man, took Abe and Sid all over Santa Fe. It was late in the afternoon when Sid returned to the wagon.

"There was mail waitin' for us here," said Ma, "a letter from Mrs. Harold and read this." Smiling, she handed him an envelope addressed to, "Mr. and Mrs. Benjamin Johnson of Alton, Illinois, c/o The Stokes Company, Santa Fe, New Mexico Territory, or hold for another company."

Sid found a place in the shade of the wagon and opened the letter.

Dear Mr. and Mrs. Johnson,

I am so very sorry to hear about Sid's death. He was the best friend I ever had. I know it must be hard for you every day without him.

My mamma and daddy and Mr. Jim Payne were killed not long after your wagon pulled out of the train. I miss Mamma and Daddy very much. Mamma had smallpox, but Daddy and Mr. Payne were murdered! Mr. Swathmore killed them and kidnapped me! It is a long, sad story, but thankfully, Old Shep followed me. He was such a good dog. I was rescued by a very nice man named Mr. Nichols. He helped Mrs. Payne, too. He said she is taking Daddy's medical books to California so someone else can start a medical school.

I live with my grandparents in St. Louis now. I am happy here, but I will never forget Sid and my time on the Santa Fe Trail. It was the best time of my whole life.

Yours sincerely,
Grace Willis

She was rescued! Except Mrs. Payne said the man was Mr. Bright. It didn't matter. And Old Shep stayed with her. He was flooded with relief. He might not ever see Grace again, but she was alive and well.

"I think you'd better write her before we leave and let her know you're alive," said Ma. "What a sad little thing she must be."

Sid crawled under the wagon and wrote:

Dear Grace,

It's me, Sid. I am alive! I refused to die, ha ha.

You'll never guess. Mrs. Payne is the same wagon

company. She has become part of our family. Or maybe we're part of her family. I drive her team. She still has lessons. I finally memorized all of Mark Antony's speech and we put on Julius Caesar for the whole company. I've made friends with a boy named Abe. We have had more adventures than I can tell in one letter. Everyone is well and Serena is still with us. What happened to Old Shep? I miss that dog. Someday I hope to have a dog like Old Shep.

When I get to California, I will write you a nice long letter. I don't know if there will be post before we get there. We still have to face the desert, but I know we will get to California. So will Dr. Willis' books.

Your friend, Sid

The Johnsons weren't the only ones to get mail. Mrs. Sinclair sent letters from Fort Bent to the place where the orphan girls' family had lived. The postmaster wrote to say there was no one to take Isla and Mazie. "But Pearl Joiner and her brother say they want to adopt them," said Mrs. Payne. "Miss Joiner started taking care of them after Mr. Joiner recovered. Mrs. Sinclair says they get on famously."

That night at dinner, Nathan said, "You boys are quiet. You might like to know that we're looking to trade in California. If the United States can keep itself out of a Civil War, there'll be all kinds of trade opportunities. Fact is, as our youngins get bigger, I want them to know what it means to be a Jew. Right now, they know more about being Apache. I'd like to locate in an active Jewish community. I was thinking San Francisco, but Kurt thinks Los Angeles. He says it is a small but growing community. We'll make a point of sending Abe to California with Kurt."

Sid felt himself grinning all over. He turned to Abe, but Abe wasn't at the table.

Suddenly it got quiet. The children, who had been eating on the patio, appeared in the dining room shushing each other as they tried to keep from giggling.

"Sid,"—Abe stood right behind him—"if you can bear to give up that battered old hat . . ." He held a new felt hat like he and Max wore.

"Try it on."

<h1>31.</h1>

<h1>SANTA FE TRAIL'S END</h1>

Thursday evening came too soon, their last in Santa Fe. Mr. Rodriguez called for them in a carriage drawn by four horses. He took them along the Rio Grande River coming to stop at an iron gate. Arching above was a sign, "Ranchero Esteban-Valdez." Ahead stood a complex of adobe buildings. Cattle and sheep grazed in the distance. The Sangre de Cristos dominated the horizon to the north, high desert plains and the faint outline of mesas and mountains stretched south from the river.

Soon they were being ushered into a building, through a hallway, and out into a patio brightened by splashes of colorful flowers. They were met by a beautiful woman, wearing traditional black. Her hair was pulled back in a tight chignon, brightened by a red flower. "I am Catalina Lucia. Welcome to my home."

She didn't ask for the letter. She seemed more interested in making everyone welcome. "I am sorry my husband could not be here to welcome you. He has been with his mother in New York these past weeks. She has lately been taken ill."

Dinner was served in the dining room. Over a meal of local foods Sid would have enjoyed more if the letter hadn't been waiting in his waistcoat, they talked about food, about Mr. Gallager's traditions and hers, about Mrs. Payne's life in New York, and the Johnson's life in Illinois.

The dishes were cleared. They retired to the drawing room where a delicious chocolate drink awaited them. "And so, Sid, you have something for me?" Doña Catalina asked at last.

"I have, Ma'am, but it has been opened." He felt red rushing to his face. "Mr. Gallagher said he would come for it or send someone. When nobody came, I . . . I began to doubt him. I asked Mrs. Payne to read it. I thought it might help me know what to do."

"And did it?" she asked, smiling, as she took the envelope.

"Sort of," said Sid, feeling like he'd been caught stealing the silver spoons. "I knew I shouldn't have doubted him. And I knew why I had to keep it safe."

The room fell silent as Doña Catalina read the letter to herself.

She dabbed her eyes with a lace handkerchief, looking up. "My mother often spoke of this letter. It was stolen long before my time. My husband learned of it and went to St. Louis where he bought it from a man there who deals. . . the man would say in antiquities. You know the rest."

"But do you, Doña Catalina?" asked Pa. He told her about how the letter had been stolen and all that had happened.

"This is why your Mr. Wood has asked to speak with me," she said thoughtfully. "I am pleased to hear this about J.J. Gordon. Bayless Sly was always a detestable man. But I was most distressed when I learned he had influenced Mr. Gordon. It must be hard to grow up between worlds. Mr. Gordon is Scottish and Comanche. He must have felt he didn't belong to either world. I'm happy to know he has found himself.

"I shudder to think how Bayless Sly learned about the letter. I daresay there was a treasure at one time, but the letter has passed through too many hands to imagine it is waiting for Bayless Sly to find it."

"I felt very privileged to read the letter, Doña Catalina," said Mrs. Payne. "It changes my conception of history. If Esteban was Moroccan, he may have been the first black man on the North American continent. The letter is a treasure, not just to your family, but for the world."

Doña Catalina nodded. "I had not thought of that. I wonder where such documents of historical significance are kept? My family will need to consider it. I am only one of many, you see. Mr. Gallagher likes to say he kidnapped me and installed me in Ranchero Esteban-Valdez. My family home is in Santa Fe, where my mother and brothers live." She sighed. "My brothers have not been so interested in the history."

"I'm very curious about the rhyme at the end," said Mrs. Payne.

"Yes. This part baffles me, too. A curse?

A deed. Toothless Crook!
Who rows life unhurt?
He who has ears, let him hear.
El que tiene oídos, que oiga.

Interesting, that part in English."

Mrs. Payne nodded. "Why in English?"

"A note of despair? 'A deed?— something done? Toothless—without teeth, no strength perhaps? Someone cowardly has done an ignoble deed. They will not go through life unpunished. Perhaps Esteban's treasure was gone before my ancestor was laid to rest, and this part added for those who have ears to hear."

"That makes sense," said Mrs. Payne. "I wish the person writing it had identified himself. Or dated the note."

Doña Catalina set the letter aside. "Now we shall have

some flan to cool the taste of so many spices. The flan is not indigenous food. It was brought from Spain. But I am ever so glad they brought it." She clapped her hands and a servant appeared carrying a silver tray laden with dishes.

"Mrs. Payne, you are a teacher? I have a school here for children of our teamsters and others who live nearby. You could stay and run my school. It is a very pleasant place to live. The hardest part of the journey is yet to come. Don't mistake my intent, it is not because you are a woman, but because the journey through the desert will be so difficult for everyone"— she gave Mrs. Payne a broad, almost mischievous smile—"and because I need a teacher."

"That is kind of you, Doña Catalina, but I made a promise to myself when my husband was killed. I am determined to go to California."

"Then go to California, you must, and God go with you."

A silence fell as the flan was served. Sid agreed. Bringing flan to the New World was a good thing the Spaniards did. Ma asked if the cook might possibly share the recipe. It would be one more thing to look forward to in California.

Pa said they must get back to the wagon train for an early start tomorrow. Loud objections rang from the patio as the children were called.

Doña Catalina walked to the carriage with them. "Sid, my husband was right to put his confidence in you. Perhaps we will meet in California one day. I should like to see the grave of my ancestor. It will be so much easier once there are trains connecting this vast land. And there will be.

"I want you to have this to remember us." She held out a silver cross set with a turquoise and suspended on a silver chain.

"But I don't deserve a reward," Sid stammered. "I didn't do anything but hide the letter and not a very good job of that. It wasn't even me who got it back."

"I see. Perhaps you would feel more worthy if you had wrested the letter from Mr. Gordon, or rescued little Cora from Bayless Sly? Then you would be a true hero. But you are mistaken, Sid Johnson. Sometimes small things are more heroic than grand acts—and harder. You didn't know Mr. Gallagher when he asked you to protect the letter to Doña Catalina, yet you trusted him. Think of all those miles it traveled safely in your care. When you opened it, you didn't think of the treasure, you thought of what the letter would mean to me. You kept the secret of Esteban's Cross. In my eyes, you are a hero."

"Esteban's Cross." said Sid, taking the cross.

"Yes. We shall call it Esteban's Cross." She smiled at him with dancing eyes.

*****

"Wagons Roll!" Mr. Wood's call echoed through the camp. The first hit of dawn was yet to brighten the eastern horizon. They were headed south into the desert. Behind them, the Sangre de Christo Mountains stood black against the lingering stars. How different it felt from that morning such a long time ago, when Sid heard Mr. Stokes call, "Wagons Roll!" and they set out on the Santa Fe Trail for the first time.

It was a hopeful morning, back then in Westport. He felt hopeful now as he waited to take his place in line. It was a different kind of hope, a hope steeled by the reality that adventure walks hand in hand with hardship and loss.

They were leaving the Santa Fe Trail, setting out on a new trail, the Camino Real de Tierra Adentro, the ancient Royal Road to Mexico. Somewhere beyond the southern horizon they would pick up Cooke's Wagon Road to California. Sid watched as wagons fell into line. He could name most of them now, the Ryckman group led. Connie walked beside his mother leaning on a walking stick. Had he learned anything from his scrape with death? Squeaker led the Warwick team—his father was giving him more responsibility now.

The Sinclair wagon pulled into line. Sid thought maybe he and Ethel had signed an unspoken truce. Frog waited with his older brother by their team. Missing were Mrs. Turney's wagon and the buggy belonging to Reverend and Mrs. Jones, who had also remained in Santa Fe. Every wagon that pulled into line had its own story to tell. *How many more stories will we have to tell when we get to California?*

Ahead the rise called La Bajada dropped 800 feet to the desert plains below. Heavy trade wagons still used its ancient trail, but the company set out on a longer, less torturous route. The vast desert gradually took on color in the pre-dawn light. It was unlike anything they had crossed before. Sandy, short grasslands were covered with low shrubs and cacti. Behind him, Matthew and Jimmy grumbled about having to be up so early as they always did. Snatches of conversation rose above the sounds of oxen and creaking wagons.

He wasn't sure how long they'd been moving when it hit him: maybe the message at the end of Mrs. Gallagher's letter was an anagram—a secret message all scrambled up so it said something else. What if it was? And what if there really were a treasure? He felt the silver and turquoise cross tucked under his shirt. Esteban's Cross was treasure enough. Still—

"Do you mind if I walk with you?" Ethel took him completely by surprise. "I thought you might be missing Abe."

"Do you know anything about anagrams, Ethel?" he asked.

Acknowledgments and Notes

First, Thank you.
I am grateful to Amelia Bolin, Noah Dunlap, c. huffman, Mitch McCoy, McWendy Pollock, Pauline Sharp, Sylvia Spratt, Marie Swaby-Rowe, and Georgianna Torres, for your careful manuscript reading and feedback on characters and setting. Leo E. Olivia, Santa Fe Trail Historian, thank you for helping me understand the history, your generous feedback, and for introducing me to Ronald D. Parks, whose book, *The Darkest Period: The Kanza Indians and Their Last Homeland, 1846–1873* was an invaluable resource. Thanks to Ronald Parks for introducing me to c. huffman and Pauline Sharp, my Kaw tutors. Wíblaha (thank you). Any errors I have made in describing the Kaw Nation are mine, not yours. Beth Schmeizer, Jon and Leslie Dunlap, many thanks for reading an early draft and your continued support. Warren Schoonmaker and Candia Thew, thank you for making the Fort Union to Santa Fe journey with me and knowing the right questions to ask along the way. Greg Baker and the Park Rangers at Fort Union National Monument were enormously helpful as was Leo E. Oliva's comprehensive resource paper, "Fort Union and the Frontier Army in the Southwest." As always, thanks to Nancy Schoonmaker for your critical eye. A special thanks to Liesl Bolin for the cover and interior design of the book.

The Kaw (Kanza) Nation
In Sid Johnson and the Phantom Slave Stealer, I dealt with the issue of slavery as seen through Sid's eyes. In this book, Sid encounters the ambiguity between going to California to settle and opposition to the displacement and near-

extermination of native people along the Santa Fe Trail. I chose to focus on the Kaw Nation because the state of Kansas takes its name from the Kaw. Our 31st Vice President of the United States was one-eighth Kanza. Yet the Kanza are barely mentioned in history textbooks, if at all.

Before the signing of the Treaty of 1825, the Kaw lived and hunted on 20 million acres of land. The treaty left them with two million acres, 35 miles wide, leaving 18 million acres to the U.S. government. The Treaty of 1830, known as the Indian Removal Act, relocated eastern tribes west of the Mississippi, crowding Kaw lands, and disrupting their traditional ways of living, family life, and sources of food. The Treaty of 1846 reduced their land from two million to 256,000 acres, with further reductions in 1859 and in 1873 when the 500 remaining Kaw were removed to Indian Territory. Congress dissolved the last reservation in 1902, giving the Kaw individual allotments. What we know of their early history focuses on them at a time of cultural adaptation and is written from the perspective of the Europeans and Americans who were displacing them.

Today, the Kaw Nation has grown from near extinction to a vibrant society. Learn more about the Kaw at https://www. kawnation.gov/history-of-kaw-nation/ .

The Letter and Esteban

Esteban de Dorantes was a Moorish slave who accompanied an expedition shipwrecked off the Texas coast in 1527. So far as we know, he was the first black man on the American continent. Of the 300 who set out on the journey, Esteban was one of four survivors who wandered across the Southwest US for eight years. Alvár Núñez Cabeza de Vaca wrote an account of their journey. Later, Esteban was sent with Fray Marcos de Niza to find the famed cities of gold. It is thought that Esteban was killed by the Zuni on this expedition, but as there were no eyewitnesses to his actual death, he remains a mystery. I borrow from the little we know of his history for the letter William Gallagher entrusts to Sid, but the family history (including Suna) is fictional. —F.S.

More information about the Santa Fe Trail and resources for learning about the Trail may be found on my website: https://fschoonmaker.com. I have drawn extensively on resources of The Kansas Historical Society and The Oklahoma Historical Society as well as The Santa Fe Trail Association in my research for the book.

ABOUT THE AUTHOR

Native of Oklahoma, Frances Schoonmaker taught elementary school in Washington, Oregon, Tennessee and Maryland early in her career. She is the award-winning author of books for teens, *The Last Crystal Trilogy* (Auctus Publishers, 2018-2019), *Sid Johnson and the Phantom Slave Stealer* (Auctus Publishers, 2022), and editor of five books in the Sterling Press *Poetry for Young People* series. Among her awards are the Agatha Award for Best Children's/Young Adult mystery, the Coffee Book Club Award for Historical fiction, and Readers Favorite 5 Stars. Professor Emerita of Teachers College, Columbia University, New York, Schoonmaker directed the graduate-level teacher preparation program in childhood education, a program drawing heavily on children's literature and storytelling. She has taught, lectured, and consulted internationally, particularly in the Middle East and Asia. She lives with family in Baltimore Maryland.

OTHER AUCTUS PUBLICATIONS
BY THE AUTHOR

THE LAST CRYSTAL TRILOGY

The Black Alabaster Box
The Red Abalone Shell
The Last Crystal*

THE SID JOHNSON SERIES

Sid Johnson and the Phantom Slave Stealer**
Sid Johnson and The Well-Intended Conspiracy
Book 3 to be announced

* winner of the Agatha Award for Best Middle Grade/Young Adult Mystery 2019

** nominee for the Agathar Award for Best Middle Grade/Young Adult Mystery 2022.